It did not begin immediately. T'
mercurial than those of earth, (
when one invoked them properl
taste, they often desired more tha
He felt the spirits contained withi
earth and the blood, considering-

The water churned, and shot
ing column, coiling around itself and forming a perfect, shimmering sphere. Ilias raised his arms, weighted with the dragging, swirling hunger of the water, and thrust his hands into the sphere, letting the visions it would impart flow over him and draw him down.

He sensed a vast distance, far greater than anything he had every felt before, a gulf of space and age that beggared his imagination. For an instant, he *saw* nothing but a great rushing darkness, the passage of many miles, and then it came to him—

Mountains... high, snow-capped mountains, higher even than the mountains of the east, standing sentinel against the deep blue sky—

Wind, cold—the air was dry against his skin—

Copyright © 2004 by White Wolf Publishing
ISBN 978-1-950565-57-3
All rights reserved. No part of this book may be used or reproduced in any manner whatsoever without written permission except in the case of brief quotations embodied in critical articles and reviews
For information address Crossroad Press at 141 Brayden Dr., Hertford, NC 27944
A Mystique Press Production - Mystique Press is an imprint of Crossroad Press.
www.crossroadpress.com

Crossroad Press Trade Edition

Vampire: The Dark Ages

CLAN NOVEL
TZIMISCE

BY MYRANDA KALIS

WHITE WOLF

Dark Ages Tzimisce

Myranda Kalis

AD 1232
Thirteenth of the Dark Ages Clan Novels

What Has Come Before

It is the year 1232, and decades of warfare and intrigue continue among the living and the dead. The Teutonic Knights and Sword-Brothers have embarked on campaigns to conquer and convert pagan Prussia and Livonia, spreading the crusading zeal into new lands. Bloodshed has, as always, followed in its wake. In the shadowy courts of the undead, the situation is no better. Lord Jürgen of Magdeburg, called the Swordbearer, has followed these knightly orders into the east with his own vampiric warriors, the Order of the Black Cross, bent on taking new territory and feasting on the blood of those he bests in battle.

During this conquest, Jürgen seized control of a monastery of the Obertus Order, an order of monks transplanted from Byzantium in the wake of that city's destruction almost three decades ago. In it, Jürgen discovered a surprising secret, and has sent that secret, along with his diplomat and consort Rosamund d' Islington, to the Tzimisce ambassador Myca Vykos.

As Jürgen continues his quest to conquer the east and Rosamund approach Vykos' stronghold in Brasov with her lord's message, Vykos himself finds himself entrenched in the centuries-old war and blood-feuds within his own clan....

Prologue

Sredetz, c. 1210

In the house of the Archbishop of Nod, a single light burned. A shielded candle-lantern sat on the corner of a long writing table, covered with neat piles of correspondence sealed in wax and ribbon, a stack of ledgers, four personal journals, and a wooden box with a complicated lock. The Archbishop would soon be departing the seat of his power for a journey of indeterminate duration, and he was putting his affairs in order accordingly. Most of the letters were addressed to various prominent members of the Crimson Curia throughout Christendom and the Levant, and would leave for their destinations on the morrow in the saddlebags of his couriers. The ledgers contained the financial arrangements he had made, to be executed in his absence by his seneschal, a record of the precise amounts of monies to be spent and how his material estate was to be dispersed.

The journals were his own most private writings, his ruminations on his existence and its most important facets, its most formative events. Each was deceptively slender; he had long ago effaced himself of the ego needed to write of himself at embarrassing length. The last lines had been written in those books years before. He would never open them again, having said all that he wished to say. Soon, they would go into the box and the box's lock would be set, to be opened only after he was gone.

The silence in the Archbishop's study was broken only by the sound of a freshly sharpened quill on parchment, as he wrote one last letter. In the servants' quarters downstairs, an

Obertus revenant waited to carry it to its destination in the south, a small nunnery in which the eldest and wisest of his surviving childer found shelter.

My beloved daughter, dearest of the comforts left to me in this world, I give greetings to you.

By the time this letter reaches your hand, I will have already departed Sredetz for the journey of which I spoke in my last missive to you. I am resolved in the course that I have chosen, and I write you this last time to thank you for the many years of companionship and wise counsel you have generously granted to me. The strength of your faith has sustained my own soul, during the darkest hours of my existence. Your calm words have soothed my heart and soul in the hours when I felt that no balm of comfort would ever ease my pain again. Were it not for the duty that I owe to my own dead, I would come to see you again, and lay a father's kiss on your brow, and wish you peace and joy in all the long years left to you.

Would that I might witness what you will become, and what you might accomplish, at your side.

But the fallen call to me softly, with voices that I cannot deny, and I must bring an ending to both their suffering and to my own.

I remain, and I shall always remain, your sire and your friend.

He gave the letter no signature. Instead, he dripped a medallion of deep red wax at the bottom of the page, and sealed it with the imprint of his house, his true house, not the signet of the Archbishopric of Nod. He tied the letter closed with a length of blue ribbon shot through with gold, his daughter's favorite colors, for they reminded her of the sky she had long ago forsaken.

Then, he blew out the light.

Part One

Dragon's Blood

Sângele apã nu se face.
(Blood is not water.)
—Romanian proverb

Chapter One

**Just outside Brasov,
Winter 1232**

The last snow of the winter was falling as the column made its way up the steep, circuitous road leading to the monastery. It departed Brasov late in the day—too late, strictly speaking, for absolute safety beneath the threatening sky—but nonetheless made good time on the frozen roads. When the last of the day's wan light failed, they lit torches and lanterns filled with fat tallow candles and continued on, albeit more slowly. They also released the diplomat traveling with them from her daylight conveyance and set her a-horse in the middle of their formation, protected on all sides yet in a position to display her importance to their mission. They refrained, however, from raising her standard into the stiffening wind. Her mount's barding, deep green silk marked with a many-petaled white rose, had to suffice on that score. A pair of senior officers, also traveling protected from the light of the sun, emerged as well and took their places near the head of the column.

From their vantage point atop the hill on which the monastery stood, the monks watched the column's progress and prepared. A message had arrived some days earlier, indicating the presence of the visitors and politely craving permission to approach concerning a matter of some urgency. After a suitable interval passed, that permission was formally and politely granted. The monks made ready, preparing pallets and sleeping spaces, and making certain adequate supplies were laid in to feed the guests and their mounts. By the time the column reached the top of the hill and came to the monastery's high, heavy doors, all was in readiness. As the column made its way into the monastery courtyard, dragging a heavy sledge loaded down with a wooden casket, those doors opened, and the superior came forth. In his gnarled hands he carried a friendship cup of blood, hot from the vein and steaming slightly in the chilly air. A half-dozen novices followed him out into the snowy courtyard and filtered among the armed and armored knights, assisting in dismounting, accepting reins and murmuring quietly to cold and disgruntled horses.

The ambassador dismounted with the aid of the column's commander and, after a fractional hesitation, handed her reins to the novice who offered his assistance. She lifted the hem of her heavy winter skirts and swept forward, her carriage regal, bending her spine only to offer the elderly superior the courtesy he was due. He responded with equal gravity, bowing carefully from the shoulders, and extending to her the greeting-cup. When he spoke, his voice was unexpectedly stentorian, showing almost no sign of his physical age. "Welcome, friends and brothers, most honored sister, to the house of God. Welcome, in the name of my Lord Vykos, who stands ready to greet you. Welcome, and be safe and sheltered within our walls."

Rosamund d'Islington rose and accepted the cup, taking the sip that courtesy required. "We accept Lord Vykos' gracious hospitality in the name of our lord and prince, Jürgen of Magdeburg, and in our own. I am Lady Rosamund d'Islington, Ambassador of the Rose, and my companions are Sir Gilbrecht and Sir Landric, of the Order of the Black Cross." Each of the knights, in turn, accepted the cup and drank of it, both being well schooled enough to hide any distaste or distrust they might harbor for the gesture. A brown-robed novice accepted the cup and, bowing quickly to his superior, carried it inside quickly. "We seek counsel with Lord Vykos on a matter of some urgency, and not inconsiderable mystery."

One elegant hand, gloved in fur-lined leather, gestured down at the sledge and its burden. The old monk nodded gravely. "I am Father Aron. Come, my lady, and my brothers, my Lord Vykos awaits you."

It had been a long journey and Rosamund was already deeply, deeply tired. Traveling rough across half the east in the dead of winter was most assuredly not how she had hoped to begin the year, much less undertaking that journey with the intent of treading deep into the lands of the *Voivodate*. The laboriously negotiated truce between Jürgen of Magdeburg and Vladimir Rustovitch held—tenuously, at times, given some of the provocations flung back and forth across the Obertus territories that lay between them—and Rosamund did not particularly relish the task of putting its elasticity to a serious test despite the love, and the duty, she bore her lord. She did not, even to herself, admit to fearing the task she was assigned. To do so was beneath her dignity as an ambassador of her clan, and a woman raised to rule. She was more than a little frightened, however, as she followed Father Aron through the halls of his monastery. She endeavored not to let it show in her posture or expression, and kept her emotions rigidly controlled, lest someone with keener eyes than most notice her discomfiture.

Even in the west, tales circulated of Tzimisce savagery, the brutality of their rule and the horrors that they wrought with their unnatural magics. Rosamund, as a youngster newly come to the blood, had listened to those tales the way mortal girls listened to their grandmothers' ghost stories, half-afraid and half-laughing, in every way certain that those tales were as exaggerated as the *lais* in a book of romances. She knew the truth now, and if the truth was more complex than the frightful tales of wandering storytellers, there was still enough horror in the reality to justify caution.

Rosamund refused to admit to fear, even inside the walls of the dragon's den – though she was forced to admit that this particular dragon seemed far more civilized than most. They had met once in Magdeburg, she and Myca Vykos. The impressions that she retained of that brief encounter were of a man whose graceful use of language nearly matched the diplomats of her own clan, whose intelligence and grasp of subtle political nuance gave a certain lie to the tales of simple-minded Tzimisce barbarity. Rosamund hoped profoundly that those impressions were true, for what she needed to deal with now was a politician and a diplomat, not a warlord.

Father Aron opened one of the doors branching off the main corridor, revealing a staircase descending in a slow, gentle curve. Rosamund lifted the hem of her kirtle and followed, summoning to mind, for the thousandth time since leaving home, everything she knew about Tzimisce greeting protocols. The sum total of this knowledge, she realized early on, was something less than satisfying and reassuring, but repetition of what she did know lent steadiness to her nerves. She also cherished a fleeting hope that a Tzimisce diplomat would be fractionally more tolerant of the lapses of ignorant foreigners than a Tzimisce warlord looking for an excuse to separate an ignorant foreigner's head from her shoulders.

The staircase terminated in a wider, shorter corridor at the end of which lay a highly vaulted doorway, lacking a door, but guarded by two towering figures swathed in heavy robes. They bore no obvious weapons or, beyond their great height, any obvious sign of deformity—both stood a head and more taller than her knightly escorts. At the doorway, Father Aron paused and nodded politely to them both. They returned the gesture, and permitted him to pass. Rosamund followed the priest's lead, offering each figure a suitable curtsey, and her escorts both bowed. They were motioned through without further ceremony. Rosamund half expected to be led to an antechamber where she would be required to wait an interminable length of time until her host saw fit to allow her into his exalted presence. It was the sort of tactic used extensively by the western princes whose means of establishing dominance she was most familiar with, and she suspected that some things held true everywhere. It was therefore with considerable surprise that Rosamund found herself stepping into a small but luxuriously appointed receiving chamber, confronting Father Aron's bent back as he knelt in supplication before a low-backed wooden chair and the man occupying it. Myca Vykos was much as she remembered him, which came as a bit of a surprise, given the Tzimisce tendency to alter their forms at whim—she could not recall another Tzimisce of her acquaintance, though there were precious few of those, who was entirely the same every time they appeared at court. The flesh-shaping arts of the Fiends could be used in manners subtle and grotesque. It was Rosamund's experience that grotesque seemed to predominate among many in the clan, and the possibility that some short-tempered barbarian might choose to warp and twist her own flesh for some imagined offense never failed to fill her with dread. It was oddly comforting to set eyes on a man who seemed to change himself so little.

Even seated, he seemed tall, though not so tall as her Lord Jürgen. He was slender and well formed, his black hair loose, unadorned, and trailing over one shoulder. His features were sharp and fine, if saturnine. His dark eyes set deep beneath slightly arched brows, the shape of his mouth suggesting he spent little time smiling. His hands, ringed in gold, rested on the carven arms of his chair, long-fingered, slender, and completely devoid of nervous gestures. Rosamund dropped her eyes before those hands, and the elegant clothing he wore, drew her in more deeply than she wished.

Next to that chair knelt the brown-robed novice, still holding the friendship-cup she had drunk from, and who now offered that cup to the object of Father Aron's veneration. It was accepted, and Myca Vykos rose in a swirl of heavy Byzantine robes, drawing her forward into the room with a languidly regal gesture of greeting. "My Lady Rosamund, my Lord Gilbrecht, my Lord Landric, I offer you welcome in the name of my sire, in the name of the house in which dwells the blood of my making, and in my own name as lord and protector of this place. Come among my people as friend and guest, and know that within my walls you shall receive all honor, peace, and safety. I swear this, in the holy names of Earth and Sky, and by the Waters of Life and Death."

And, so saying, he raised the cup to his lips and drained it. Rosamund, recognizing a ritual cue when she saw one, offered her deepest court presentation curtsey. After a moment's hesitation, her companions offered their honors, as well. Lord Vykos, she noticed, actually acknowledged those gestures with a formal, ceremonial inclination of his head, before gesturing them to rise. Father Aron and the cupbearer both rose as well and took the opportunity to excuse themselves, returning the way they had all come.

"My Lady Rosamund," Lord Vykos stepped forward to claim her hand and kiss it quite properly, "no amount of graceless flattery on my part could truly encompass my pleasure at seeing you again. Our conversations in Magdeburg remain one of the finest memories I possess of that time. That you have traveled so far while winter still lay on the land, however, suggests much to me concerning the urgency of your mission—and the chill in your hands suggests much about the lack of comfort on the road. I suggest," his dark eyes flicked back to gather up the two knights, whose expressions Rosamund could clearly imagine during this little speech, "that we repair to more pleasant quarters, where we may take our comfort and break our fast."

"What a delightful suggestion," Rosamund felt diplomatic honey coating her tongue again, and her feet on decidedly more solid ground. "Sir Gilbrecht and Sir Landric are—"

"Entirely welcome to join us, I assure you." Lord Vykos bowed from the neck. "The needs of your men are being tended to above. I doubt the matter requires the oversight of these illustrious gentlemen. Though if you prefer...?"

Rosamund half-turned; Sir Gilbrecht and Sir Landric exchanged a speaking glance. Neither knight, she knew, was particularly comfortable entrusting the welfare of their men to Tzimisce hospitality, and with good reason. In another season, the truce might be a thing of smoke and history, with fire and bloodshed taking the place of relative peace. Rosamund privately hoped it would not be so, for entirely selfish reasons. She and Jürgen had already been separated for quite long enough, and a lengthy campaign against an entrenched, intractable Tzimisce enemy would simply add to the distance between them. She also knew that her escorts harbored no such hesitancy, and in all likelihood regarded their presence here as the perfect opportunity to engage in a bit of espionage by way of diplomacy—in such ways were wars won and lost. By such ways were Tzimisce lords offering hospitality also insulted beneath their own roofs and Rosamund hoped that her escorts were adroit enough to realize that without an actual lecture from her.

Sir Gilbrecht, the senior of the two knights, bowed stiffly after a long moment and spoke. "My lord, my brother and I are pleased to accept your gracious hospitality."

Rosamund was pleased. He managed to get the entire sentence out as though he weren't holding a dead fish in his mouth, and the somewhat pained grimace that followed Lord Vykos politely chose to ignore.

Chapter Two

"We are entertaining no other Cainite guests this season, my lady, or else I would have had a larger dining chamber opened and aired." Lord Vykos informed her, as he guided them down a gently curving side corridor that, unless her senses were entirely deceiving her, actually slanted deeper beneath the hill. "It is my hope that you will not consider this setting untoward in its intimacy. The halls can be cold and damp in the winter, and I ordered this chamber specially warmed. My advisor warned me last evening that the weather was likely to turn, and it might even snow. I see that he was correct."

"Indeed," Rosamund agreed, allowing a certain amount of rue to color her words. "While there are many natural things of beauty here in the East, my Lord, I find that one can rapidly grow weary of the sight of snow falling, particularly when it begins falling in October and does not cease falling until April."

They spoke, of course, Latin, the one language that Rosamund was certain they had in common. Her many months assisting Jovirdas, her lord's renegade Tzimisce vassal, improving his literacy and penmanship had taught her some small amount of his native tongue, though she in no way felt herself conversationally fluent. Likewise, she was uncertain if Lord Vykos spoke French and she rather doubted that he spoke English. She knew that he spoke German well enough to not insult Jürgen with his efforts, but if the choice came down between Latin and German, well, Latin won, each and every time.

"The winters have been unusually harsh of late." The statement was bland, but something in it caught Rosamund's ear, and she gave her host a covert look out of the corner of her eyes.

"Such things come and go, of course, but that does not prevent one from wishing for the warm breath of spring—or from wishing that the spring might never end."

There was some subtle double entendre couched in that statement, Rosamund was certain of it. She would have to interrogate Jovirdas about Tzimisce customs regarding the seasons when she returned to Kybartai. For now, however, she simply temporized. "Or even for the crisp autumn nights by the fire, with the floor scattered in colorful leaves..."

"Even so." They came to the end of the corridor, a tall square door draped in a long woolen hanging, which he graciously lifted to allow them entry. A warm breath of air rushed out to meet them. "Come, my lady, my lords. Your rest awaits."

Rosamund stepped inside, and understood immediately Lord Vykos' remark about untoward intimacy. The room was small and roughly semicircular, and its shape focused attention into its center, where sat a low wooden table, a profusion of colorful cushions, and a young god. Rosamund recognized him immediately—the companion that Lord Vykos had brought with him years before when negotiating the cessation of hostilities between Jürgen and Rustovitch—and struggled to recall his name in an effort to avoid falling into his beauty. He did not make it easy, rising from his nest of cushions and furs, unashamedly naked but for the heavy length of his red-golden hair and a few tasteful pieces of jewelry, beaten gold set with red amber from the north. The firelight gilt his flawless skin and revealed the depth of color in his hair as he bowed politely and greeted her by name. "Lady Rosamund."

Rosamund could *feel* her aura flushing. "My Lord Ilias," she managed, after a moment of awkward silence, and offered a courtesy of her own. "It is... quite excellent to see you again."

He laughed, the sound holding a genuine mirth untainted by any trace of mockery, and he crossed the room to claim his kiss, ignoring her hand completely in favor of kissing her once on each cheek. Rosamund closed her eyes and sent a brief but heartfelt prayer to the Virgin to lend her strength. "You cannot fool me, cousin. You entirely forgot about me, and I can hardly fault you for it. Much... excitement surrounded our last meeting, after all. Come, those robes you wear might as well be ice, and we've guest-robes for you warming in the next room. By the Mother, your hands are half-frozen!"

He caught her thoroughly chilled hand in his warmed one and led her into the room, a small voice of caution in the back of her mind—which sounded suspiciously like Jürgen—reminding her urgently that a Tzimisce's most terrible weapon was often his hands. It was not, however, a very loud voice and easily ignored against the chatter of her guide and the opulence of her surroundings. The floor, what little she could see of it, appeared to be cut stone beneath its covering of cushions and furs. The walls were likewise stone hung with panels of fabric, alternating between deep, rich jewel tones and the patterned fabrics that reminded her of Lord Vykos' Byzantine origins. Only where a large fireplace, burning a merry blaze, pierced it was the dark stone of the walls clearly visible, and there the flue was carved into a kind of relief, what seemed to be two figures twining in a decidedly erotic fashion. Rosamund couldn't decide if she was amused or appalled by that, or entirely what to make of either her host or his companion. Jürgen was almost entirely indifferent to such things as cold or relative comfort, and rarely bothered with the time or the expense of warming himself unnecessarily, usually only choosing to do so when interacting with the mortal brethren of the Black Cross who were ignorant of their lord's true nature. The preservation of ignorance did not appear to be a motive here. Comfort? It crossed her mind that the Tzimisce adhered often to pagan faiths that enshrined sensuality and self-indulgence as virtues.

"My Lady Rosamund!" Sir Gilbrecht's voice was quite strangled, cutting across Ilias' cheerful banter and ringing off the walls like the lingering sound of a slap. "Are you certain this is... appropriate?"

In fact, Rosamund was not at all certain of the proprieties involved, but had no idea how to communicate that information to Sir Gilbrecht without looking an absolute fool. Lord Vykos' companion saved her both the effort and the embarrassment. He turned and swept a single glance over the knight, replying, coolly, "My lord, you are a guest in the house of *stapân* Myca

Vykos, childe of Symeon of Byzantium, childe of Gesu, childe of the Dracon, first prince of the blood, most-beloved of the Eldest. You, your brother, and my Lady Rosamund have traveled far in a harsh season to visit us. Do you suggest that we show you honor less than we would our own kin, who had undertaken such a journey and sheltered within our walls?"

Sir Gilbrecht's mouth tightened and, for a moment, Rosamund actively feared that he was about to say something abysmally foolish. He was saved from that fate himself by the timely intervention of Sir Landric, who stepped firmly on his foot and hissed something at him in a colloquial Germanic dialect, so quickly and so slurred with accent that even she couldn't catch it completely. Sir Gilbrecht glanced over his shoulder at their host, who had entered quietly at his back, and sketched a stiff, ungraceful bow. "My... apologies. I meant no offense."

"And no offense is taken," Lord Vykos accepted the apology, smoothly, for what it was and, Rosamund guessed, what it was not. "Your ways are not ours, and some confusion is, regrettably, inevitable. My advisor, Ilias cel Frumos, merely wishes to do Lady Rosamund the honor she deserves. I trust this is acceptable?"

"It is," Rosamund replied firmly, before either of the two knights could respond, "completely acceptable. Lead on, my lord."

"Of course." They crossed the room to the left of the enormous fireplace, and Lord Ilias lifted one of the profusion of hangings to reveal a small antechamber, lit by an oil lamp bracketed to the wall. Its furnishings were simple, a wooden bench, a wooden chest, and a small table on which stood an earthenware basin and a steaming earthenware pitcher, along with a selection of cloths. Against the wall closest to the fireplace a number of wooden pegs held what appeared to be several lengths of cloth. A young woman clad in a simple tunic rose and offered a shallow bow by way of greeting; Rosamund guessed her to be a body-servant. She recalled Jovirdas' commentary on and instructions for dealing with such creatures, the sum of which indicated they should be regarded and treated almost as furniture. Most of them were, in Jovirdas' estimation, likely to be young revenants—the hereditary ghouls bred by some Tzimisce families—being taught some lesson concerning the nature of humility and service. Rarely were they merely human.

"Guest-garments. Refresh yourself as you will, my lady, and place your clothing in the chest. It will be cleaned and returned to you before you depart."

Lord Ilias let the hanging fall at her back and, beyond it, she heard him addressing her knightly escorts in a German so flawless it could hardly fail to provoke them. Rosamund could not help but smile, somewhat wryly, as she shed her cold-starched kirtle with the aid of the servant and waited as she poured a basin of warmed water. She wished, not for the first time on this journey, that it was her brother Josselin traveling with her and not two knights of the Black Cross for, while they were reliable in a fight, they lacked polish otherwise, and were far too naked in their distrust of Tzimisce notions regarding hospitality, despite everything they knew about how seriously such things were regarded by their hosts. Josselin she could have trusted to take this entire situation in stride and, in all likelihood, enjoy himself enormously. Josselin, unfortunately, remained in France at the command of their sire, Queen Isouda, and Rosamund was forced to make do with what she had.

The girl silently sponged Rosamund's neck, breasts, arms, and back, then patted her dry carefully. The water was lightly perfumed, and the ambassador thought she caught the scent of a sweet spring flower clinging to her skin. *Linden blossom*, she realized after a moment, and recalled a rhyme she had heard the girls singing even in Magdeburg, about linden blossoms and their power to summon the love of one's heart. She rather doubted she would step through the curtain to find Jürgen waiting for her, but the romantic fancy of it made her smile anyway. The girl took the first of the "guest-garments" down from its peg and dropped it over Rosamund's head, aiding her in finding the arms and draping it correctly. She nearly purred in pleasure as the cream-white silk—or linen so fine it felt like silk—ankle-length tunic settled against her body with its tightly fitted sleeves and a woven-in decoration of leaves and vines at neck, hem, and wrists. A second, looser garment went over top, also silk but in a deep, flattering shade of green, heavily decorated at the throat and its trailing sleeves, thick gold thread stiffening the fabric and holding a small fortune in amber and pearls. A girdle of carved plaques, solid gold and bound together with lengths of fine golden chain, went around her waist and slippers of silk embroidered in more gold and tiny seed pearls went onto her feet.

I believe there are some Tzimisce customs that I will suggest my Lord Jürgen adopt at once, Rosamund thought, running a finger over the embroidery gracing her breast, stepping out into the dining room at the servant's motion, holding aside the hanging. To her amusement, she emerged to find Sir Gilbrecht and Sir Landric similarly clad, having been separated from their cross-marked surcotes, if not their weapons, sitting uncomfortably cross-legged in a nest of cushions and black bear-furs on one side of the small table. Lord Vykos sat at the head of the table, entirely at his ease, his legs tucked neatly beneath him on one large, flat cushion, apparently unconcerned, conversing quietly with the knights and receiving minimal responses to his gambits. Lord Ilias reclined at the opposite end of the table, still adorned in his many fine pieces of jewelry but covering the finest of them in a long, loose, sleeveless tunic, dark red in color and nearly as heavily decorated as Rosamund's own. The maidservant guided Rosamund to the table, where she was seated in a nest of silk-covered cushions and her lap covered in a warmed fur of brindled ermine; the servant then bowed to her lord, received a quiet word of instruction from him, and excused herself, leaving through the same door by which they'd entered.

"The refreshments will be with us presently," Lord Vykos informed them. "I trust that all is to my Lady's satisfaction thus far?"

"Entirely, my Lord. You are almost too gracious." Rosamund assured him, arranging her legs in such a way that the layers of her clothing concealed all but the tips of her slippers from view. "We were, I admit, expecting a much cooler reception given the…nature of the events that caused us to travel here."

Lord Vykos held up a hand in a dismissive gesture. "A guest

is to be treated with all honor, and welcomed freely whether he is a much-loved kinsman or a dire foe. It is one of the oldest customs of the clan, which we, at least, hold dear even to this night."

"At least?" Rosamund inquired delicately, running her hands through the furs to warm the joints of her fingers.

"What *stapân* Vykos means, my lady, is that you chose your route well." Ilias' tone was tinged, again, with a certain amusement. "You managed to skirt quite nicely through the territories of those who continue to honor the old ways of the clan. Ioan Brancoveanu may have no love of your Lord Jürgen, but he holds his own honor too dear to defile it by mistreating a traveler who walks his borders bearing a flag of truce. Had you been brought before him, he would have hosted you the three days and three nights hospitality required of him, and escorted you unmolested to his border. You did, however, come rather close to crossing into territories that might have greeted you in a somewhat less than civilized fashion. You are fortunate to have avoided that fate."

"And it is equally fortunate that we do not have to explain to Lord Jürgen what became of you in such an eventuality." Lord Vykos added, in a tone so neutral as to be expressionless. "I suggest, my lady, that you not leave your return route to the sort of fortune you enjoyed traveling to us. If it is not offensive to you, I will have a detachment of my own guide you back to friendly territories when you depart."

Rosamund realized that she had her hands clenched in the furs draped across her lap, and forced her fingers to relax. "It was my understanding, Lord Vykos, that you are a vassal to the *voivode* of *voivodes*, Vladimir Rustovitch, and that it was by his authority that you secured the peace between my Lord Jürgen and the *Voivodate*. Is that not so? Would that agreement not protect an emissary, no matter whose territory she might travel through?"

Lord Vykos gazed at her for so long, his face so carefully empty of response, that for a moment she was certain she had mortally offended him. When he spoke, his voice was likewise flawlessly expressionless, the mask of diplomacy fitting even over his words. "That perception, my Lady Rosamund, is entirely incorrect. I am in no way a vassal to Vladimir Rustovitch. He does not command me, nor do I bend knee to him. I serve my sire, Symeon, the head of the Obertus Order, and I serve the interests of my line. I acknowledge no other master." A smile so faint as to be little more than imagination touched the corners of his mouth. "Vladimir Rustovitch has enough lickspittles among his own lineage to salve his wounded pride. And as to the *Voivodate?* Lord Jürgen made his agreement with Rustovitch and myself—I did not, at any point, claim to speak for any of the other elders who hold territory in this region. Even Rustovitch does not claim to speak for more than himself and his closest blood-kin, no matter what titles he chooses to gild himself with."

"I see." In truth, Rosamund *was* beginning to see, and what she perceived she did not like at all. "Do you mean to say that—"

A soft chime sounded from outside the room, and the door-hanging lifted, admitting a double handful of comely youths, male and female, none apparently older than sixteen and all clad in the most minimal of coverings. They arranged themselves in a loose semi-circle around the table and waited silently. Out of the corner of her eye, Rosamund caught a glint of color as Ilias shifted, and sat up. "Oh, good. Conversation is always so much better with dinner. Do you not agree, Lady Rosamund?"

"At court occasions in the west, that is, indeed, how we prefer to dine." Rosamund replied, with as much serenity as she could muster, her mind racing as she considered, and reconsidered, the situation.

"Excellent. Since it is too late for me to suggest no politics at table, I will instead suggest no religion." Lord Ilias, Rosamund realized, was the only Cainite she had ever met whose default expression actually seemed to be a smile.

"I believe we all find that suggestion agreeable." Lord Vykos interjected, dryly, with another bow from the neck to the two knights. "It is the custom among my people that guests receive first rights to sustenance. Choose as you will."

Both knights glanced at Rosamund and she, realizing their deference in this matter was wholly appropriate, examined the offerings. While they were all somewhat young, none appeared to be fearful, and none showed any obvious signs of maltreatment or deformation. In fact, they had the definite look of being well fed and freshly scrubbed and, in several cases, almost excited. Impulsively, Rosamund chose one of those, a well-favored young man with crisp brown curls and smoke-gray eyes, who in no way resembled or reminded her of her lord. He slipped beneath her fur with a slightly crooked smile and a bow from the neck, though he did not speak. Sir Gilbrecht curtly motioned to a tall frost-blonde boy, who joined him with extraordinary grace and dignity, and Sir Landric selected a plump girl whose black hair and smooth brown skin suggested a foreign origin. Lord Ilias chose a small, slender, dark-haired boy, apparently a favorite of some standing, for he quite boldly laid himself across his patron's lap. Ilias laid a hand on his hip and murmured something to him that made him smile. Lord Vykos also appeared to prefer blondes, as his selection was a girl with sun-golden curls who sat herself very carefully at his side, neither touching him nor making any effort to do so. The remainder bowed politely and filed out without comment.

"A blessing, I think, is in order." Lord Ilias suggested genially, tracing a pattern on the white flesh of his companion with the tip of one finger. "We give thanks to all the gods who care to listen for the presence of our guests, their safe journey and joyful stay, and for the service of those who offer themselves for our sustenance, in the name of Earth and Sky, and the Waters of Life and Death."

A heartbeat passed, then, making the best of it, Sir Landric uttered, "Amen." Rosamund and Sir Gilbrecht echoed him an instant later. Rosamund's companion proved to be both enthusiastic and helpful, silently offering her a variety of areas from which she might feed, though she required him to leave his tunic on. She drank lightly, once from his throat and thereafter sipped from the veins in his wrist, being careful not to take too much. His blood was beguilingly sweet and unusually strong. His warmth pressed against her beneath the furs was almost as pleasant as tasting him. A moment passed in which no conversation passed as everyone sampled the fare. Sir Gilbrecht bit deeply and without ceremony into the wrist of his ice-colored companion, who closed his eyes as though enduring stoically rather than experiencing the pleasure of the Kiss. Sir Landric's pretty brown girl giggled, the first sound to escape any of their companions. Lord Ilias' boy quivered and moaned softly, his cheeks flushed rosy, visibly aroused and pleasured before fang pierced flesh. Rosamund had no idea how Ilias accomplished it, since he did nothing but keep a hand resting lightly on the boy's shoulder. Lord Vykos' companion offered a wrist with an air of ceremony and, just as formally, he drank lightly of her, let her take her hand back, and did not touch her again.

"I trust our humble offering suits?" Lord Vykos asked, pitching the question to the table in general and receiving a chorus of quiet affirmatives in reply. "Excellent."

"The only thing we seem to be lacking is appropriate dinner music," Lord Ilias observed, in a tone of one musing aloud. "If I recall correctly, Lady Rosamund, your honorable brother, Sir Josselin, has quite a lovely voice."

"That he does." Rosamund admitted, thinking, *Would that he were here.*

"Would that he were here," Lord Ilias echoed, and Rosamund had to physically suppress a start of surprise. "I had hoped to see him again under civilized circumstances." And, so saying, he finally took his companion, bending to suckle gently at the boy's throat. Sir Gilbrecht's companion's eyes locked on them and refused to let go until Lord Ilias leaned back again, licking a rich red drop from the corner of his lips. "And I heard, just recently, a song that would suit his voice perfectly."

Rosamund cast a quick, quelling glance at her knightly escorts and replied, evenly, "You may yet meet him under civilized circumstances, my lord. No one knows what the future may bring."

"You are, indeed, a diplomat, cousin." Lord Ilias twined his fingers in his companion's hair and stroked gently. "But even you must admit that the future is unlikely to be scattered with rose petals and filled with song. Especially given your mission to us, which I doubt was motivated by any happy circumstance."

"I admit, the cause of my mission is not entirely... pleasant... but that does not mean the end results must be destructive.

I seek, in fact, to avoid a breach in the good will that exists between the Obertus Order and my Lord Jürgen." Which was, she thought, one of the finest bits of extemporaneous deceit she had ever managed. "My Lord Vykos, if it pleases you..."

He made a slight gesture of assent. "Say on."

"The cause that brings me here is simply this: my Lord Jürgen, operating under information from a source he deemed reliable, was forced to assail the walls of an Obertus monastery in Ezerelis." Lord Vykos' posture stiffened, subtly but unmistakably, and Lord Ilias sat up fully. Across from her, Sir Gilbrecht looked grimly pleased at that reaction, and Sir Landric kept his own face as still as possible. "Intelligence had come to him that this monastery had been suborned in service to the *voivode* of *voivodes*, and was passing information on the movement of my lord's men in the area, thus placing them at great risk. My Lord Jürgen determined to remove this threat and, lacking the time necessary to contact my Lord Vykos, raided the monastery and took it."

"I see." Those two words held a world of knowledge, indeed. Rosamund could nearly see the thoughts running behind the Tzimisce's eyes and she wished she dared look at his colors.

"My Lord Jürgen wished to give the Obertus Order as a whole no insult, nor do it any harm, but he had no choice other than to act." The look that Lord Vykos gave her in response to that was utterly opaque; Lord Ilias' mouth was set in the wryest of smiles, as though the disaster he'd been expecting had finally struck, and now he could relax. "And, in truth, he found something quite interesting at the monastery itself."

"Proof of rampant Obertus perfidy, justifying his action, perhaps?" Lord Ilias asked and earned himself a glare from Sir Gilbrecht.

"Hold your tongue," the knight growled, only barely managing not to add a string of descriptive epithets, Rosamund was quite sure.

"Sir Gilbrecht." Rosamund layered equal parts steel and reproof into her tone. "Lord Ilias is one of our hosts. If we expect the laws of hospitality to be honored, it is best that we not breach the laws of comity, do you not think?"

Sir Gilbrecht tendered a relatively graceless apology, which Lord Ilias accepted with the slightest inclination of his head. Rosamund continued. "What my Lord Jürgen found was a high-ranking Cainite heretic who had, evidently, suborned the monastery and its residents to his service." She paused to allow that time to sink in. Out of the corner of her eye, she caught Lord Ilias casting Lord Vykos a genuinely startled look, before he disciplined his face. Lord Vykos himself inclined a single inquiring eyebrow, for him a dramatic display of surprise. "In fact, the Heretic was none other than the Archbishop of Nod himself, Nikita of Sredetz."

Chapter Three

Myca Vykos read the letter Jürgen of Magdeburg sent along with his envoy for perhaps the fifth time, as though another repetition could extract more sense from it. He was, frankly, perplexed by the entire situation—the sudden arrival of Rosamund d'Islington with the torpid body of Nikita of Sredetz literally in tow, the delicately worded half-accusation he held in his hand, vis-à-vis the presence of a known Cainite heretic in a monastery belonging to the Obertus Order. It took all his self-control not to grind his fangs as he considered it. He could almost picture, could, in fact, *feel*, the satisfaction with which Jürgen had dropped this problem in his lap. That satisfaction was rendered doubly obnoxious by the fact that the grasping self-righteous bastard had the unadulterated *gall* to squat in the very monastery he had seized on the thinnest possible pretext, sending forth letters and envoys like a prince in truth and not the minion of a creature even more avaricious than himself; namely, his sire Hardestadt. The strength of the sudden antipathy was breathtaking and, for an instant, Myca allowed himself to savor it, enjoying the sensation of hot, perfect loathing churning beneath his breastbone and the desire of his Beast to smite the arrogant little warlord and remind him of his place.

Perhaps later, he promised, and the Beast subsided into a quiet contemplation of the havoc it might be permitted to wreak. Jürgen of Magdeburg's envoy was defended by traditions far older than the present conflict but Myca had no doubt that his sire, Symeon, would be at least as displeased by this current turn of events as he was. And Symeon was a past master of the sort of protracted personal and political vengeances that would make even Hardestadt, who dared name himself *monarch*, yield rather than continue suffering them.

The door thudded quite deliberately against its stops, drawing him from his contemplation of the missive laid out on his writing table. Ilias smiled faintly and shrugged out of the tunic he'd donned in deference to their guests' modesty. "I somehow feel, my flower, that Lady Rosamund's bodyguards do not like me very much."

"They are Teutons, Ilias. They have no taste. Pay them the same heed you would an ill-mannered lout of our own blood." He refolded the letter and set it aside for the moment. "Our guests are settled? The accommodations are to their liking?"

"Our guests are settled. Lady Rosamund, at least, accepted the bed-servant warming her sheets in the spirit that the gesture intended." Ilias rolled his eyes heavenward, in a silent plea for strength and tolerance in the face of stiff-necked vampires of few redeeming qualities. "I suspect our knightly friends were offended that we didn't strip the guest quarters to bare walls and floors, and provide them with a rock for a pillow."

"I have never claimed to understand the manias of the desperately righteous." Myca extended a hand and Ilias took it, allowing himself to be drawn close against the side of his lover, bending to claim the kiss he had denied himself all evening. When they broke apart, Myca took up the letter and handed it over. "Here. I crave your thoughts on this matter."

With great ceremony, Ilias seated himself on the comfortably padded bench and leaned a bit closer to the candle lamp to examine the missive, reading it once through quickly, then going back over it again, more closely. After a long moment of consideration, he looked up and remarked, conversationally, "I think it quite obvious that Lord Jürgen has sold his soul."

Myca felt the corners of his mouth twitching and sternly told them to behave. "Dare I ask what brings you to that conclusion?"

"Only a man gifted with the most diabolical fortune could break a treaty on a pretext this thin, and still find a provocation like Nikita of Sredetz to justify his actions. Therefore, his soul can no longer be his own. It is the only logical explanation." Ilias refolded the letter and placed it in the open correspondence chest, shaking his head. "That, and I marvel anew at the rampant ignorance of the Ventrue. You, Rustovitch's *vassal*? The man has spent the better part of the last twenty years at war with the illustrious *voivode* of *voivodes*. One might think he would learn something from that."

"I fear that Lord Jürgen's logic has always been rather susceptible to the sway of self-interest." Myca replied, dryly. "And while I cannot speak with authority concerning the disposition of his soul, I think you are fundamentally correct. Lord Jürgen felt himself unduly constrained by the strictures of the treaty he and his honor agreed to uphold, and so found an excuse in his own mind to justify breaking it. It is either diabolical good fortune on his part, or malignant poor fortune on ours, that put Nikita of Sredetz there for him to find. What, precisely, the Archbishop of Nod was doing in our territory is a… separate and distinct consideration."

"Your sire will no doubt be thoroughly displeased."

"No doubt. I shall write him tomorrow, after I have interrogated Lady Rosamund more fully. May I rely on you, my heart, to entertain our other guests while she and I speak privily?"

Ilias smiled, his cat-smile of greatly anticipated pleasure. There were, Myca knew, few things Ilias enjoyed more than tormenting the sanctimonious minions of the Black Cross. "I am quite certain that I can provide some appropriate activity to while away the long winter hours. And, speaking of appropriate activities…"

"Yes?"

"Nico and Sergiusz are keeping the bed warm for us. I, for one, would like to end this evening in a much more pleasing fashion than it began." He offered a hand, and a smile of invitation.

Myca accepted both, with a small smile of his own. "Lead on, oh my teacher."

Myca Vykos knew this was a dream. He had never walked the streets of Constantinople by day.

The dark waters of the Marmora shimmered in an endlessly shifting pattern of golden radiance, rushing past the Blachernai sea walls, beating against the marble breakwaters, throwing gilt spray and churning up gilt foam. Beneath his long-fingered hands and his silk-slippered feet, the stones of the sea wall were warm yet with the captured heat of a high summer day. They shone, as well, pale marble veined with gently pulsating golden light. He looked about, and found the Blachernai palace garden spread around him, every plant and every fountain, every graveled path and exquisitely placed statue, burning from inside with a fierce and holy light that should have wounded him, but did not, that should have reduced him to ash, but left him whole.

He walked, each stride consuming miles. He passed harbors filled with ships and bustling with their passengers and crews, he passed quiet piers where fishermen dragged ashore their catches. He passed monuments to imperial glory that had endured since the fall of Rome and the humblest tenements in the poorest corners of the city and the houses that belonged only to God. He passed through the marketplaces great and small, and he walked the length of the Mese, from one end of the city to the other. He saw everything there was to see of it—everything sacred, everything profane.

And all of it was perfect. It burned from within, so perfect was the city and all who dwelt in it. Its light shone through the skin of stone and the skin of flesh—imperishable, eternal. He knew it for absolute truth when he came before the great walls of the Hagia Sophia, and saw its dome shining with the light of the rising sun, filling the arch of the heavens with the city's glory.

He wept then, and fell to his knees, and bowed down in homage that he would offer to nothing and no one else.

Myca came back to himself slowly, warned by the heaviness in his limbs and the sluggishness of his thoughts that the sun was not yet below the horizon. The bedchamber was wholly dark, the night lamp no doubt extinguished hours before by the bedservants. All around him, darkness pressed in, thick and damp with winter chill. His cheeks were wet, and his skull swam with equal parts uneasiness and exhaustion. He felt as though he had not slept at all. It took all his concentration to raise his free hand and wipe away the tears. His lover slept pressed against him beneath the bed-furs, head pillowed on his shoulder, golden-red curls spread across his chest and throat. His hand found those curls and tangled itself in them; despite the inner disquiet that woke him, he found himself soothed by their softness, the gentle scent of linden blossom that rose at his touch.

Ilias stirred slightly in response, curling closer, his face tilting up though his eyes still refused to open. After a moment's effort, he managed to form words. "Myca? Is something wrong?"

For a moment, Myca seriously considered lying, and lulling Ilias back to sleep with a kiss, but such a thing was unworthy of the bond between them. Ilias *knew*, with perfect certainty, when someone he loved was in pain, and when he himself was being deceived. "I dreamed again. It is nothing. Truly."

A ripple of tension ran through Ilias' body, shaking away his lethargy; he lifted his head and whispered, "Do you remember what you dreamed?"

"No." He paused, reconsidered, answered again. "No, that is not wholly true. I remember that there was...light. A great light, terrible and glorious. Not the sun. It was not a death-dream. It was... something else."

"Something you feared?" Another whisper.

"Yes." Until Myca spoke the word aloud, he had not realized it was true.

"My flower." Ilias caught the hand tangled in his hair, and brought it to his lips. "Sometimes dreams are only dreams. Here and now, you have nothing to fear."

It was an attempt to distract and soothe him, and Myca knew it without the need for thought. Within himself, he was unsettled enough to do as Ilias wished, and let himself be comforted. A line of cool kisses crept up his arm and across the flat planes of his chest; a small, strong hand stroked his ribs gently, coaxed him to shift himself over, to lay on his side. It took a moment of effort, for daylight lethargy was only just leaving him, but once it was managed, he found it wholly pleasant to lie with his face pressed against a mixture of silken pillows and impossibly soft furs, while Ilias kissed every inch of his body between throat and navel. Ilias, Myca thought, was exceedingly fond of his navel and paid it generous attention with lips and tongue and jewelry when given permission. Ilias knew precisely where and how to touch him to arouse first the ghost of pleasure and then its reality. Ilias knew how to turn mere pleasure into blinding, soul-consuming ecstasy, a union of blood and spirit, flesh and mind.

This evening, pleasure was enough, comfort was enough. Soft kisses, gentle caresses, the delicate pressure of fangs behind lips and the sweet pain as they pierced his skin, then Ilias holding him as he sobbed quietly in reaction. Gentle words of endearment that he did not quite hear. Silence as they lay tangled together, furs and silks and naked skin blending.

Myca had absolutely no desire to move and Ilias' arms wrapped around him, Ilias' legs cupping his own, further discouraged him. "I should..."

"Should what?" Ilias pressed the last of the space from between their bodies. The warmth that he was so fond of had bled away some hours before, but tonight it hardly seemed to matter to him. Tonight there were better things than borrowed heat to make him feel less like a corpse on waking.

"Rise. We have guests. I should at least pretend to care about their welfare." Inwardly he admitted that seemed a distant concern.

"Nnn. Teutons. Invaders." Ilias perked up slightly. "Let the servants take care of them. That is why we have servants, after all."

"We have servants to take care of *us*, my heart." Myca began the protracted process of extracting himself from both Ilias' embrace and the bed-covers.

Promptly, a quiet scratch sounded at the door and two of those servants entered, one bearing a lit lamp and towels, the other carrying a basin and warmed wash-water. They laid their offerings out on the low table, retrieved clothing from the presses for both of their masters, and silently excused themselves, graceful, elegant, and swift in their competence. Myca completed the process of escaping and made use of the water while Ilias continued lounging in the nest of cushions, furs, and mingled earths that constituted their bed. "I am almost jealous."

"Jealous?" The servants had chosen well. The *tunica* and

hose they brought out were a deep and flattering shade of Tyrian purple bordered in thickly pearled golden embroidery, and the dalmatic itself was of purple and golden silk brocade. He suspected strongly that he would have Lady Rosamund's undivided attention.

"Yes, jealous. You are going to spend the evening entombed in the convivial company of the Lady Rosamund, while I will be preventing her bodyguards from making floor plans of the haven." Ilias sat up and stretched, and Myca paused to enjoy the sight. "Perhaps I should demand some form of recompense for my sacrifice."

"Perhaps you shall receive recompense, with or without a demand." Myca crossed the room, bent and kissed him quickly. "Have a care, my heart. I know you enjoy taunting them, but I suspect our knightly guests will endure such games poorly, and I mistrust their ability to control themselves in the face of… provocation."

"You and I are of one mind in this, I assure you," Ilias replied, wryly. "I think I will wear red. And confine my taunts to the game-table."

"Good." Myca turned to go.

"I have also decided what I desire for my reward, since I am to have one." The laziness in Ilias' tone was both tease and warning.

Myca paused at the door and glanced back over his shoulder. The cat-smile was still in place, and he was very much reminded of a great golden cat preparing to toy with its dinner. "And what might that be, my teacher?"

"Ah. An excellent choice of words." An indolent, fangs-baring smile. "A rite, I think. A girl resides in the larder, who I have been keeping for such an occasion. I selected her for her hair, which is a most unusual shade of red, and her age. Her family had one too many daughters." A pause, then, softly, "The Lady Rosamund is quite a lovely creature, do you not think?"

Myca closed his eyes for a moment, and contemplated the possibilities.

Chapter Four

"It was not, of course, present when my Lord Jürgen raided the monastery and only visited it well after the fact," Lady Rosamund informed him as they descended the staircase that led to the lowest levels of the monastery, beneath even the storage rooms and the windowless sleeping chambers of the resident Cainites. "From what I saw, there was very little damage though my lord's men were… a bit less than wholly respectful, I must admit."

"Conquerors are generally not respectful of the conquered." Myca replied, offering no reassurance and, in truth, feeling no need to make that offer.

Lady Rosamund was, for a moment, visibly uncomfortable before her diplomatic mask reasserted itself. "I would hardly define my Lord Jürgen as—"

"My Lady Rosamund, with all due respect, your Lord Jürgen has offended against the Obertus Order, the house of my blood, and the honor of myself and my sire. He has seized our territory on the thinnest pretext and murdered our chattels. He breached a treaty that he swore upon his own honor to uphold, for no logical reason that I can perceive beyond the satisfaction of his own relentless ambition." They came to the bottom of the stair, and he brought out a heavy iron ring of keys, one of which fit the lock of the door they faced. It swung open with a screeching complaint of rusty hinges. "Your Lord Jürgen has much to answer for, but it is not to me that he will answer. My lord sire Symeon will no doubt take a great interest in these events, for it is his honor as the ultimate guarantor of the treaty that Lord Jürgen chooses to defame, and he does not endure such insults kindly."

"Do you deny, then, that the Obertus Order had aught to do with the knowledge displayed by the *kunigaikstis* Geidas?" Lady Rosamund asked, with deliberate formality. He had no doubt that her temper was roused.

"That claim is, indeed, denied and, moreover, you have presented no evidence of its truth, Lady Rosamund." And, so saying, he stepped across the threshold and went about lighting the handful of lamps and candles that provided the illumination for Nikita's prison.

"Nikita..."

"Nikita is not a member of the Obertus Order. Nor, to my knowledge, does he serve Vladimir Rustovitch. The *voivode* of *voivodes* may be no Christian, but he is most assuredly no Heretic, either." A pause. "And Lord Jürgen was not hunting Heretics when he saw fit to violate the Obertus demesne."

The room was originally constructed as an adjunct to Myca's own private study, a storage room for the overflowing contents of his library, perfectly square and lined in bookshelves, several of which were as-yet empty. The small worktable was pushed back against one of them and the heavy wooden casket Nikita traveled in occupied the center of the room. Lady Rosamund stepped inside and looked curiously about; the three servants they had brought with them for protection, appropriate chaperonage, and heavy lifting entered behind her. They were all Obertus brothers, tonsured and simply clad in brown wool robes, and each was quite capable of protecting himself and the Lady Rosamund against most normal dangers. One of them carried an iron pole to open the casket, and the others carried a selection of stakes, most of them carefully carved of rowan, the wood deeply incised with pictorial symbols that Myca himself did not know how to decode. Ilias had made them earlier in the winter during an apparent fit of constructive boredom; Myca sensed the power invested in them, could not define its providence personally, but trusted the wisdom of their creator.

Myca motioned to the monk carrying the prybar. "Open it."

"My Lord Vykos, I do not think it entirely wise to free the... Archbishop." Lady Rosamund used the term with considerable distaste.

"I have no intention of freeing him. I wish to look on him and I wish you to confirm that he has, in fact, been delivered and received unharmed." Myca opened a drawer set in the edge of the table and extracted a half-filled workbook, flipping to a blank page. A handful of decent quills and a tiny blown-glass bottle of ink came out, as well. "Did Lord Jürgen locate any of the Archbishop's personal effects?"

"Yes." Lady Rosamund crossed the room and stood, somewhat uneasily, at his side as the monks went to work with the pry-bar. "He was, evidently, carrying a small correspondence chest, and a somewhat larger box with a rather complicated lock. No one managed to puzzle it out, and my lord thought it unwise to break it open. I brought them both in my own baggage."

"I will, of course, wish to see them." The iron spikes used to hold the casket's lid in place began giving with a screech that put his teeth on edge.

"If you wish, we can retrieve them now." Something in Lady Rosamund's tone suggested she would be glad to rid herself of those particular artifacts. Myca nodded, and one of the monks hurried out to accomplish that task. "My Lord Jürgen made certain to review the Archbishop's documents before we departed. It is his personal opinion, I know, that they will be of little use. Unless a very subtle and well-hidden cipher is involved, most of it was of relatively mundane nature, and much of it was also unfinished."

"No journal?" Myca inked his quill and began taking notes in his fine, careful hand.

"None that was found. No clothing, either, oddly enough—no vestments of office or anything of the sort." He cast a glance at her, and found her expression distant with recollection. "It is very odd. He dressed plainly when he passed through Chartres, more plainly than the Bishop St. Lys, at least, but he wore a cassock, and a ring. It is passing strange that he would travel without the symbols of his office."

"Unless he was making some attempt at secrecy, but, even so, you are correct. The ring, at least, he should have kept in his possession, even if he traveled otherwise incognito." Myca noted that point. "Could you describe the ring?"

Lady Rosamund shook her head. "I never saw it closely enough to make out details, but it was a heavy gold signet, and large. It took up most of the last knuckle on his ring-finger, and his hands were long."

"I should hate to imagine what you would notice if you *were* observing for detail, ambassador." He made a quick sketch and, as he finished, the last of the nails came free and the casket lid came off. "Come, my lady… let us see."

The Obertus brothers backed away, crossing themselves and murmuring quietly to each other in Greek. Myca offered Lady Rosamund his hand to clasp, if she wished, an honor she declined, and they stepped closer to view their prisoner. Nikita of Sredetz, Myca reflected distantly, had clearly not gone down without a fight. The Archbishop of Nod was not a tall man, but every inch of his body was rigid with tension, his hands hooked into rending claws, his face twisted in a rictus of emotion. A cascade of dark hair wound beneath his head. The robes he "wore" were wholly organic, the product of his own blood, flesh, and bone, and Myca recognized the work of a master flesh-sculptor in the elegant functionality of their lines despite the rents and tears of the violence done him. "My Lady Rosamund, is this the same man you saw in Chartres?"

"It appears so, yes. But appearances, as we both know well, can be deceptive." She hesitated fractionally, then drew closer, her expression becoming somewhat abstracted as she studied him closely. "I thought he might be wearing the ring, if it was not among his possessions, though my lord made no mention of it."

Myca let his own vision expand and refine, examining Nikita's physical shell closely, the shape of the bones in his face and his hands, the tension of the skin across his cheeks, brow, and throat. "He has been shaped but… the markings are very fine, almost invisible. I do not think he alters his form very often, or his flesh would show more obvious signs. Perhaps he chooses not to confuse his congregation on a nightly basis."

"Perhaps." The ambassador echoed. "My Lord Vykos, if there is nothing more you desire of me I fear I am finding this quite unsettling."

"No, my lady, I have no further questions of you, for now." He caught her hand and kissed it, properly, and bowed low to her, as well. "Brother Milos and Brother Antol will escort you to the oriel."

She curtseyed deeply, and departed, one monk leading and one monk following, with the perfect obedience to which they had been bred. Myca himself remained, alone and thoughtful, contemplating the man lying helpless before him. He did not, in fact, have any intention whatsoever of setting Nikita free, despite Lady Rosamund's fears to the contrary. Honoring the ties of blood kinship was a wonderful idea in theory but, in practice, it was substantially more convenient simply to keep the man as he was until some decision was made about what to do with him. Word had come to him from nearly all points west and east where he had colleagues and correspondents that the Cainite Heresy had fallen on hard times since the final destruction of Narses and Nikita's assumption of the Archbishopric of Nod. Heretical temples looted and burnt, heretical congregations put to the sword, heretical officials stumbling fatally in their efforts to win the hearts and minds of their fellow Cainites. The Archbishop of Nod himself apparently felt the situation dire enough to risk traveling from one end of Europe to the other in order to show his support for his struggling faith.

"When did you leave Sredetz, Nikita?" Myca murmured aloud, noting the question in his book, beneath a swiftly detailed sketch of the man's twisted face. "What induced you to leave the very bosom of your little nest of serpents? What is to be gained from keeping you safe?"

He refined his vision still further, pushing his sight past the bounds of the purely physical, until the concrete objects of the room became flat and lifeless, and only the torpid body of Nikita retained any reality, that reality defined by his soul. He was deeply withdrawn into himself, the essence of his being concentrated into a tiny, egg-shaped pool of radiance, shining faintly from deep within. His halo was so pale and weak, so devoid of emotion, that Myca nearly thought he imagined its existence. He absently laid aside his notebook and came closer, gaze drifting from Nikita's contorted face down the length of his body—and it was real. The Archbishop's halo was there, just impossibly faint, and deeply scarred in black. Relief welled up inside him, for some reason he could not adequately name, even to himself and, almost involuntarily, entirely impulsively, he rested his hand on the Archbishop of Nod's pale brow.

Nikita's hair was soft beneath his fingertips and the skin beneath his palm had the cool dryness of one who had spent freely of his strength without a chance to replenish himself. As Myca stood contemplating this, *something* leapt between them, a spark, a shock that sent itself all the way up his arm, and, in the instant, he knew precisely what he should do. He ran his hand over Nikita's face and throat, across his chest and the length of his body to his pale, unclad feet. When he finished, a shudder passed through him, nearly as strong as the sudden burst of understanding that possessed him, and he jerked his hand away, startled and disturbed. His grip on his sight shattered and his vision dissolved into normal realms of sensory perception.

Nikita's face, when he looked, was still and peaceful, emptied of its welter of emotions, and his body was eased of its painful tension, his hands lying open and empty at his sides. He looked as though he slept nestled in the earth of his own grave, beyond pain or fear, wholly at rest in body and spirit. Myca slowly backed away, his fingers working into his palms, feeling, for a moment, as though his hands belonged to someone else, the blood still stirring in his veins with the echo of what had passed between them. A silent communion.

He turned, and fled.

The oriel room was not really an oriel, but the residents of the monastery haven called it that for the touch of the exotic the term lent. It was not part of a tower, nor did it extend anywhere above ground. It was, however, perfectly round and the product of the architectural genius of the engineer-monk who designed the private dining chamber, and who had a passion for oddly shaped rooms. It consisted of two stories, the main floor and an upper gallery that connected to both the guest chambers and the private suites of the monastery's Cainite residents by means of a single corridor. The main floor was lit by lamps burning gently perfumed oil and warmed by strategically placed braziers, and its walls were draped in panels of heavy fabric that fell from the edge of the deeply vaulted roof to the floor. A gaming table and chairs occupied the center of the room, while large, flat floor pillows occupied the periphery for spectators and idle conversation. The second floor gallery doubled as a stage for the monastery's resident musicians.

Nicolaus, Ilias knew, would be completely useless for any task more arduous than lounging about and looking pretty given his exertions of the previous evening, and so that was the task he was given. Bathed and oiled, painted and perfumed, clad in red silk and gold, he was the very picture of beautiful indolence among the cushions of the musicians' loft where he sat, coaxing a sweet tune from a long wooden flute. His lover, fair silver Sergiusz, sat with him, a harp imported from the west in his lap, teasing accompaniment from its strings. They were both, Ilias admitted to himself, pale from the evening before but musical entertainment was well within their capabilities, and they rose skillfully to the challenge. He was quite pleased with both of them, and showed his pleasure by granting them both an extra taste of him. It put the bloom back in their cheeks. The oriel itself was constantly attended by four of the comeliest youths in the monastery's service, two male and two female, all of whom had also been freshly bathed and scented, were flawless in their comportment and excellent in their service, and under strict orders to give the masters' guests anything they required.

It was obvious from the start of the evening that Sir Gilbrecht had no particular interest in actually enjoying any of the many pleasures—or, for that matter, basically pleasant services—available to him. He lingered in the oriel only long enough to play a single round of draughts with Sir Landric, eye the servants with naked distaste, and request, somewhat brusquely, that he be permitted to speak with his mortal lieutenant. Ilias granted that request, but required a brace of Obertus brothers to accompany him at all times, a stipulation that irritated the man's already choleric temperament even further. Ilias failed to care, having little love of Teutons in general and even less for most of the minions of the Black Cross. Sir Landric, at his superior's gesture, remained behind and proved to be much more congenial company out from under the eye of Sir Gilbrecht, curious and talkative, while discussing nothing of substance. Ilias returned that favor, thinking it all to the best. They played two quick games of draughts, Sir Landric besting him soundly both times, and Ilias had just suggested backgammon when Lady Rosamund entered in the company of her Obertus escorts.

Ilias noticed at once that Lady Rosamund appeared a bit unsettled, which, considering that she'd just been subjected to Myca at his no-doubt less than diplomatic best, was not entirely surprising. He recalled also that the lady had a pronounced poor reaction to ugliness of any sort, and he didn't doubt that Nikita of Sredetz was not the most pleasant thing to look upon. He surrendered his seat at the table to her and begged her pardon, on the grounds of minor matters of a domestic nature requiring his attention. As it happened, there were, and he ended up instructing the brothers sent to retrieve the Archbishop's belongings from Lady Rosamund's baggage to place the two boxes in the main study, dispatching two more brothers to monitor the activities of Sir Gilbrecht and his men, and almost going downstairs to check on Myca.

He restrained that last impulse, knowing that, should his lover require him, he could make that need known silently and efficiently through the blood they shared between them. He almost whispered a question through that bond, but checked that impulse, as well; whatever he was doing, Myca was clearly, fully engaged in it, and disturbing him unnecessarily when he was absorbed was one of the surest ways to put him out of sorts. Ilias sensed stillness and concentration emanating from below, Myca's intellect very much at work, and decided to leave him alone. He would come upstairs when his initial rush of curiosity quenched itself.

Lady Rosamund, he had been told, was supposed to be very good at backgammon, which was more than could be said for Myca.

The night wore on. Lady Rosamund proved to be as skilled

at tables as she was in diplomacy. Ilias was privately glad that they weren't playing for more than boasting rights, as she bested him slightly more than half the time. As the night passed, her unease gradually left her, as well, and once or twice he thought he coaxed a real smile and a genuine laugh from her. It was difficult to tell, for her charming manner was the most perfect of her many masks. He observed her closely, but kept his hands to himself. It would be easier to sculpt her likeness into the flesh of another if he had liberty to touch her, to sample the texture of her skin and the shape of her bones, but he rather thought Sir Landric and the lady herself would respond rather poorly to such an act on his part. As dawn approached, Sir Landric made quiet noises about returning to their chambers and Ilias, exercising his rights as host, escorted them back, then sought out Sir Gilbrecht and saw him safely to his chamber, as well.

Myca was no longer downstairs. Ilias realized that at once, as he disengaged himself from thoughts of guests and entertainments and future pleasures in the dark. Myca was no longer downstairs, and he was no longer coolly centered, tightly intellectually focused; a disquiet close to fear vibrated in the bond between them, and Ilias nearly ran through the corridors, suddenly disturbed, as well. He found his lover sitting in the study at his writing desk, the room dark but for the guttering stump of a single candle, staring blankly. His elegant, patrician face was empty of expression and the way he sat, half-slumped in his chair, sent a jolt of fear up Ilias' throat. He crossed the room in three strides, and caught one of Myca's limp hands in is own. That elicited a response. He felt, deep inside himself, Myca's instinctive urge to pull away from the contact, and his deliberate refusal to do so. Ilias released his grip, and instead laid his hand next to Myca's own, close enough to take if he wished.

"My flower," Ilias kept his voice low and soothing, "Myca. What troubles you?"

Myca's head lifted slightly. In the uncertain light, his dark eyes were emotionless, reflectionless, yielding no clues to the direction of his thoughts or what he was feeling in those few places Ilias could not touch. "I... have had a rather unsettling experience. No—I do not wish to speak of it yet."

Ilias held his tongue and nodded silently.

"Can you…" Myca stopped, moistened his lips with the tip of his tongue, and continued. "I know that it is within your power to cast protections on a place, to ward it against harm. Can you bind a place, as well? Close it against entry."

"Yes. Or, rather, I do not think it beyond me."

"Then I wish you to do this for me. I wish the downstairs study barred against intrusion. I want no one to enter there without my express permission. Not even you." He clasped Ilias' hand suddenly, his grip bone-crushingly fierce.

Ilias inhaled through his teeth, and whispered. "It shall be done, my flower."

Chapter Five

Ilias spent the next three nights preparing, secluded in his own sanctum, making himself a pure vessel for the magic he planned to work. He slept alone and fasted. He bathed nightly in water in which a selection of astringent herbs had steeped, and forced himself to breathe in the aromatic smoke his censers spilled into the cool air. He knelt before his small carved-bone altar and meditated deeply, summoning peace and serenity, contemplating the tools he would need to accomplish what his lover asked of him. On the second night of his vigil, he began grinding salt and dried herbs together, mixed with a handful of earth taken from the monastery garden and nine drops of his blood. He left the mixture in its earthenware bowl on the altar over the day to continue strengthening, and that day dreamed strange dreams in which a mighty tower of stone and glass rose from the crest of the hill on which the monastery sat, shining by both night and day. On the third night, he rose and, before he engaged in any of his rituals of cleansing, he went to his lover and begged a small bone cup of his blood, which was given without comment or objection. They did not touch, though they each wished to do so, and Ilias returned to his labors, his cleansing, and his lonely bed.

On the fourth night, Ilias rose feeling that he still lacked something to make the spell complete, but uncertain what that thing was. He sent a note to Myca, requesting that the halls between his sanctum and the lower study be cleared that he might travel between the rooms undisturbed, in the hope that Nikita himself might hold some answer to that uncertainty. He received a prompt reply, a note indicating that this would be done, and a small leather pouch containing, Myca said, a sample of Nikita's grave-earth.

It was what he needed, and Ilias knew it at once.

Nikita looked as though he were sleeping, his face still and every inch of his body utterly relaxed, by all visible indications utterly at peace. Given the violence that Ilias imagined attending his capture, the witch-priest found that apparently peaceful repose odd and disturbing, and avoided looking at Nikita whenever possible. In truth, he had not much time to waste on idle curiosity: the ritual would consume time as well as strength, and the length of the night waned.

A fat beeswax candle burned in each quarter of the room, incised with symbols of elemental correspondence, their bases marked with a drop of his blood, the very action of their burning forming the first layer of the invocation. In the silver censer that once belonged to his sire a selection of incenses beloved of the spirits smoldered, filling the room with the sweet-bitter scents of amber and myrrh, hazing the high ceiling in a pall of fragrant smoke. Ilias himself wore gold and amber, braided into his hair, set in two cuff bracelets and a heavy necklace that hung nearly to his navel, metal and stones worked into a pattern that was itself a subtle invitation to the little spirits and greater gods of Earth and Sky. He was otherwise naked, cleansed in salt water, bare areas of skin painted in a mixture of myrrh oil and his own blood.

He used that same mixture to mark Nikita of Sredetz as one of the objects of his spell. The Archbishop of Nod was utterly helpless. Ilias knew that intellectually, and yet he could not deny the fear he felt in the man's presence—the visceral, instinctive fear of laying hands on a thing that could destroy him at will. His own fear roused a hiss of terror from his Beast, which was many things, including a good deal more craven than the man who owned it. He felt that blind terror clawing at the dark places of his soul and reached out to clasp it, admitted it for what it was—the knowledge that, somehow, Nikita of Sredetz was a thing to fear even immobile and incapable of defending himself. He knew it for truth, but did not permit that knowledge to stay his hand or turn him aside and his Beast, recognizing the acceptance of its wisdom, subsided, watchfully subdued but not quiescent.

Ilias touched the tip of one finger, moistened in blood and oil, to Nikita's brow, drawing a sigil that his sire had taught him before her destruction, a word encapsulated in a single sign, to draw the notice of gods and spirits. It was a language no longer spoken by any mortal tongue, his sire had taught him, a language older than that of the Romans and Greeks, handed down through their line and, possibly, only the other *koldun* lineages. It was properly used for only a few purposes—written or spoken entreaties to the Eldest or its *bogatyr*-childer, invocation, propitiation, thanks, or praise to gods and spirits. Tonight, Ilias invoked. He requested the attention of the ethereal beings of Earth to Nikita of Sredetz, to himself, and to the room in which he stood, for the purpose his will defined. His deft fingers traced sigils on Nikita's brow, eyelids, throat, hands, feet, begging a binding of the Earth upon him, to hold him in his place, even should he, through some agency, manage to rise. He spelled out a similar request in blood and oil on the floor, in a tight circle around the casket, then laid in place a fine circle of the mingled salt, earths, and blood that he had prepared earlier. A second circle went around this one, and then a third. All the while, he incanted softly in the tongue of spirits, singing praise and offering petition, his voice sweetly seductive.

Ilias could feel his request being answered. The attention of the earth-spirits, deep-rooted and strong but sluggish yet from winter's grip, turned to focus upon him, hear his words, sample the offerings he held up for their delectation. They favored the perfume of amber and myrrh, scents derived of tree-sap and earth-life, and the rich taste of salt and blood spilled in their honor. The stones of the floor rippled slightly as the earth beneath them stirred, the spirits stretching up stony fingers and rocky tongues to taste of the essences provided and consider his request. Dimly, around the sensations that assailed him, the caress of spirit hands and the slow, deep sound of spirit voices, he realized that the whole of the monastery was trembling gently in response to his call. It seemed a touch excessive, and he altered his incantation slightly, to weave in a question…

And received an answer. A numbingly intense sensation washed over him and through him—age, incredible age, married to a vast expanse of sorrow and regret, a grief as infinite as the sky and as deep as the roots of the earth. Ilias swayed and fell to his hands and knees as the sensation filled him, tears washing his face and a sob locking in his chest, choking off his voice and his invocation. He found his lips forming a word, two words, but he lacked the air to give them sound.

Fortunately, no more words were needed of him.

Blood and oil, salt, earth, and blood, sank into the stones of the floor, leaving behind traces that gleamed with the light of the magic that formed them. He felt his strength drawn from him in a single great rush as the spirits accepted the bargain—to bind Nikita of Sredetz and ward his place of rest against all comers but the *magnat* of the land, its rightful ruler, and to endure until such a time as the bonds were dismissed. Earth was always amenable to such arrangements, for it was earth's purpose to endure, and the offerings he made were rich and sweet. Ilias let his forehead slump to the floor and he whispered a word of thanksgiving to the stones of the floor, remaining in his posture of deeply submissive honor until he felt strong enough to move. His face was stiff with tears, his soul still quivering with the pain he had experienced, and his body felt as though it were a statue cast of solid lead. His Beast was roused, and lashed hungrily inside him, woken by the sudden drain on his strength.

And the stairs were many and high.

Setting his feet on them, leaning hard against the wall to support himself, Ilias promised his Beast the first thing they met on the way up. Fortunately, the first thing they met was an Obertus brother, and not a guest.

Ilias found Myca in the oriel room with Lady Rosamund, Sir Gilbrecht, and Sir Landric, evidently doing his duty as host. He came to the door still naked and bloody, his chin and hands coated with the remnants of his meal, mentally exhausted from his efforts if full again. Sir Gilbrecht, unfortunately, saw him first and leapt to his feet with an emphatically Christian exclamation of shock and disgust, reaching for the sword he was not permitted to wear. Ilias found he had neither the inclination nor the lingering tolerance necessary not to smirk at him in response. "Myca."

Myca sat with his back to the door, opposite Lady Rosamund who, after a single, startled glance kept her eyes modestly averted. He rose slowly, with the perfect elegance of carriage and bearing that Ilias found so attractive, and motioned Sir Gilbrecht to sit. "Please, my lord... do not be alarmed. My companion will do you no harm."

"*Alarmed?*" Sir Gilbrecht yelped, the affront so obvious it was almost comical. "I'm not alarmed by that filthy heathen —"

Myca turned sharply, and the Teuton's voice choked off just as quickly. Distantly, Ilias felt Myca's cool fury sweeping the room and washing off the walls, silencing Sir Gilbrecht as effectively as a slap. He smiled tiredly, but gratefully, at his lover. "Myca, I fear that Brother Istvan is somewhat indisposed."

Myca's dark eyes swept over him in a single, assessing glance, then he turned fully to Lady Rosamund and bowed deeply to her. "My lady, I fear that I must leave you, for a moment, to your own devices. If there is anything that you require in my absence, ask it of the servants. There will also be brothers outside to attend your needs and see to your safety. Please excuse me."

He did not remain to accept Lady Rosamund's polite murmur in response, but turned, Ilias by the elbow and guided him out into the hall. Silk-clad arms closed around him and swept him from the floor, carrying him with the ease of an adult hefting a sickly child, and Ilias let his head fall against his lover's shoulder, his eyes drift closed and weariness to claim him for a time. He came back to himself as he was laid on a length of silk and a mass of furs, a cushion beneath his head, as gentle hands removed his necklace and bracelets, took the ornaments from his hair. He lacked the ambition to force his eyes open or move in any way, and passively submitted to the care he was being given. A cloth dipped in warm water scented with bath herbs washed the blood from his face and hands, and the remnants of the oil from his skin. A warmed towel blotted away the water. Then those wonderful, glorious, gentle hands poured a stream of lightly dampened earth down the center of his chest and began massaging it in, stroking slowly and deeply, spreading it across his chest and belly, down his arms and over his thighs. He moaned softly in pleasure and found, for the first time, the will to open his eyes as the strength of his own earth suffused him, restoring him in a way that even blood could not.

Myca leaned over him, naked to the waist, hair bound back in a loose knot, his hands coated in grave earth and an expression of undisguised concern on his face. "Ilias?"

"I am here, my flower." Ilias pushed himself up on his elbows, and from there into a boneless sitting position, half-slumped over his own legs. Myca stroked a muddy hand down his spine. "Did the whole monastery shake, or was that just me?"

"We felt a tremor, yes. But it did not last for very long." Both hands now, working loamy earth into the muscles of his back, and Ilias felt *immensely* better, all at once. "It seemed different for you?"

"Yes. Much stronger. It shook everything in the realms of spirit, I felt for quite some distance. It should *not* have done that." He lifted his head slowly. "And I felt very odd in Nikita's presence, and the impressions I received while I was working were stranger still."

Myca's hands went still against his back, and through that contact Ilias felt a sharpening of the tension inside him. "Odd?"

"Yes. I feared him, completely, immediately. It was all I could do to work in his presence. And during the spell…" Ilias paused to consider both the memory of it and his words. "I felt a sensation of great sorrow, a terrible pain, the beginning of which I could not see, nor its ending. I could not tell if it came from Nikita himself, or the spirits of his earth. It might have been both."

Myca's hands restarted their soothing motion, but his tension persisted. "When I was alone with him I felt impelled to lay my hands on him. The desire was not my own, and I cannot explain where the need to do so came from, or why I obeyed it."

He fell silent. Ilias turned his face to watch his lover's expression as he worked, and found it alarmingly empty. "He appeared to be in pain when he arrived. The Ventrue was not gentle with him. When I lifted my hands away, he was as you saw him, as though he had been soothed and comforted, somehow."

"Who is he, Myca?" Ilias whispered, unnerved. "Who is Nikita of Sredetz that he can command such power, even helpless?"

"I do not know." Softly. "But I *will* find out."

Chapter Six

"*Stapân* Vykos." Father Aron bowed as deeply as his arthritic joints would allow. "A man has come to the gates, and craves an audience with you."

Myca lifted his eyes from the letter he was reading for the half-hundredth time. "Tell me of him. Is it a messenger from Jürgen of Magdeburg, seeking after his missing ambassador?"

"No, my *stapân*, it is not. He is dressed roughly, in the garments of a knight-pilgrim, and he claims to be a traveler," the old monk hesitated slightly, "from Constantinople. He gives his name as Malachite."

"Malachite." Through a heroic application of willpower, Myca managed to keep his tone cool and level. "By all means, Father, show our illustrious guest to the small receiving chamber, and make certain that he is offered any refreshment he requires. I shall join him presently."

Father Aron bowed again and departed as swiftly as his legs could carry him. For a long moment, Myca sat at his writing desk, unmoving, his thoughts winding around themselves as he considered what this development meant. Malachite, the Rock of Constantinople. It strained credulity to ascribe his appearance, so soon after the arrival of Nikita of Sredetz, to mere coincidence. Malachite, when last Myca had spoken with him, was on a quest, chasing the tattered remnants of the Dream to which he had dedicated his unlife, seeking the last survivor of its founders, Myca's own not so distant ancestor, the Dracon. When they met in Magdeburg, Malachite had enjoyed little success in his effort thus far, having traveled from Constantinople to Erciyes, seeking the wisdom of the ancient Cappadocian oracle who dwelt there and receiving ultimately little guidance from that effort. From the holy mountain temples of Erciyes he traveled much of the world, seeking some clue or sign that would lead him further and, evidently, coming across that clue in Paris. Malachite had admitted, somewhat tersely, that he felt there was a connection of some kind between the Dracon and the heretical Archbishop of Nod, an assertion that Myca himself was not immediately prepared to credit without significantly more evidence than Malachite had been able to provide.

Michael the Patriarch, the first founder of the Dream, had possessed an absolute detestation of the Cainite Heresy and all that it stood for. Myca could not imagine much sympathy for it lying hidden in Michael's last surviving lover. He was, however, at an impasse in his own investigations, and as Lady Rosamund had indicated, the papers in Nikita's possession at the time of his capture consisted entirely of mundane correspondence. If there was a hint contained within it of Nikita's plans or intentions, he was deeply loath to admit it was too well hidden for him to puzzle out. Not even a lingering sense of the man's mood as he wrote remained clinging to the paper. The correspondence, the chest it traveled in, and the cleverly locked box containing Nikita's grave-earth had all been cleansed, somehow, of any personal impressions belonging to the man himself. A patina of other emotions clung to it—Jürgen's, Rosamund's—but Nikita's own were sponged away so completely not even the faintest echoes remained. Ilias had suggested interrogating the spirits of Nikita's earth, but Myca was not wholly comfortable taking that approach. The witch-priest remained somewhat weakened from the effort it took to bind Nikita and ward his place of rest and admitted, somewhat reluctantly, that there was some risk involved in the course he proposed. Myca did not outright reject the possibility, but neither did he give Ilias his consent, preferring to reserve that option should more mundane researches fail.

Unfortunately, they had. And then came Malachite.

Myca rose, put his clothing in order, and went forth to meet the Rock of Constantinople, to see what might be learned from his sudden, unannounced arrival.

Malachite's travels had clearly not treated him kindly. His body, already twisted by the curse of his blood, seemed to stoop far more than Myca remembered. Newly arrived in Constantinople, he had found Malachite intimidating, the vastly competent and unswervingly loyal supporter of Michael the Patriarch, in his own way as much an incarnation of the Dream and its principles as any of its founders. Now, almost in spite of himself, he felt a profound sympathy, an upwelling of mingled compassion and repulsion as the Rock of Constantinople bowed to him, the edges of his road-worn clothing swirling with the motion. Here was the man who clung to the remnants of the Dream, who refused to admit that the Dream was dead, who struggled still to breathe life back into it, no matter the effort.

Admirable. Cleanly, utterly admirable. And still so very pathetic. Myca gestured a servant forward, to bring his guest a chair. "Malachite, please sit. You have no doubt traveled far."

"I have. And I thank you for your hospitality." Malachite, his gravelly voice tinged in gratitude, sat in the chair, leaning back against the cushions with a muffled crackling of bones and sinews. He was masked by the illusions his clan often used to disguise their ugliness, and the face he chose to wear was that of a man in his middle years, craggy and worn around the edges, but still strong for all of the hardships written on his flesh. Myca made no attempt to see beyond that face.

Myca settled himself, as well, and motioned the servants outside the door. For a moment, he and Malachite merely regarded one another steadily, with no words passing between them. Finally, pure hospitality brought words to Myca's lips. "Dare I ask what induced you to make the journey here to Brasov?"

"Nikita." Malachite replied, so bluntly that, for an instant, Myca was at a complete loss for how to respond. "I know that he is here. I learned that much in Magdeburg, when I returned there from the north. I wish to speak with him."

"I fear, my lord, that I cannot, at this time, answer your request." Myca managed, after a moment of silent consideration.

Malachite fixed him with an unblinking dark-eyed stare, the sort of look that Myca had seen provoke hysterical confessions of wrongdoing from half the shiftless younger childer in Constantinople. "Are you saying that you do not have him, Lord Vykos?"

"No. I am saying that he is in no condition to speak with anyone, and that is how I prefer him to remain for the time being." Myca replied, evenly. "Jürgen of Magdeburg did not treat the Archbishop very gently."

"Ah. But you could wake him, if you wished." There was no question in the Rock's tone.

"Perhaps." In a tone that clearly stated, *But I will not.*

"I see."

"Myca, I see we have another guest." Ilias' clear, quiet voice drew their attention; he stood framed in the doorway, clad in his long wine-red tunic and a shapelessly loose pair of trousers in the same hue, offering a serenely pleasant smile of greeting. "Father Aron just informed me."

Myca made a mental note to have a word with Father Aron and rose, gesturing for Ilias to join them. "For tonight and the morrow, at least. My lord Malachite has traveled a considerable distance already, and has many more roads yet to walk before his journey is done."

Ilias caught the hint, almost visibly toyed with it, and decided not to take it. "Ah, the famous Rock of Constantinople, of whom Myca has told me so much. Surely you will be staying for longer than a night and a day? What tales you must have to tell!"

Myca made a mental note to have a word with Ilias, as well, and turned to face Malachite, who was regarding the colorful apparition that had appeared before him with clear bemusement. "My lord Malachite, I have the honor of introducing you to Ilias cel Frumos, *koldun* and priest, and the first of my advisors."

"Ilias the Fair. Your name suits you, *koldun*." Malachite rose, with some effort, and offered a short, but polite, bow of greeting. "I would, of course, accept whatever hospitality this house offers, with gratitude. I am, as my Lord Vykos has mentioned, long on the road and weary from my toils."

"Excellent. I shall have a guest apartment prepared at once."

Ilias smiled his lazy cat smile and Myca felt, quite distinctly, his lover's amusement through the bond they shared. "A houseful of guests for the first time all winter, my *stapân* Vykos. We are, indeed, fortunate."

"Indeed," Myca echoed, though he failed to appreciate how Ilias could consider this development a good one. "My lord Malachite, we will, of course, extend to you three nights and three days, and all safety and welcome within our walls."

Malachite bowed low and rose with the ghost of a smile lurking at the corners of his mouth. "My lord is too gracious."

Malachite's arrival put edges on the tension that had begun building in the monastery over the four nights of Ilias' seclusion and the subsequent, fruitless investigation of Nikita's correspondence. Sir Gilbrecht was positively champing at the bit. Now that it was obvious that the roads were clear enough to travel, and their duty as he felt it was done, he saw no reason to linger. Lady Rosamund was better bred and more thoroughly diplomatic in every respect, but even she was beginning to show signs of restiveness and a desire to be gone back to the arms of her lord. Only Sir Landric, of the original trio of visitors, seemed at all inclined to delay leaving and his opinion was solicited by no one but Ilias, who suggested quietly that the boy might be worth cultivating as a friendly, or at least not entirely hostile, ear in Jürgen's court. Myca accepted that possibility while keeping in mind he had Jürgen's ambassador—and, if rumor were true, his would-be consort—in hand, and that he ought to deliver her to his sire to answer personally for the actions of her lord.

Myca wrote his sire, Symeon, nightly and, each night, put the letter away unfinished, uncertain of how much he wished to say. It was urgent that Symeon be informed of Jürgen's incursion into Obertus territory, that it might be dealt with swiftly, but Myca was deeply, almost instinctively, unwilling to commit words concerning Nikita of Sredetz to parchment. He told himself he did not yet know enough about Nikita's mysterious presence or how he suborned an Obertus monastery to his service to comment intelligently on it, and did not wish to lead his sire astray with poor advice, or erroneous suppositions. He had no evidence. He had nothing he could yet tell Symeon of a conclusive nature. Malachite's assertions were equally unsupported, and quite possibly the ravings of a crumbling and deluded mind. Myca wished, more than anything, to have the opportunity to fully and completely investigate the mystery of Nikita, in his own time, and make a decision only when his curiosity was satisfied, all his questions answered. He felt also this would almost certainly cease to be an option once he informed his sire of Nikita's activities and continued existence.

Symeon also detested the Cainite Heresy, and would likely seize any opportunity to damage it further. Myca did not spare two thoughts for the Cainite Heresy, in general, but found Nikita to be an intriguing, frustrating puzzle.

On the second night after Malachite's arrival, Myca sat in his study attempting, yet again, to write the sort of letter that would inform Symeon adequately without telling him too much, too soon. It was slow going, especially with the periodic traffic of servants delivering fresh supplies of parchment and ink, replenishing the supply of charcoal for the braziers, engaging in the sort of homely tasks that he otherwise found completely ignorable but which tonight grated on his last nerve. After two hours' effort, he realized, with disgust, that he had more crossed-out lines than he did coherent thoughts, and threw down his quill in annoyance, splattering the page with ink. He rose and walked the lower halls of the monastery, receiving gestures of homage from servants and Obertus brothers whose existence he barely acknowledged, restless and severely out of sorts. His path took him, eventually, to the oriel, where he found Ilias and, to his irritation, Malachite passing what appeared to be quite a friendly evening together. As he entered, they were engaged in a game of draughts, or rather, Malachite was engaged in utterly massacring Ilias at draughts, while Ilias wheedled stories of his travels out of the Rock of Constantinople. Neither Lady Rosamund nor her valiant knight defenders were anywhere in evidence.

"No, do not let me interrupt you." Myca waved Ilias and Malachite back down, as they made ready to rise in greeting. "I fear that I have done all the thinking I care to do tonight. If you do not object, I will watch."

One of Ilias' brows flicked towards his hairline at that statement, but he offered no counterargument, gesturing instead for Myca to join them at the table. He selected a chair and sank into it, observing the havoc that Malachite had wrought on Ilias' game pieces, smiling wryly.

"Not a word," Ilias remarked, in an undertone, and made his next move.

"None whatsoever," Myca agreed, feeling just bad-tempered enough to offer no reassurance.

"And *you* play next." Ilias continued, in a slightly exasperated tone as Malachite took an opening, and removed yet another of his pieces from the board.

"If you insist," Myca replied, his temper beginning to migrate in the direction of mildly amused.

Malachite actually chuckled. For an instant, Myca was struck by the complete unreality of the moment. An elder Byzantine Nosferatu of solidly Christian temperament, a former exile returned home at last, and a pagan Tzimisce witch-priest, sitting comfortably around the table, playing a game that did not involve the manipulation of human pawns. It brought a faint smile to his lips to contemplate it, and for a moment he felt almost warm towards Malachite, despite their differences in opinion, and obsession. Much that was worthy of respect still dwelt in the old Nosferatu. Myca admitted, very much to himself, that he did respect Malachite for all that he had been, and could yet be, and silently hoped he would free himself from the chains of his past and find a new way to continue on. Beneath the surface of the table, Ilias' free hand found his own, and clasped it gently, his lover eternally sensitive to the flow and texture of his moods.

The relative peace of the moment was broken by a soft clap on the door, followed by the entrance of Father Aron, who looked as though he'd been rousted from his bed rather peremptorily. "My *stapân* Vykos... I crave forgiveness for my interruption, but a matter of some urgency has come to my attention."

Myca exchanged a glance with Ilias. "Do not apologize for matters of importance, Father. What has passed?"

"A messenger arrived from the north, some few minutes ago,

my *stapân* Vykos. He is in the refectory now, being refreshed, for he was weary from the road and unfit to be seen." Father Aron hobbled forward, a heavy leather document case beaded with moisture in one gnarled hand. "He says that he has come from the court of Oradea."

Myca rose, and Father Aron placed the case in his outstretched hand. Within was a single parchment, folded and sealed with the arms of his sire, Symeon of Constantinople. Myca broke the seal without ceremony and scanned the brief message. After a moment of silent contemplation, he refolded it, and replaced it in the case. "Father Aron, have this placed in my study, at once."

The old man accepted the case and retreated. Myca turned to sweep a glance over his companions. Ilias, as usual, was not troubling to conceal his curiosity. Malachite's illusory face was completely, professionally devoid of expression.

"My sire," Myca said softly, "My lord sire, Symeon of Constantinople, summons me to court in Oradea. It seems he has a task which he wishes me to perform."

Chapter Seven

It was at times like this that Myca Vykos truly appreciated the existence of well-trained servants and silently obedient Obertus brothers. The preparations for a journey involving five vampires, a dozen knights of the Black Cross, and suitable transportation for all was the sort of logistical nightmare that he was entirely glad to leave in someone else's hands. He privately wondered how Andreas Aegyptus, the most famous transporter of Cainite passengers he knew of, managed it year in and year out, as it was consuming the attention of most of the senior servants and monks just to handle it once. Fortunately, they were also rising to the challenge, providing fodder for the horses and food for the mortal attendants who would accompany their masters, acquiring sufficient light-proofed vehicles, and assembling all the other oddments that a party on the road for some length of time might require. Even the knights of the Black Cross willingly offered their aid and expertise, grateful to be finally escaping the severely oppressive atmosphere of the not-entirely-Christian east.

Myca invited Lady Rosamund to accompany him to Oradea, on the very edge of the Great Plain, over which she could travel with ease through friendly territories back to her lord. Lady Rosamund, after taking counsel with Sir Gilbrecht, accepted that offer, and the course was laid out accordingly. Their route crossed the Olt River below Sibiu, skirting the territories of both Ioan Brancoveanu and the Prince of Sibiu. They planned to cross the Mures River at Alba Iulia, where they could replenish their supplies in relative safety, as the local *stapân* was an ally of the Obertus, very much to the annoyance of Nova Arpad, the

Ventrue prince of neighboring Medias. The final leg to Oradea was a long one but, thankfully, descended out of the high country into the rolling hills and lowland forests that bordered the Great Plain.

Myca kept to himself the opinion that, once Lady Rosamund was actually *in* Oradea, Symeon was unlikely to permit her to depart again until some restitution was extracted from the hide of Jürgen of Magdeburg. The results of his silence would no doubt be educational for all concerned and perhaps succeed in teaching Jürgen, once and for all, that some things were outside his grasp and always would be. Unsurprisingly, Malachite also invited himself along on the journey and, after a day and night of severe inner struggle, Myca acquiesced to the Rock of Constantinople's desire. There was not, after all, anything he could effectively do to forbid or prevent it, short of staking the man and shoving him in a neglected storage room somewhere for a year or ten, and that was the sort of breach in hospitality that Ilias would never condone. Malachite could follow their route or make his own with minimal effort. It was much better to have the man where an eye could be kept on him at all times, and they would arrive in Oradea together. Myca was still not certain how much he wished to tell Symeon concerning Nikita of Sredetz, but he was entirely certain he didn't want Malachite giving his sire that news in his place.

In public, and to his guests, Myca presented his most pleasant face, approving travel plans and the choices of the men responsible for organizing the expedition, telling Lady Rosamund and the knights of the sights they could expect to see along their intended route. Malachite added his own remarks, having traveled the region extensively himself, and between them they managed to paint a coherent portrait of the terrain they would travel through, and the people they were likely to meet. Their route included stopovers at three Obertus monasteries and passed through the territories of a half-dozen Cainite lords of consequence. Myca wrote to them all, announcing his intent to travel through their domains without lingering unnecessarily, requesting what hospitality they might choose to offer and the unfettered use of the roads passing through their lands. It was a formal nicety rarely observed any longer, Ilias had told him once, but it would likely make a good impression on those lords who kept faith with such gestures and would hardly damage his reputation with those who did not.

In private, to Ilias, he did not bother to conceal his irritation.

"I dislike the timing of this summons." Myca paced the length of his study, a windowless room fully wide as it was long, lined in the bookcases that contained the documents and artifacts that he personally preserved from the Library of the Forgotten in Constantinople. It was a very satisfying room to pace in, with a fireplace to keep the mountain damp from the books, and a minimum of furnishings, creating a relatively warm and open space in which to work out tension. Myca paced when he thought, which Ilias found quite helpful when reading his lover's occasionally opaque moods.

Ilias sat cross-legged on one of the few pieces of furniture, a backless padded bench next to the writing desk, and watched silently, waiting for his companion's train of thought to come to its next utterance. After a moment, it did.

"It is almost too coincidental, given all the other factors at work." Myca returned the way he'd come, the pearl-encrusted hems of his dalmatic swaying gracefully with the motion. "'A matter of diplomatic importance,' he said. Jürgen? There are nights when I believe that man was put in creation *solely* to vex me. The Tremere? Unlikely. Something else? The last Symeon wrote to me, he was playing peacemaker with Noriz' little brood of monstrosities… Could that be it? Ilias, my correspondence chest."

Ilias already had the little lacquered wooden box open and extracted Symeon's most recent letters, which had arrived late in the previous summer. Myca accepted the bundle and began paging through it, scanning the closely written lines. "Lukasz and Rachlav. He was entertaining envoys from them last autumn. Do you know anything of either of them?"

"Childer of Noriz, both of them." Ilias remarked as Myca paced back past him, rubbing his chin thoughtfully. "Lukasz,

I do not know personally. Rachlav the Unquenchable I have… met. His name suits him." He cast a glance over his shoulder at Myca, who had come to a complete halt. "He and his sire have a startling number of similarities in temperament, including the inability to hear the word 'no.'"

Myca came back to his side and lingered silently for a moment, running a caressing hand through Ilias' hair. "You served him?"

"For a time. He desired the honor that would accrue to him, hosting a *koldun* in his domains. That he believed his tastes matched mine was merely an added advantage, in his mind." Ilias' tone was coolly impassive. "Our desires were not as complimentary as he wished."

Myca raised a handful of red-golden curls to his lips, and said nothing, not knowing what to say. After a moment, Ilias continued. "I departed his domains after a year and a night, as was my right, and he chose not to pursue me. In that, at least, he was wise." He shook his head slightly, pulling his hair tight in his lover's grip. "Rachlav is a favorite of his sire, inasmuch as Noriz actually has favorites, though it has not done him much good. He has been at war with his brother Lukasz since before my Embrace. There is some sordid little humiliation at the heart of it, something about a mortal favored by them both, and quite a bit of bloodshed and mutual provocation since. They detest each other thoroughly, of that I have no doubt."

"But apparently they detest the Tremere more." Myca laid the most recent of his sire's letters in Ilias' hands. "And are of the mutual opinion that not enough is being done on that front."

Ilias shrugged slightly. "The impression I received while I was at Rachlav's court was that Noriz himself found their little quarrel amusing, and had no intention of doing anything to halt it. Noriz favors bloodshed as an entertainment, so long as the blood being spilt is not his own." A thoughtful pause. "Of course, if he wishes to regain the respect of the clan, and the honor he believes should be his, he is going to have to crack the whip on that revolting brood he has spawned over the centuries. It is all well and good to talk a fight against the Tremere—but that is no different from what Rustovitch has been doing for the last handful of years. Otherwise he will never reclaim what he lost."

"Reclaim...?" Myca asked, an appalling revelation stealing over him. "Wait. Are you suggesting to me that Noriz was once considered *voivode of voivodes*?"

Ilias laughed out loud at the naked horror in Myca's voice. "Once, a very long time ago, Noriz, Damek, the eldest childe of the *bogatyr* Ruthven, and Valeska, the priestess of Veles, were considered first among equals. And, for a time, the clan prospered after the fall of Rome and beneath their leadership. But Damek Ruthven turned to scholarly pursuits, Noriz fell to decadence and dissipation, and Valeska turned her back on the depravity he helped foster, passing her mantle to a *veela* shield maiden when the time came. Noriz was content to subsist on the honor owed him as an elder prince of the blood and tales of his past glories—and discovered the hard way that past glories availed him little in the face of a new foe."

Myca shook his head. "It is almost beyond belief, but it does make sense, if Noriz truly cherishes some ambition of humbling Vladimir Rustovitch, to let my sire make peace between his childer. That way, if the effort fails, he can wash his hands of it, and if it succeeds, he can claim some reflection of the credit." He resumed pacing as he thought. "The gods, I hope Symeon does not expect me to travel all over the mountains, making diplomatic sounds at the behest of Noriz. It would likely kill me."

"I doubt it would kill you, my flower, but I cannot claim it would be very pleasant." Ilias smiled wryly. "If you wish, I will accompany you, should it come to that."

"No." Myca addressed that answer to the far wall and its case of delicate papyrus scrolls standing against it. "No... I wish you to stay here."

"Myca," Ilias said softly, "you cannot keep your sire and me from meeting forever. The world is not large enough for it."

"I know. But I am also not in a hurry to rush the arrival of that night," Myca admitted frankly, turning around and pacing back toward the bench. "My motives are not entirely altruistic in this matter, my heart. I do not trust Malachite, and I do not wish to leave Nikita's body unattended, even warded as it is. It... I feel that would be the wrong thing to do. I wish you to remain, and make certain that Nikita continues to rest peacefully."

"This is not beyond my powers," Ilias assured him, with a hint of wry humor. "Given that I doubt he will rise on his own any time soon. Do you wish me to do anything else, in the absence of our so very pious guests?"

Myca hesitated. "If your strength is recovered, and you feel the risk not too great, I would not object to your plan to discover what you may from the spirits of Nikita's grave-earth. But I do not wish you to risk yourself unnecessarily."

"My flower, I assure you, I *never* risk myself unnecessarily." Ilias caught his companion's hand, and brought it to his lips. "Some risks are necessary, after all, and worth the price one pays for them."

"Yes," Myca agreed quietly. "Some are."

Chapter Eight

Oradea, like most of the towns along the edge of the Great Plain, made its living through trade. The city lay along the banks of the Crisul Repede, the river responsible for much of its prosperity, at the junction of the Great Plain and the low hills extending down from the high range of the Apuseni Mountains. Its location was fortuitous in all ways for the people who dwelt there and the merchants who traveled to do business there. Its marketplaces were bustling even into the night, and in its streets a dozen languages collided as folk came together from points all over the East, to converse, to trade, to drink and share tales.

Symeon's haven lay a short distance outside of the town proper, perched atop a thickly wooded hill and reached by means of a steep, unpaved road that horses and pack animals traversed far more easily than even the lightest sledge or cart. By day, the party waited in the city itself. They took lodgings in a traveler's hostel run by the sort of professionally uncurious landlord who thrived on the business provided by night travelers. Windowless rooms were available upon request, and adjoining chambers for body-servants. Lady Rosamund, of course, slept by herself, on the finest bed in the establishment. Myca, Sir Gilbrecht, Sir Landric, and Malachite shared the chamber next door. When they rose in the evening, the mortal members of the party had already prepared for the last leg of the journey, procuring extra horses and pack animals, and shifting the majority of the baggage over in the hours before sunset. For an extra fee, and the knowledge that the lord of the house on the hill would reward him well for his services again, the landlord agreed to store their sledges and the carts. They departed Oradea an hour after sundown, outriders with torches and pole-mounted lanterns lighting the road, a letter having preceded them during the day via the best rider among the Obertus brothers. They did not pause to repair their hunger, in the knowledge that Symeon would greet them well, and provide for their needs before the night was done.

Despite the foul dampness that dogged them the whole of their journey, the road leading to Symeon's house was, while muddy, not an actual bog. He had, in Myca's opinion, made clear and thoughtful use of Obertus engineering expertise, improving the road's drainage and, in some places, raising its level considerably above the surrounding plain. The area was prone to flooding as the streams that fed into the Crisul Repede rose in the spring with snowmelt and rain. Those streams were high now, and the night was full of the sound of rippling water as they rode. In the distance, lights occasionally came into view through the trees—torches, Myca thought—showing the way up the hill. As they came closer, his supposition was borne out. Stone pylons bearing torches heavily soaked in pitch stood at regular intervals, hissing and popping in the light rainfall.

As they reached the top of the hill, the steepness of the road leveled off and the forest thinned. Symeon's house loomed out of the darkness, a Byzantine villa that appeared as though it had been lifted whole from Constantinople and placed on the hill by some giant hand. Symeon was prepared for their arrival. As the party clattered over the cobblestone courtyard, a dozen house-servants emerged and, with the sort of quiet competence Symeon favored, began assisting the travelers. Baggage was unlashed and carried inside, horses led away to the stables for appointments with dry blankets and warmed grain. After a brief consultation between Sir Gilbrecht and Lady Rosamund all but three of the mortal complement of Black Cross knights were led away to the guest quarters that had been prepared for them.

Myca dismounted for himself and handed his reins to the stable-boy who came to collect them, patting his great-hearted mount on the nose in passing. The most senior of the servants at hand, a man Myca recognized as the mortal seneschal, approached him and bowed deeply, speaking in Latin for the edification of the westerners. "My *stapân* Vykos, my lord *stapânitor* Symeon gives you his fond greetings and welcomes you home with all honor and felicitation. He asks that you and our illustrious guests, the Lady Rosamund d'Islington and my lord Sir Gilbrecht and my lord Sir Landric, as well as my Lord Malachite, forgive that he is not present to greet you. My lord *stapânitor* Symeon is detained by diplomatic affairs of a highly sensitive nature, from which he cannot yet separate himself. He asks that you accept his hospitality, in his stead, and quarters have been prepared for all, as well as comforts to ease the weariness of the road. Please, come with me."

Lady Rosamund, her knights, and Malachite were accorded quarters in a guest-wing of the villa that had not yet been finished the last time Myca was in residence. They were not alone in it, Myca could not help but notice as he passed by. The doorways leading to the upper gallery staircases were guarded by two small mountains, giant Cainites in their *zulo* war-shapes, armed with weapons shaped of solid bone longer than Rosamund was tall. She recoiled at the sight of them, and Myca could hardly blame her. They had not been chosen for their comeliness to anything but Tzimisce eyes. The first was night-black, its skin rippling with a pattern of scales that caught the light of the torches and glistened as though wet, its vaguely reptilian maw set with such a multitude of tiny, sharp teeth its mouth could not close all the way. Its eyes were a flat yellow and slitted like a snake's, and never seemed to waver from the object of its attention. It seemed to find Lady Rosamund quite magnetic. The second was salt-white and parchment yellow, its brittle-looking skin pierced by bony extrusions across the backs of its many-fingered hands, the lengths of its arms, the crest of its skull-faced head. Its shoulders, legs, and chest were massive with corded muscle, and it looked strong enough to swing the maul it held with mountain-shattering force. A moment of uncomfortable silence passed, as the seneschal unlocked the doors leading to the lower level guest chambers, during which no one spoke but everyone's thoughts were clearly in evidence. Myca got the distinct impression that both the *zulo* guardsmen found the reaction they provoked very amusing, indeed.

Myca was escorted to his own apartments, which were kept for his visits, and as a silent invitation should he ever wish to dwell in Oradea permanently. The rooms had been cleaned recently and thoroughly. No trace of dust remained on any surface, the bed and bed clothing were both fresh with the scent of herbs, and a hint of lemon oil still hung in the air. When he checked, he found the wooden base of his bed filled with freshly turned soil, his own grave-earth, a generous supply of which Symeon always kept to hand. A wooden bath lined in linen waited for him in the next room, still steaming hot, next to the fire crackling in the grate. Myca thankfully shed his sopping and muddied traveling garb, and sank into the water for a long, soporific soak. He lowered himself until the point of his chin touched the water and closed his eyes as the warm, wet heat began chasing the chill from his flesh, inhaling the sharp scent of the steam, rich with bath-herbs.

Lavender was Symeon's favorite bath-scent. It was traditional, conservative, entirely Roman. Much of his house reflected those values, from its rambling size and structure, to its magnificent Byzantine architecture, to the mosaics on the floor and the furniture and fabrics used in its decoration. Normally, Myca did not find this jarring at all, for he had dwelt in Byzantium for decades, and found its glories beautiful, as well. Tonight, however, he found that it robbed him of the peace he should have felt at what was, after all, a homecoming. He found himself violently, wrenchingly homesick for a place that was not Oradea. He ached for the sight of steep snowcapped mountains against the moon-washed sky, silent forests of evergreen on the hillsides, wide-spreading oak in the valleys, the misty plunge of waterfalls down sheer rock faces and mossy streams flowing through the narrow places in the mountains. He longed even more for a slender, strong body against his own in the bath, a body to twine with beneath the linen sheets and fur coverlets of his bed. It occurred to him, with a sharp pang, that he had not been this far apart from Ilias for more years than he could easily count. He wondered, with an even sharper inner pain, what his lover was doing tonight, and whom he was doing it with. He did not, he informed himself and the small, insidious voice in his soul that he knew to be his Beast, doubt Ilias' faith; he was not jealous, for no such petty emotions existed in the bond between them. He was, however, lonely, and he no longer knew how to deal with his loneliness as easily as he once had.

He opened his eyes and found that soft-footed servants had come and gone while he warmed himself. Thick, warmed towels sat on the bench next to the bath, and clothing hung warming next to the fireplace. Simple clothing, of silk and richly colored, but lacking the elaborate decorative flourishes of garments made for public scrutiny. Myca surmised that Symeon would not call him, or the guests, into open counsel any longer tonight. He dressed himself and stepped into his bed chamber—and there, to his surprise, he found his sire waiting, seated in a low-backed chair next to his reading table, the candle-lamp lit, reading from a slender, leather-bound folio. Myca paused, and caught his breath, struck, as always, by the patrician beauty of the Cainite who had chosen him, the fine bones of his face, the dark eyes, the spill of raven's wing hair, neatly confined in an enameled ornament, the elegant carriage of his body, even in relaxation. For many years, he had almost feared to look upon his sire with sensual eyes, to view him as a sensual being, but now he felt no such inhibition. A curl of desire wound its way through his belly and he wondered what it might be like to feel Symeon's hands on him, rough with longing, and Symeon's mouth against his skin, desperate with want. He knew that his soul was colored vividly with that fantasy when Symeon looked up and his thin-lipped mouth relaxed in a smile of pleasure and greeting. "My childe."

"My lord sire." Myca remembered his manners and bowed deeply, heartily glad he could no longer blush.

"Such formality." Symeon sounded faintly amused. "Come… sit. You have traveled far to answer my summons and brought me a gift of great worth, as well. I am very pleased with you, Myca." The praise warmed him more than the bath, and he rose from his bow smiling slightly, taking the chair across from

Symeon's own. "It pleases me that I was of service to you, my lord. I wish only that I might have accomplished more."

"You will, I do not doubt, have the opportunity to act on that sentiment before all is said and done in these matters," Symeon assured him, dark eyes playing over him thoughtfully. "You are very drawn, Myca. Have you dined yet?"

"No, not yet. My lord—" Symeon paused in mid-reach for the brass bell, hidden on the other side of the lamp, that he might use to summon a servant. "There is a matter that I did not feel it safe to commit to parchment, which impacts closely on this situation. If I may…?"

"You may not. Not tonight. I do not wish to speak of politics and stratagems and incidents with you tonight." He lifted the bell and rang it once with a languid flick of his wrist. "It has been too long since I last saw you, my childe, and tonight I wish only the pleasure of your company. I trust you do not object?"

Myca realized he *was* surprised by that sentiment, coming from his sire, and experienced a momentary tangle of emotions in response. "No, my lord, I do not object. It has, indeed, been a very long time since… we simply sat and spoke."

"Then that is what we shall do. There will be time enough for politics tomorrow night."

Golden light. Golden light was all that he could see. Radiance filled his world, blinded him to all other perceptions. It was magnificent, glorious—he felt himself bathed in a wonder that was truly divine.

From out of that divine light, the voice of an angel spoke to him, ringing with the clarity of a silver bell, sweeter than the finest music. "Beautiful. I had… almost forgotten how beautiful you are."

He heard the words and knew that they were true. He was divine himself, or touched by divinity, beautiful enough to make angels weep. He felt it, deep within himself—perfection, soul and flesh in flawless union, finding its expression in the smoothly muscled symmetry of his limbs, the elegance of his features, the silken expanse of pale skin and night-dark hair. Luminous hands, glowing with the pure soul-light of their owner, touched him gently, running fingers through the extravagant length of his hair, caressing his thigh with a knowing touch. He shuddered with a joy that penetrated to the core of his being and he ached to be one with the glorious being gracing his flesh with its hands.

A whisper, in that clear and sweet voice. "I knew, my love, that you would return to me in the end..."

Myca woke in the cool blue twilight, curled around himself and shaking with a terror he could give no name to. He knew that he had dreamt again, and something in that dream filled him with a fear, with a horror, so deep his mind refused to hold the memory of it, and even his Beast cowered away from the knowledge. For a long, miserable moment as the weight of sleep faded from his limbs, he longed silently for Ilias and for Symeon, for someone whose presence would lend him even an instant's comfort. Then, almost miraculously, it came to him, faint with distance but strong and warm despite that limitation, the gentle brush of his lover's presence over his soul. He closed his eyes against the rush of grateful, relieved tears, and simply drew strength from the sensation, the feeling that, no matter how much distance lay between them, Ilias was and would always be at his side.

Chapter Nine

"Myca," Symeon's tone was regally distant, the voice of a prince speaking to one of his courtiers, "tell me of Nikita of Sredetz."

Myca restrained the urge to swear. He stood with his sire in the antechamber behind the villa's main receiving hall where, if the sounds making their way beneath the door were any indication, a number of guests awaited their attention. Symeon was clad in the deepest hue of imperial purple, so dark it verged on black, bordered in white and cloth of gold and all of the most impressive accouterments of his station, the heavily decorated ritual garments of Byzantium. The weight of the gold alone would have bowed the shoulders of a lesser man, but his sire stood perfectly straight, radiating calm strength and ineffable patience, waiting for his answer.

Malachite, Myca realized with a silent, cool fury. Malachite must have taken the opportunity, the night before or earlier this evening, to tell Symeon of Nikita's presence in Obertus territory, and how he came to be in Myca's own hands. The urge to twist the miserable leprous dog's head off was sudden and fierce. It took all of Myca's concentration to force his fangs back and to speak calmly in response. "My lord sire, Nikita of Sredetz was the matter I did not wish to commit to parchment, which I mentioned last night."

"Ah. I should have listened to you, then, for this is a matter of some significance. Forgive the selfishness of an old Cainite, my childe." Symeon shifted the drape of his garment into a more comfortable position over his left arm, and gestured for Myca to continue.

Myca thought rapidly and condensed his thoughts in a quick sketch of the situation. "Jürgen of Magdeburg captured Nikita of Sredetz at the Obertus monastery he assaulted. He appears quite willing to use Nikita's presence there as his justification after the fact for the attack. The Swordbearer was not hunting heretics when he violated our territory, but was operating under the assumption that the monastery was somehow in league with, or suborned by, Vladimir Rustovitch or his agents. How he came to this conclusion is not entirely clear—comments that the Lady Rosamund has made to me suggest that some provocation Jürgen encountered while in the territory of the late *kunigaikstis* Geidas may have led him to that belief. He produced no proof of that allegation, nor was Lady Rosamund able to provide an adequate justification of it, nor any connection between Nikita of Sredetz and Rustovitch."

Symeon nodded fractionally. "And the illustrious Archbishop of Nod himself?"

"Restrained, my lord sire. I thought it unwise to wake him." Myca hesitated fractionally. "There is something very odd about him, even sleeping."

Symeon looked at him sharply. "What do you mean?"

"It is not something I can describe logically, my lord." Myca admitted, with some difficulty. "He—I believe that he is more than he seems."

His sire regarded him steadily for a moment, then nodded again. "Malachite believed that much, as well."

"Malachite told me, when we met in Magdeburg, that he believed there was some connection between Nikita of Sredetz and our ancestor, the Dracon. I am not certain that I am prepared to credit that, my lord sire. It seems unlikely on its face." Myca was privately grateful he managed to speak Malachite's name politely. "But I believe the matter requires more investigation before it may be disposed."

"We shall discuss this in more detail, later."

The door of the antechamber swung open without even the most peremptory of knocks and a woman whom Myca had not seen before entered. She was extraordinarily tall for a woman, within a hair or two of Symeon's height, and Myca was immediately struck by her severe plainness, her perfect posture, and the icy hue of her eyes. She bowed, deeply, first to Symeon and then to himself, holding the gestures at the perfect depth and for the perfect length of time, and when she rose, she kept her brilliant eyes on the floor at Symeon's feet. "My lord *stapânitor*, court is assembled, and the westerners await your judgment."

"Thank you, Eudokhia." Symeon smiled grimly, and strode past her, Myca trailing a respectful three paces behind.

Most of the central portion of the villa was given over to rooms of a public nature—receiving chambers, Symeon's office in which he received petitioners, the long second-floor solar overlooking the inner courtyard and garden, a number of smaller rooms used for meetings and conversations of a more intimate kind. The room they entered was the largest and most lavish of the public receiving chambers, a fine example of Byzantine architectural beauty and excess, all green marble floors and gilt mosaic walls, sculptured friezes and columns whose capitals were clearly the product of a demented sculptor's wildest imaginings. Myca felt a momentary, minor twinge of pity for Lady Rosamund, who was standing in the middle of the room flanked by her knightly companions, her eyes fixed on the most innocuous feature in the room, the mirror-polished floor at her feet. There was virtually nothing else safe for her to look at for any length of time. Sir Gilbrecht, his Toreador nature almost wholly suppressed by the general unpleasantness of his personality, was dealing with the problem by glaring around the room at the assembled Tzimisce courtiers and their not inconsiderable entourages, clearly wishing for his sword. Sir Landric, on the other hand, was making no effort to hide his appreciation of his surroundings, or much of his curiosity.

On each side of the room, clustered in front of the green marble support columns for the high, frescoed roof, the Tzimisce court had assembled, nearly ringing the three westerners. The envoys of Lukasz and Rachlav, Myca realized without surprise, surveyed them with a critical eye. Both were male, or at least male seeming. One was almost inhumanly tall and slender, bone white in the coloration of skin, hair, and, most disturbingly, eyes, clad in what appeared to be hundreds of yards of translucent white silk that pooled on the floor around him and which his entourage was very careful to avoid treading on. Nothing about the way his clothing hung on him suggested femininity, nor the way he carried himself, as though he were a statue carved of ivory, easier to break than cause to bend. His entourage showed their allegiance through ornaments carved of bone, tunics or belts of the same pale fabric as their lord's extraordinary robe. By contrast, the other side of the hall was a riot of color, rich garments and ornaments chosen with only the most minimal guidance of taste or restraint. It was difficult to pick out the envoy from among the bright flock of his entourage, but Myca eventually decided it had to be the stocky one clad in a confection of wine red silk and cloth of gold, embellished with a long coat of heavy black fur and square hands bearing more rings than he'd ever seen on one person before. His hair and beard were a deep shade of auburn and well tended, and beneath his thick brows, Myca caught a glimpse of eyes glittering red and hungry. Both entourages were equally bloated in size, a round dozen each, only a few of whom seemed to be other vampires, the majority being revenant lickspittles of one house or the other.

As they emerged into the room, the herald waiting on the opposite side of the door announced them in his deep voice, carrying the length of the room without effort. "Attend the presence of lord *stapânitor* Symeon Gesudin syn Draconov! Attend the presence of *stapân* Myca Vykos syn Draconov! Attend the voice of the first prince of the blood!"

Eudokhia, Myca noticed, was not announced, but joined them on the green marble dais to which they repaired, Symeon taking his seat with the regal grace of a true prince, and Myca taking a position standing at his right hand. Eudokhia crossed to the left, and stood behind both Symeon and Myca, her eyes modestly downcast though the iron in her spine did not ease a fraction.

"I give you greetings this night, my honored guests, the kin of my own blood and travelers who have come from afar." Symeon's voice reached every corner of the room, and provoked a polite murmur in response. Myca attended closely, watching reactions. "My Lady Rosamund of Islington, Sir Gilbrecht and Sir Landric of the Black Cross, approach."

By western standards of presentation, Myca knew, this was somewhat irregular. By Tzimisce standards of presentation, it was extremely irregular, and set the entourages of both ambassadors buzzing quietly among themselves. Normally there would be a good half-hour of letting any western visitors adequately abase themselves before a Tzimisce ruler would even start speaking of important matters. Neither envoy deigned to comment, though Myca sensed a sharpening in their attention as Lady Rosamund and her armored shadows approached the dais to a respectful distance and offered their courtesies. Symeon accepted the gestures with a stately inclination of his head, and waved them up. Lady Rosamund was far too practiced a courtier herself to display confusion and so her face was a lovely mask when she rose from her curtsey. Both Sir Gilbrecht and Sir Landric hung back two paces and closed ranks behind her, as though guarding her back.

"My Lady Rosamund of Islington, I have read both the letters of your own hand and taken counsel with my ambassador on the matter of Lord Jürgen of Magdeburg's unlawful intrusions into the lands of the Obertus Order." That statement, blandly delivered, silenced the entire hall. "And I have found Lord Jürgen's explanation of the matter... most severely wanting. I confess myself disappointed, Lady Rosamund, by your lord's obvious and unsupportable cupidity in this matter, the seizure of my lands and the murder of my chattels, resting upon no basis of fact for which you have chosen to offer evidence."

Sir Gilbrecht bristled, and nearly opened his mouth, only to be literally stepped on by Sir Landric, who put his foot on his superior's instep and pressed sharply. He fell silent, but his hands remained balled at his sides, clearly longing to hurl himself at anyone who dared defame the man he had chosen to follow. Lady Rosamund composed herself more quickly in the wake of this blunt statement, and spoke gently. "My lord Symeon—"

"My lord prince," Lady Eudokhia coolly corrected her, to Rosamund's very visible consternation.

"My lord prince," Lady Rosamund began again, a little strain showing in her voice, "my Lord Jürgen feels that he has proceeded in good faith with the Obertus Order—"

"No, my Lady Rosamund," Symeon interrupted her bluntly, "Your Lord Jürgen has proceeded with the rapaciousness of a jackal to seize my territory, alleging a breach of treaty for which he cares to offer no proof. Good faith, my Lady Rosamund? When Lord Jürgen and Vladimir Rustovitch were on the verge of transforming this entire region into an abattoir with their ambitions, *I* took the risk of coming between them, to warn them of the danger they both faced should they continue with their reckless folly, and gave them both a means of withdrawing with their domains and their precious honor intact. *I* guarantee the treaty that Lord Jürgen has so casually broken in the name of his own unquenchable lust for dominion, and it is to *me* that he will answer for his actions. Lord Jürgen may *call* himself an honorable warrior and a walker on the road of all true rulers, my Lady Rosamund, but has a great deal to learn concerning the conduct of kings."

Symeon's words rang off the walls; he hadn't even raised his voice. One slender hand rose from the arm of his throne, the purple gems in his rings catching the light as he gestured Eudokhia forward, holding an elaborately ribboned and sealed document, which she presented to Lady Rosamund without comment. Lady Rosamund was, herself, pale and speechless, almost visibly fighting the urge to kneel as the force of Symeon's personality swirled around her, bright and fierce in his own anger as an offended prince among princes.

"I demand restitution." Symeon's tone was cool and hard, and no one in the room failed to notice the steel in it. "Lord Jürgen will remove himself from my territory *immediately*. He will make recompense for the murder of my chattels and the property he has seized and abused for his own sustenance and that of his minions, preferably in kind as no amount of bloodmoney would be sufficient to replace the minds and hands your lord's brutality stole from me. To ensure that the ever so honorable Lord Jürgen executes these demands with appropriate haste, one of you will remain here in Oradea as the guarantor of your lord's *good faith*. You will have the remainder of this evening to determine which of you will stay, and which of you will go. If you cannot decide, I will choose for you." His gaze lingered pointedly on Lady Rosamund. "You are dismissed."

"My lord prince," Lady Rosamund recovered herself enough to protest, "my Lord Jürgen will not accept *demands*. There must be some degree of negotiation—

I do not negotiate with oath breakers, Lady Rosamund." Symeon replied, flatly. *"You are dismissed."*

The next evening, Lady Rosamund informed Symeon that Sir Landric had honorably volunteered to remain hostage in Oradea. The night after that, she, Sir Gilbrecht, and the full complement of their knights departed, escorted to the border of Obertus territory by a detachment of Symeon's personal guard. No one was particularly sorry to see them go.

Chapter Ten

"It seems that we have two difficulties—two *unrelated* difficulties—before us just now, my childe." Symeon, like Myca, paced when he thought. They were in his study, and the door was barred and guarded against interruptions, though they were not alone. Lady Eudokhia sat silent in one corner, hands folded on her lap, listening to their discourse. After several nights of association, Myca still did not know how to take her, how to read her, or what to make of her. She appeared to be Symeon's advisor on matters of clan etiquette and culture, but he kept her near to hand even when such matters were not a topic of conversation. Quiet inquiries among the resident courtiers indicated that she was a war-prize, the victim of Tzimisce dynastic struggles in the dominions to the north and east, the last survivor of her line given to Symeon as gift and slave by her family's conqueror. Her demeanor appeared to bear out that truth.

Myca nodded slightly in response. "The diplomatic matter you summoned me to attended and… Nikita of Sredetz."

"Even so." Symeon irritably tugged open the heavy wooden shutters blocking the view of the garden, admitting a breath of cool, rain-scented air and the sound of yet another shower. "The diplomatic matter will, I fear, not wait another season for resolution."

"Lukasz and Rachlav have agreed to a truce?" Myca asked, trying not to sound too clever and schooling his expression to perfect neutrality as his sire turned to face him.

Symeon surveyed that lack of expression and nodded. "More than simply a truce. They have all but agreed to cooperate on a mutual goal beyond the lofty aim of not randomly slaughtering each other's chattel and childer any longer. I admit, when they came to me, I thought the truce alone would be an uphill battle against the impossible. It seems that I, too, can be pleasantly surprised." He reclaimed his chair behind the wide expanse of his writing table, heavy dark wood polished to a high sheen with beeswax and lemon oil. From one of its many drawers he drew out a thick sheaf of parchment, as of yet unsigned and unsealed, which he handed across to Myca, who reviewed it silently.

"The wording is very precise." Myca glanced a question at his sire.

"Precision was insisted upon." Symeon tossed a faintly amused glance at Lady Eudokhia, who ignored it. "They are, after all, agreeing to let bygones be bygones. It seemed only sensible to innumerate precisely what they were letting fall by the wayside and why, in exhaustive detail. The matter lacks but one thing to bring the issue to successful resolution."

Myca glanced up from an eye-wateringly unpleasant paragraph detailing Lukasz's specific intent to forgive his brother for a colorful series of ravishments and beheadings stretching across approximately two centuries. "And that one thing would be...?"

"Ioan Brancoveanu, childe of Lukasz, childe of Noriz. Ioan had just cause, a century ago, to declare his own intent to separate Rachlav from his head and made a very dedicated attempt at collecting on that vendetta. Rachlav escaped by the skin of his teeth, and by virtue of hiding behind his sire's skirts. Ioan never declared his honor satisfied, and has not rescinded his intent to murder his uncle. He has simply moved on to matters of greater importance." Symeon laced his fingers together. "Rachlav has indicated to me, through his envoy, that he requires a declaration on the part of Ioan Brancoveanu that his honor is satisfied by the blood that has already been shed between the families and will pursue the matter no further, in order for the provisions of the truce to be wholly satisfactory. Lukasz has indicated that this demand is acceptable to him. Ioan himself has not yet been consulted."

"And you wish me to… consult with him on this topic?" Myca asked, neutrally.

"Yes. You may use whatever resources you require on the journey and in the process. You may offer Ioan whatever reassurances he requires, in my name, to sweeten the prospect. But his acceptance is essential, and his refusal is not an option that may be seriously entertained." Symeon's tone was likewise neutral, but Myca knew a command when he heard one.

"It will be done." Myca replied, quietly. "And Nikita of Sredetz?"

"I can see that the Archbishop of Nod has captured your imagination." Dryly. "Very well. For now, Nikita of Sredetz may keep his head. And I trust that *you* will keep your grasp on yours."

Myca bowed from the neck. "Of course, my sire." When he looked up, Symeon's expression had softened an almost imperceptible fraction.

"You have done well for me, these many years, Myca. I am more proud of you and your accomplishments than I find it easy to express." Symeon glanced away from him, turning to look through the shutters at the night-darkened garden beyond. "You have done your duty and more for me without fear, without compulsion, for my ambitions and your own. And you have done me the great honor of not pretending toward ingenuousness or a lack of personal ambition. I found, and continue to find, your honesty very refreshing."

Myca felt a pang and forced his face to remain still, pushing down a surge of guilt and dismay that almost moved his tongue to speak of Ilias.

"I think it is time that I permitted you a touch more freedom than I have in the past, to pursue such interests as you have developed, independent of my own." Symeon turned his dark gaze back on Myca, and smiled slightly. "Complete this mission for me, my childe. Ensnare Ioan Brancoveanu in a web of diplomacy from which he cannot escape, and end the blood feud between Lukasz and Rachlav. When this is done, you have my permission to investigate the matter of Nikita of Sredetz until you are fully content. Only when you are satisfied will I act, and

I will do so in accord with your recommendation. Do we have an agreement?"

Myca bowed again, more deeply, from the shoulders and fought down a triumphant smile. "Yes, my lord. This thing will be done, as you wish it."

"Good. Now, come. We will dine together in the solar and tomorrow, you will begin your mission."

The rain stopped sometime after midnight, and Symeon of Constantinople repaired to his small garden to walk and to think. In the wing of the villa given over the private quarters of the family, his childe was making ready to depart, selecting the members of the staff who would accompany him, setting the packing of his baggage in motion, and, no doubt, writing letters. Myca had a ritual that he observed faithfully at the beginning of every enterprise, and tonight he was doubtlessly doing so with the intent of starting and finishing quickly. A certain fondness warmed Symeon's heart—he could not truthfully call the emotion "love," for the last of everything he truly loved had crumbled to ash in Constantinople—but it was a tender sentiment nonetheless. Myca reminded him very much of himself at that age, at times, and that realization never failed to stir nostalgia for a time before pain, before betrayal and fire and death.

A shadow materialized before him, beneath one of the pitch-soaked torches that lit the garden path, tall and lean and straight, clad in a heavy woolen cloak that failed to disguise his deformity. Malachite bowed, deeply, carefully, and straightened. "May I walk with you, my lord?"

"I shall always welcome your company, my Lord Malachite, and your wisdom." Symeon offered a polite bow of his own, and together the two vampires continued their perambulation in silence for several moments.

Malachite broke it, with his quiet strong voice, as they passed the bright-lit wing of the villa that housed the family quarters. "Your childe, my lord, young Myca... I fear for him. I fear that he has fallen into... bad company."

"You are referring," Symeon replied dryly, "to his plaything, the so-called *koldun*, Ilias cel Frumos."

Malachite hesitated fractionally, then nodded. "He claims the heathen as his advisor."

"And I am certain that the heathen does, in fact, advise him. I am not ignorant of the little *koldun's* presence in my territory, Malachite, or his service in my childe's bed. Myca is not the only one with eyes and hands in many places." A faint smile touched the corners of Symeon's mouth. "I do not, however, fear his influence. Myca belongs to me, and always has, and the freedoms I allow him make him placid in the jesses. He flies where I will, and does as I wish."

"For now," Malachite murmured, the contradiction in his tone mild.

"Forever." Symeon plucked a green bud off a bush in passing, rolling it between his fingertips. "For now, I am content to let Myca keep his plaything. It ultimately does no harm, and may even do some good. The *koldun* lineages are few, any longer, and sheltering a *koldun* within one's court is a mark of some honor among the clan. In this way is this creature useful to me, as well. So long as he continues to be useful, and Myca continues to do his duty as he should, there need be no quarrel between us."

Malachite nodded silently. If he had any other thoughts, or any other objections, he kept them to himself.

Interlude

Michael came to me at a time when I was simultaneously weary and restless, discontent and unsettled in my existence and as without peace as it was possible for me to be. I had, in truth, been restless and without peace for many dozens of years, if not centuries; decades passed in which I thought myself content in my loneliness, in the absence of companionship, living the ascetic life of the mind. I might even have been content, for solitude is not abhorrent to me when solitude is what I truly desire. It is not, however, always what I desire.

One would almost have to have been there to appreciate the impact that Michael had upon me when we first met. It was like watching the sunrise over the sea and not being burned when he came into my presence that first night on Cyprus. Rarely had I met anyone his equal—his equal in beauty, his equal in wit, his equal in passion. We were not lovers, not at first, though it was not for want of desire between us. I had been alone for so long, alone and wretched in my loneliness, in my self-imposed exile, in my desire to touch nothing and let nothing touch me, that it took a great deal of time and effort to coax me out of myself again. Michael was not insistent, nor demanding, nor over-eager. He was patient and gentle, and at first he gave me only what I needed—a friend, a compassionate ear, and a voice of wise counsel. He seduced first my mind and my heart. Then he claimed my body and my soul. Laying in his arms, making love to him, was like being touched by love itself, joining with something greater than I could ever hope to be alone, becoming part of something vaster and more permanent than any act or work that I could myself conceive.

It is odd, now that Michael is gone, that I can recall so much that *was good in him, and forget all else as I choose. I loved him then, and I love him still, and I can remember the things that made me love him without pain, without shame, without feeling manipulated, misused, and betrayed. I loved him, even when he turned to Antonius solely to cause me pain. I loved him, even when I saw what he was becoming in his madness, what he would do when that madness finally consumed him. I loved him even when he did not truly love me any longer, for I could not help myself—he had become a part of me, inextricable as my own flesh, my own bone. A part of me died when I turned away from him, when I left him as much to save myself as to save him. My presence could not save him, but I hoped against hope that my absence could. I knew that staying would drag me down in madness along with him, and destroy everything that I tried to create.*

I loved him, and I abandoned him to his destruction. There are not enough words in all the world to define how much I despise myself for that cowardice.

Part Two

Dragon's Eyes

*Odio et amo: quare id faciem, fortasse requiris.
Nescio, sed fieri sentio et excrucior. (I love and I
hate. You ask me why this is so; I do not know, but I
feel it, and it torments me.)*

—Catullus

Chapter Eleven

Winter released its grip on the mountains grudgingly. Three weeks passed from Myca's departure before the weather warmed enough for rain to fall regularly, and the snowmelt to begin in earnest. The ground in the monastery garden began thawing, and the trees in the monastery orchard grew red with sap and began to bud. Ilias, witnessing this from within the confines of a cloister belonging to a faith not his own, grew restless, wanting to be out among the trees, listening to the quickening rhythms of the earth. He remained at the monastery only because the road was still too chancy to rely upon, being covered most of its length in a revolting mixture of mud and rapidly disintegrating slush, unfit for the feet of men or beasts.

Three more weeks passed, and the worst of the rains eased, though it remained windy. The monks told Ilias that the forests on the lower slopes were fully in bud, a beautiful sight during the day, and he silently envied them their ability to witness that sight. Snow lingered now only on those heights that were always snowy, and the darkest, coolest parts of the valleys. Another week, and the road was almost dry enough to ride, consisting of only three inches of mud instead of ten. Ilias decided to give it another week, and put his servants to work grinding salt and herbs, packing ritual implements, and acquiring equipment sufficient for the purpose he had in mind. Father Aron was somewhat bemused by a few of the requests he received that week, but provided all the buckets and floor-scrubbing implements they required.

Ilias and his four most favored servants departed the monastery early one evening, descending the hill carefully, and made for a traveler's hostel maintained by the Obertus brothers on the road that led to Brasov. The hostel, forewarned of their coming, had rooms prepared for their daylight rest, which Ilias at least took advantage of. The four mortals napped for a few hours, accepted the meal that the Obertus brothers offered them, then rode off again along a track that the hostler-monks knew led into the dense forest to the west, rather than into the city itself. They departed carrying much of the baggage and a supply of their own food. They did not return as the day grew late, making the brothers a bit fearful for their safety. When Ilias awoke at sunset, they broached the matter to him and he, touched by their concern, informed the brothers that his servants were in no danger. They had ridden ahead to prepare his house for him, which was only a short distance into the forest. Then he also departed, amused beyond the capacity for words.

Ilias was not at all alarmed by the failure of his servants to return, for he realized there would be a great deal of work to do at the sanctuary. The winter had been harsh, and detritus had no doubt accumulated accordingly. He also knew that those he had chosen were up to the task, the most dedicated of his personal followers. He rode in their tracks, lighting the way with a lantern on a long pole, following the route he had mapped out for them and the way-markers he himself had placed. Here, a tree split by lightning, still standing despite the ferocity of the winter wind; there, a huge mossy boulder, almost precisely triangular, jutting out of the leaf-mould like a fang. The trees were, indeed, all in bud, their branches lashed by the blustery spring wind, last autumn's damp leaves drifting across the path. The forest thickened as he approached the sanctuary itself, and the path grew narrower. He dismounted, and led his placid and well-trained mount the last stretch. Though the thick-clustered trees, he caught a glimmer of light from the candle-lamps outside the small structure of the sanctum itself and heard the sound of horses whickering from the animal enclosure behind it.

The temple of Jarilo was not an elaborate structure, but it was adequate for its purposes. Its sanctum was a low, round building of wood and stone, roofed in wooden tiles, lacking windows, containing little besides an open space of floor for a small congregation to sit and a low wooden altar for offerings. For most of the year, Ilias left it untended, that those who wished to come and make their offerings and devotions in privacy could do so. During the months from planting to high summer, he spent most of his nights there, acting in the position for which his sire had Embraced him, the immortal witch-priest, servant to the god of the reborn earth, the bright beauties of spring. The rest of the sanctuary he let grow wild, a forested expanse of hidden glades and quick-running streams, with only one large assembly area, the wooden circle where the rites of high summer, the feast of Kupala, were usually held.

From what he could see, his servants had done well, gathering up the deadfall wood and stacking it beneath a heavy leather covering in the lee of the sanctum, and sweeping clean the stone walkway leading up to the building. He took his horse to the animal enclosure, and there found Miklos on watch, tending the beasts and guarding against predators, for wolves prowled the woods. The boy leapt up to help him, and Ilias gave him the reins and a cool-lipped kiss of thanks, which he blushed to accept.

"The cleansing goes well?" Ilias asked, glancing about the enclosure. It, too, appeared swept clean, the hay and oats fresh, the water troughs well filled.

"Very well, *koldun*. We finished the sanctum and the area around it first, as you asked. There wasn't as much damage as we feared—the roof didn't lose any tiles this year." Miklos smiled, his gray eyes alight with humor. "Nico complained about the dust, but he always does, and there were a great many offerings left. We saved them in the chest you gave us."

"Excellent. The others are asleep?"

"Yes, *koldun*."

"Then I'll not wake them." Ilias reached up and removed a woolen cloak lined in fur from the pannier of his saddle. "Someone is going to replace you?"

"Yes, *koldun*. Sergiusz made Nico and Teo promise to take turns before we did anything else." Again, his little grin lit his face, and Ilias patted his cheek gently.

"Good. I shall return before dawn. Do not forget to sleep, Miklos."

And, so saying, Ilias went to walk beneath the trees of his own sanctuary, the place that was his and his alone.

That day, as he slept safe in the windowless darkness of the sanctum, Ilias dreamed strange dreams. In his ears, a solemn voice spoke a language he did not know, softly but with great urgency. In his mind's eye, images flickered but refused to come into focus, smears of color spreading across the inside of his thoughts, indistinct but profoundly disturbing. He woke unsettled in his nest of sleeping furs behind the altar, screened off against stray light passing through the seams of the door, and lay for a moment trying to convince his mind to yield up a single coherent thought. As he did, a single image came to him: a tall figure, dark of hair and lithe of form, clad all in red silk, his hair trailing nearly to the floor, walking between columns of blue marble, as though he were in a dream, or dreams made flesh himself.

Ilias sat up slowly, and took several deep, deliberate breaths to calm himself. He felt, for no reason that he could name, that he should know who that man was, should know him as he knew his own blood and flesh, but could not see his face. It chilled him to the bone.

It took four days and nights to prepare the sanctuary to Ilias' satisfaction. By day the four boys labored physically, sweeping paths clean, gathering fallen wood, carting away last year's ashes from the several fire pits scattered about the sanctuary. By night, Ilias offered a spiritual cleansing, scattering the paths with herbs and fragrant oils, renewing the circles of salt and blood that delineated the boundaries of the wooden circle, its carven plinths cleansed with saltwater. Slowly, he felt the presence of the spirits and the gods returning, waking after a long winter's rest. The trees murmured to each other in their own tongues and, out of the corner of his eyes, he caught the bright flicker of their souls and their attendant spirits as the air warmed and the buds began to unfurl.

Ilias brought his tools with him, and by day had them placed in the clearing outside the wooden circle—a small altar carved from the heartwood of a lightning-struck beech tree, a carved stone bowl, a wooden bucket of water drawn from a spring in the sanctuary. When he rose that night, he bathed himself in salted water and dressed in a long white tunic and a circlet made of beaten gold in the shape of flowers and vines. Sergiusz and Nicolaus, having slept much of the day, were awake and accompanied him as he walked the path to the circle, barefoot, carrying the symbols of his office, a human skull in one hand, and a sheaf of last autumn's wheat in the other. Sergiusz went first, carrying an iron candle-lamp in one hand and a bag of salt and herbs in the other. Nico followed behind, carrying four beeswax candles and the bag containing two handfuls of Nikita's grave-earth.

Overhead, the sky was clear and star-strewn, and the moon was dark. Sergiusz's lamp provided the only light as they stepped into the clearing. He stood, a silver-gilt sentinel, as Ilias carried the altar and the bowl into the circle of wooden plinths and laid the skull and the wheat upon it. Nicolaus gave him the candles, which he lit and placed on the altar; the water, he poured into the bowl. Sergiusz gave him the salt, and Nicolaus gave him the earth; he kissed them both in thanks and murmured, "Go back to the sanctum. I shall return before dawn."

They went. Ilias stepped across the lines of blood and salt sanctifying the circle, and knelt before the altar, soaking his tunic and his legs in dew. The salt, ground together with visionary herbs, he used to trace a circle around the bowl, and lay a bit beneath his tongue. He left it there to melt, savoring the bitterness, closing his eyes and feeling the power welling up within him. The words came to him easily, the invocations of water and earth, calling upon the spirits to open wide his eyes, to show him what he needed to see. With his thumbnail, he slit open his wrist and dripped nine drops of his own blood into the waters filling his vision-bowl. With that same hand, he reached into the bag of Nikita's earth, and added to the water nine pinches of that earth, dark and grainy, oddly textured against Ilias' fingertips.

It did not begin immediately. The spirits of water were more mercurial than those of earth, cool and changeable, and even when one invoked them properly and gave offerings to their taste, they often desired more than one would be willing to pay. He felt the spirits contained within the bowl swirling about the earth and the blood, considering—and then felt them accept.

The water churned, and shot upwards in a steaming, swirling column, coiling around itself and forming a perfect, shimmering sphere. Ilias raised his arms, weighted with the dragging, swirling hunger of the water, and thrust his hands into the sphere, letting the visions it would impart flow over him and draw him down.

He sensed a vast distance, far greater than anything he had every felt before, a gulf of space and age that beggared his imagination. For an instant, he *saw* nothing but a great rushing darkness, the passage of many miles, and then it came to him—

Mountains... high, snow-capped mountains, higher even than the mountains of the east, standing sentinel against the deep blue sky—

Wind, cold—the air was dry against his skin—

Home. He felt it in his blood, in his flesh, in his soul. This place, this high and stark and beautiful place, was Nikita's home. There was no sea. There was not even much forest, the heights given over to scrub and stone and snow. There was nothing put mountains as far as he could see, mountains and a great starry arch of sky, the ancient bones of the earth exposed beneath the eyes of heaven. He felt the age and the strength of the spirits of this land, their beauty and their cruelty, and their strangely absolute mutability. Fire was fire but intermingled with earth and air in a way that defied his ability to fully perceive it. The spirit of this land itself seemed to have been shaped somehow, worked, blended together in a manner suited to a will not its own. It was like nothing he had felt anywhere in the east, and he had, in his time, traveled many of those lands and spoken with their spirits. He knelt, and ran his hand over the earth, cool and dark and frozen, and tried to bespeak the spirits—

Chaos exploded before his eyes, within his mind, a howling maelstrom of pain and rage and grief that clawed at the core of his own essence. He screamed and tried to pull himself back, hurl himself away—

And came back to himself, flat on his back, his skull swimming with pain and exhaustion, his throat raw from screaming. There was no light but starlight. The water had fallen, and doused the candles. For a long moment, Ilias could do nothing but lay there in shock, watching explosions of painful color pass before his eyes as the aftermath of the vision faded slowly. He rose to his hands and knees, wearily, acknowledging to himself that the spirits were getting a bit too avaricious in their demands on his person, and perhaps he should be less tolerant in the future. He crawled to the edge of the circle and pulled himself to his feet with the aid of a plinth, his knees weak and the muscles of his legs ropy from the drain on his blood and spirit. It took far longer than he liked to reach the sanctum, leaning on trees and crawling when he had to, the sky growing gradually grayer as the dawn approached.

Miklos and Teodor were waiting for him when he reached the door and helped him inside, removing the crown from his tangled hair and the muddied tunic from his body. As they bundled him into his nest of sleeping furs, the last thought that came to him before exhaustion claimed his mind was that Nikita did *not* come from Sredetz.

Chapter Twelve

Ilias' party returned to the monastery two weeks later, after he had officiated over the rites of returning spring, accepting the offerings of those who knelt to the priests of the Christ by day, but acknowledged that earth and night were full of gods, as well. There, he found a letter waiting for him from Myca, requesting that he join him in Alba Iulia as soon as could be arranged. Before that week was out, Ilias was on the road again with his mortal entourage and the six members of Symeon's personal guard who delivered the message in the first place. The guards were all *szlachta*, warrior-ghouls who concealed the modifications to their flesh beneath armor and clothing, a fact for which Ilias was grateful. Symeon of Constantinople did not waste any tender aesthetic sensibilities on the men he expected to die in his service.

The Obertus house in Alba Iulia was not a religious establishment, but one like many others clustered around the town's market square, two modest stories high with a cluster of storage buildings behind it. The first floor was given over to a genuine business, owned and operated by a family long in Myca's service, who dealt in luxury goods, furs and spices and the fine amber and pigeon's blood rubies of the east. The second was the Obertus "embassy," Myca's offices and windowless sleeping chamber, perpetually scented with the fine spices residing in the first floor storage rooms. Ilias, who normally disliked most towns on general principles, found little to detest about Alba Iulia, small and picturesque along the banks of the Mures.

They arrived close to midnight, detained only briefly by

the men of the town watch. They were permitted passage after the captain of Symeon's guardsmen showed the captain of the watch a letter affixed with an enormous waxen seal. It was clear that not a one of them had the letters to read it, but the seal itself seemed to contain all the information they needed. Ilias was, not for the first time, grateful for the efficiency with which Symeon of Constantinople bought or intimidated his lessers. Some few people were still about the market square, scattered with puddles from a recent rainfall, most of them the patrons of a tavern on the corner, its doors and lower shutters thrown open to let in the pleasant evening air. A light burned in the ground floor study of the Obertus house, and a sleepy servant answered their summons at the door. Ilias, his attendants, and their baggage were ushered inside, while the guardsmen went in search of a place to stable the mounts.

The servants slept in a small room off the kitchen, and pallets were already prepared for Ilias' servants, as were soup and cheese to repair their hunger, and Ilias sent them off to dine and rest. The master of the house himself rose, wrapped in a rich brocade sleeping robe, to see Ilias upstairs, where Myca waited. A smile touched the *koldun's* mouth as he beheld his lover for the first time in many weeks, completely oblivious to his arrival, hunched over a slanted desk on which was spread his leather-bound journal and a handful of loose parchment sheets, writing in the light of two low-burning candle lamps. Ilias bowed shallowly in thanks to the sleepy merchant, and crossed the room on cat's feet, resting his hands on Myca's shoulders and murmuring, "I suppose if I must share you with any other lover, at least that lover is a book."

Myca did not start or otherwise show the slightest trace of surprise. Instead, he straightened in his low-backed chair and leaned his head against Ilias' breast, inviting a caress, which Ilias was quite pleased to give. A low sound, almost a purr, escaped Myca's throat as Ilias stroked his hair, worked his thumbs into the tense muscles of his lover's neck, the taut, slender shoulders clad in silk. They kissed in greeting, lingering over each other's lips. When they broke apart, Myca murmured, with a soft smile, "You are entirely superior to a book, my heart."

"I should hope so, if for no other reason than the fact that books lack hands." Ilias found a second stool, backless and shorter in legs, and pulled it close. "I trust your business with your sire went well?"

"Very well, indeed." The smile did not fade; in fact, it grew a shade more satisfied, and Ilias inclined a questioning brow in response. "My lord sire wishes me to ride south to the domain of Ioan Brancoveanu, to summon the Hammer of the Tremere to council in Oradea, and entreat him to add his voice to the accord of peace and brotherhood being built between his sire and his uncle-in-blood."

"Well," Ilias replied phlegmatically, not certain how to respond. "That sounds like an exercise in futility, and a disaster waiting to happen."

"Possibly both. In the time I was in Oradea, I did not receive the impression that Lukasz and Rachlav's followers waste much brotherly amity on each other, and I am not convinced that we can trust even self-interest to keep them from reopening hostilities at the first available opportunity." None of this seemed to be bothering Myca in the slightest, which Ilias found faintly amusing. "However, the intrinsic untrustworthiness of Lukasz and Rachlav is not really my problem, nor will it be in the future. I need only to inform Ioan that his sire desires him to give his approval to the alliance and convince him that doing so is in his best interest, which, given that the man is not a fool, should not require too much effort."

"You *have* noticed that Ioan is not a fool," Ilias pointed out, delicately.

"Yes. I have also noticed that he is bogged down in his current position and has been for almost a decade, and that any potential change in that status quo can, for him, only be a good thing. Even if the alliance between Lukasz and Rachlav proves to be fleeting, Ioan may be able to reap some benefit from it. After all, their forces could defect to *his* service, without damaging their own honor in the eyes of the clan."

"Are you thinking out loud," Ilias asked, "or practicing your arguments on me?"

"Both." Myca reached out and caught his hand, running a

thumb along Ilias' knuckles. "You made good time. I was not expecting you for another week, at least."

"The rites were somewhat sparsely attended this year." Ilias admitted. "I suspect that I'll come back to a number of offerings in the sanctuary. The roads were disgusting after you left. Do not change the subject."

Myca pressed a kiss to his knuckles. "I am not changing the subject. I do not intend to fail with Ioan—for when I am finished with him, Symeon his given me permission to investigate Nikita to my own satisfaction."

Ilias' eyebrows rose slightly in surprise. "Now, that is a surprise."

"I agree, but Symeon seems genuinely concerned, and wishes to know how Nikita managed to suborn an Obertus monastery to his service. I have already written to the prince of Sredetz, requesting permission to travel there as part of my investigation and begging whatever assistance he may wish to provide." Myca leaned forward in his chair, placing a stopper in his bottle of ink and closing his journal. "By the time we are finished with Ioan, we may have even received a reply. I wish you to accompany me, if you desire."

"Of course. You could not, I will tell you now, successfully make me stay behind." Ilias smiled, somewhat crookedly. "I did as you asked, and interrogated the spirits of Nikita's earth. Or, to be more precise, I attempted to interrogate them. I did not receive much concrete information, but I feel quite strongly that Nikita does not come from Sredetz. When we go there, I will know for certain if that intuition is true or not."

"I felt within myself, some time ago, that you were very weary and… possibly injured?" Myca's tone was coolly neutral, a request for information rather than an expression of concern. Ilias felt the anxiety underlying it, anyway, but answered the question instead.

"I was not injured. The pain was not my own, but Nikita's—it invaded my being when I attempted to bespeak the spirits of his earth. It was, however, a rather tiring effort." A pause. "Nikita is much stronger than he should be, Myca, and perhaps much older, for a man so little renowned within the clan."

Myca nodded fractionally. "I have thought as much myself. In any case, we will soon be free to pursue the mystery of him, and, until then, your magics hold him well. Malachite will also be accompanying us, at my sire's request, though he remains in Oradea until my mission here is complete."

"You trust him to do so?" Ilias asked.

"I trust my sire to keep him in check." Myca replied, grimly. "And I trust Malachite to abide by the will of the last surviving ruler of the Trinity families of Byzantium."

Ilias nodded. "You wish, I take it, for me to accompany you to see Ioan, as well?"

"Yes. It is my understanding that he holds the *koldun* lineages in high esteem and that he himself hosts a *koldun* in his court, such as it is..." Myca trailed off, his tone faintly questioning.

"I have heard that, as well. In fact, I have heard that he harbors no less a *koldun* than the Shaper priestess of the Mother herself, Danika Ruthven, childe of the eldest of the *bogatyri* kinlines." Ilias smoothed his tunic over his knees, somewhat nervously. "She attended at my Embrace, and neither her power nor her wisdom can be overstated. She is certainly one to cultivate as an advocate, and was a friend of my sire for many centuries."

"Then I will leave the fearsome Lady Danika to your charms, my heart." Myca rose, and doused the lower of the two candles. "Come. I will have a bath drawn. You have traveled far, and I am very pleased to see you again."

Ilias rose, and smiled, teasingly, at the eagerness that underlay his lover's brisk tone. "Oh, good. I was beginning to wonder if I would have to wait all night."

Once Ilias arrived, the preparations for departure were rapidly completed: There were a sufficient number of horses , and a heavy cart in which the two Cainites would travel by day, protected if not wholly comfortable. Myca had already been in contact with Ioan, requesting permission to travel into his domain, and Ioan's stipulations in agreement to that request were several. They were not given permission to travel directly into his territory. They were to meet his envoy at the edge of the lands he claimed, and travel on from there under that envoy's guidance.

They would also depart from his domain under guard, and they would not travel anywhere within his domain without an escort. He could not, he emphasized pointedly, entirely guarantee their safety while on the road, as his domain consisted almost entirely of territory contested with varying degrees of pugnacity by the Tremere. They were to come prepared to defend themselves as necessary, but should limit their numbers sensibly, the better to make speed. Myca ultimately decided to bring the entire complement of guards lent to him by his sire, and Ilias' half-dozen attendants, as well, reasoning that some would no doubt be sent back, anyway. They rode almost due south from Alba Iulia, and as they went the terrain grew steadily rougher and higher in elevation. Despite the fact that spring was well advanced, the nights continued cool enough that the warmth of fires and mortal attendants was a necessity, not a luxury—at least insofar as Ilias was concerned. By day, the party traveled, Ilias and Myca together in their single light-proofed conveyance, knowing that soon the road would run out and they would be traveling rough across country.

The party arrived at the meeting place Ioan had stipulated at midday, setting up camp beside the crossroads and waiting patiently for night to come. The forest had not been cleared back far from the edge of the road, though several small clearings were clearly used by travelers forced to camp rather than continue to their destinations. Ilias and Myca, cramped in their accommodations, rose as soon as the last sliver of sun passed behind the mountains, found the majority of their servants in a pleasing state of watchful preparedness, and settled in to wait, as well. They did not have to wait long.

Ioan Brancoveanu's envoy heralded her own arrival with a lupine chorus. Pale-furred shapes emerged from the foliage at the edge of the wood, their eyes catching the light of cook-fires and low-burning lamps, their voices filling the night with a sound both fearsome and oddly mournful. A nervous young guardsman reached for his bow, only to be restrained by an older, more experienced colleague. Myca, seated on a low bench next to the cart in which he and Ilias had traveled, rose and closed the book he had been reading with the aid of a candle. Ilias came instantly to his side, standing back a pace, profoundly calm and watchful. Deep inside himself, Myca felt the essence of Ilias' thought—that the envoy was among the pack of wolves slowly ringing their camp, and was watching to see how they would react. Myca nodded fractionally in agreement with that assessment, and laid aside his book, letting his hands fall to his sides and striding to the edge of the encampment where the guards now stood, watching tensely. He could hardly blame them, with this impressive number of wolves playing hide and seek with the camp's fires.

He stopped just outside the perimeter of the camp itself, beyond the ring of tents and the cart, but not inside the wood itself, and spoke clearly into the darkness beneath the trees. "I am Myca Vykos, childe of Symeon, childe of Gesu, childe of the Dracon, childe of the Eldest. I come in the name of my sire and my house to seek speech with Ioan Brancoveanu, childe of Lukasz, childe of Noriz, childe of Djavakhi, childe of the Eldest. I come in the name of peace, so I swear by Earth and Sky, and the Waters of Life and Death."

"Do you?" The voice was soft, husky, wholly feminine, and came from his left. "It was my understanding that we were merely seeking a new way to make war."

Myca turned and bowed smoothly to the woman who stood before him, rising after an appropriately respectful moment. "Perhaps we are, my lady, and perhaps we are not. I bring word to your lord of peace among his own kin, at least, and if that leads to another sort of war," Myca shrugged gracefully, "it is not my place to pass judgment."

"Diplomats." Her appearance indicated the woman was a Gangrel, one of the feral Cainites who made their homes in the wild places of the world. She was by no means *hideous*, Myca thought, but she showed her acquaintance with her own Beast quite clearly. Her eyes caught the light and reflected it in points of gold, much like her lupine pets, and her tawny hair had more in common with an animal's pelt than anything else. She did not, however, appear to cherish any particular bias against clothing, and wore a long pale tunic, belted at the waist, and sturdy leather boots. "I am Lukina of the *Veela*, and my lord has sent me to be your guide."

They departed the next night, considerably reduced in numbers and weight, at Lukina's insistence. The cart they had always intended to send back, but with it went four of Ilias' six attendants and half the bodyguards Symeon had assigned. Packed inside it was the majority of the unnecessary clothing, bedding, and supplies of food they had carried with them from Alba Iulia. Lukina informed them that the traveling and sleeping would be rough, and anyone who could not keep up would be left behind. She only permitted them to take sufficient horses and two pack animals after Myca urgently pointed out that he had no intention whatsoever of walking halfway across the mountains, and there was no room for flexibility in his position on that issue. Lukina snarled and made a number of uncomplimentary remarks about the dainty tenderness of the Tzimisce these nights, but ultimately relented.

They made decent enough time on the ascent through the lower slopes, where the roads were better and a number of villages huddled in the highest valleys, eking out a living in the shadow of the peaks. Most of the people were shepherds or goatherds, or foresters making their living on the chancier trades of trapping and hunting. There were few fields to be found, and what fields there were grew only enough for subsistence, not trade or taxes. Most of the folk had also been taught not to welcome chance-met travelers who arrived by night, likely by harsh fortune. Unlike their lowland cousins, their hospitality was purchasable by sufficient weight in silver, but was generally not free for the asking. Soon, even the modest comforts of a lightless storage cellar for the day's rest were a luxury as they climbed higher into the mountains.

The roads became little better than goat tracks winding through the high, narrow passes, continuously swept by cool, dry winds. By day, they slept in closely grouped camps, buried in the rocky earth beneath canvas tarps and heavy furs, or in caves when such amenities were close enough to the trail. Broad-leafed trees vanished entirely, replaced by dark forests of fur and pine that swallowed the light of their lamps and torches as they traveled by night. Lukina's wolves dogged their tracks, keeping watch and, occasionally, sounding warning. Things moved among the trees, their footfalls softened by the carpet of fallen needles, avoiding the reach of the brightest firelight, their presences apparent only with the infrequent glimpse of something huge and misshapen slipping past the corner of the eye, or the lingering sense of malignance they left hanging in the air. When Myca questioned Lukina on the issue, she informed him that not everything stalking the mountains belonged to Ioan or the Tremere. Some things darker still came to feed on the remnants of the war, and it was best to avoid crossing paths with such things. She spoke those words with the first hint of genuine fear he had seen in her, and so he was inclined to give them credit, for the woman was nothing if not hard minded and capable.

Myca had expected Ilias to fare somewhat poorly on the journey, relatively soft as the last few years had been for him, but the *koldun*-priest of Jarilo rose to the challenge with ease. Myca had to remind himself, somewhat wryly, as he watched his slender, seemingly delicate lover negotiating narrow trails and the hardships of the road with perfect ease, that not so long ago Ilias was a wanderer who traveled from one end of the east almost to the other, rarely settling in one court for any length of time. Even Lukina was grudgingly impressed with his stamina and his woodcraft and, more importantly, his complete failure to whine about any inconvenience, no matter how obnoxious. He was, however, more quiet than usual, nearly withdrawn, and Myca endeavored to remain as close to him as possible, sensing some inner uneasiness. When Lukina announced, five days into the mountains, that they were nearing the territory directly under Ioan Brancoveanu's rule, Ilias shivered slightly, and Myca saw it.

When they retired late that night to their shallow pit-bed beneath the pines, Myca wrapped his arms around his lover and drew him close. "What troubles you?"

Ilias was silent for a long time, winding their fingers together and leaning his head back against Myca's chest. Amazingly, his hair still smelled faintly of linden. Finally, he whispered, "I have never been this close to a place where war has been fought with magic. It feels..." Another shiver. "It does not feel right."

"No," Myca replied, softly. "I do not imagine that it does. Are you well, my heart? Can you continue on?"

Ilias lifted one of Myca's hands to his lips. Against his palm, he could feel his lover's wan smile, then a cool, gentle kiss. "I am not well. Can I endure it? Yes. I will not send you to face Ioan by yourself, with only ghouls to defend and advise you. We shall come through this together, and we will be the stronger for it."

After that, they spoke no more of the matter, and if the blight of sorcerous war scourged Ilias' soul, he kept his pain to himself.

Chapter Thirteen

Two nights later, they crossed the border into Ioan Brancoveanu's domain. No physical barrier that Myca could perceive marked the transition, but the change was palpable nonetheless. Lukina and her wolves, all of whom had prevailed snappish and temperamental, perceptibly relaxed a fraction, tension lessening as they re-entered their home range. The forest itself almost seemed less unwelcoming, better suited to the passage of travelers. Darkness still lurked beneath the pines, but it was a natural darkness, cool spring night rather than the twisted remnants of baneful magics. Ilias brightened up, as well, his discomfort lessening so dramatically that Myca remarked on it.

"Something protects this place, more powerfully than the route we took to make it here," Ilias replied, thoughtfully, as they bedded down for the day.

"Lady Danika's work?" Ilias' pain had manifested in such a way that, for the first time since Myca met him, he was completely disinclined to be touched. Now, he was entirely content to be held as they curled together on silken mats filled with grave-earth.

"Possibly. She is very strong. I remember her as being very strong." He rested his head beneath Myca's chin. "But, even so, she is only one and she must spend her strength wisely."

Myca nodded wordlessly and drew his lover closer, feeling, for the first time, the fragility that lurked beneath his strength, and wondering if the consequences were worth the power the *koldun* called their own. He himself had felt not a trace of discomfort traveling through the mountains, but rather had felt strangely exhilarated, as though he were coming home for the first time in ages, almost as powerfully as he had felt it when he first set foot on the soil of his homeland after fleeing Constantinople. Beyond the mountains to the south lay Ceoris, where he had spent his mortal youth. A small part of him still regarded it with an emotion similar to affection, though he had few good memories of the place itself, or the people who dwelt there. It was, nonetheless, still a part of him, an admission he made without difficulty or guilt—Ceoris and the Tremere had in part made him what he was, but they were not the whole of him, a truth that he had struggled with in silence for many years. One night, he would possess in full the power they claimed, and he would do so on his own terms. For now, he was content with their place in his past, and what he had become since he left them, however involuntarily.

Holding that contentment close, he closed his eyes, and let sleep claim him.

Myca woke to a chorus of howls, Lukina's pack singing with full-throated gusto, and he wondered blearily if the moon was full tonight.

"Moon-rise will not be for hours yet." Ilias replied aloud to the silent question. "The sun is only just down."

"So I feel." It took a moment for Myca to work up the energy to push himself to his elbows, particularly with Ilias draped across his chest yet. "What do you suppose it is?"

"I have no idea." Ilias reached up and lifted the tarpaulin covering their resting place a few inches. "Alin?"

A pair of hands slid under the edge of the tarp and lifted it, allowing the light from a candle-lamp to fall over them, the younger of the two attendants Ilias had brought with him peering in. Myca noticed that the boy was unusually pale and seemed more nervous than usual; Ilias generally chose his servants for their steady temperaments as much as for their aesthetic appeal. "Master?"

"What is going on? The wolves…"

Alin licked his lips and replied, as steadily as he could, "We were joined during the day by a patrol from the *voivode*'s manse.

They say their captain will be joining us shortly, to guide us the rest of the way in."

Myca and Ilias exchanged a glance as Alin, aided by the older, taller Isak rolled back the tarp and assisted them in rising, then rapidly began breaking down and packing away the tent that stood over them, as well. The rest of the camp was already broken down, the men clearly prepared to move at a moment's notice, tending to their restive horses and making certain that all the baggage was lashed down properly. Scattered among them were a number of men (and some few women) not originally of their company, clad in light leather armor and what appeared to be reinforcements of pale bone, armed with short, powerful bows, short wasp-waisted swords, and, in several cases, single-edged hatchets. Lukina stood in the center of the clearing in which they'd camped, next to a low-burning fire, deep in conversation with a hulking figure that could only be loosely described as human-seeming. It was at least seven feet tall—the top of its spike-tipped helmet brushed the lowest branches above their heads—armored and armed, its face covered in a mask of shaped bone, its eyes dark pools within the sockets of the mask. Myca glided forward across the soft bed of pine needles to join the group. Lukina nodded shortly to him in greeting and the giant bowed low, dark hair braided together with bone ornaments spilling over its shoulders.

"*Stapân* Vykos, this is Vlastimir Vlaszy, lieutenant to my lord *voivode* Ioan Brancoveanu cel Macelar," Lukina introduced them, with a passable attempt at formality.

Very properly, the *voivode*'s giant lieutenant waited until Vykos acknowledged his obeisance before rising. "*Stapân* Vykos." The voice that emerged from behind the twisted beast-face of the mask was deep and rich, cultured. "I give you greetings in the name of my lord *voivode*, Ioan Brancoveanu cel Macelar, and welcome you to his domain. He will be joining us presently."

"The *voivode* is gracious. I did not expect him to greet us personally. I and my house are honored." Myca bowed himself, shallowly, in response to this, and rose to find Ilias at his shoulder. "My advisor, Ilias cel Frumos, *koldun*-priest of Jarilo."

All about them, the lupine chorus swelled, and abruptly ceased. Lukina raised her head and listened tensely then announced, "He comes."

A stir began at the edge of the camp, many of the new arrivals coming forth to give obeisance to their commander as he joined them. Ioan was preceded by two enormous warriors in their *zulo* shapes, mottled ghost gray and night black, almost invisible in the near-total darkness but for the bright yellow sparks of their eyes. He was otherwise unattended and wore no other form. Myca was startled to realize that Ioan was actually shorter than himself, standing only a finger or two taller than Ilias. The force of presence he exuded gave him the illusion of much greater size as he joined them, quietly and without ceremony, at the fireside, his giant lieutenant bowing to the ground and being waved up with barely a pause.

Myca was not entirely certain what he had expected, but Ioan did not seem to fit the general image of the ravening Tzimisce warlord he had constructed over the years. Certainly, he was clad in armor, the same dark leathers and pale worked bone reinforcements, and certainly he was armed, the pommel of the weapon at his hip a snarling dragon's head of shaped bone. A bone mask that fit so closely it seemed crafted in place gave his face a vaguely reptilian image. The eyes behind that mask were a shade of brown pale enough to seem amber-golden in the firelight and his pale blonde hair fell to his waist in a multitude of slender braids wound with bone beads and ornaments. A necklace hung to mid-chest, also strung with carved and polished bone charms. He *looked* appropriately feral, but force of personality that rolled from him did not bespeak a creature of mindless destruction. Myca received the impression of great calm, a questing mind, curiosity tinged with interest.

Ilias and Myca bowed simultaneously and their host waved them up as quickly as he had his servant. "No ceremony now, my lord *stapân* Vykos, my lord *koldun* Ilias cel Frumos. There will be time enough for it later, and we must make speed tonight. I wish to reach the bastion before dawn. I trust you are prepared to travel?"

Myca absorbed this lack of formality with barely a blink. "Of course, my lord *voivode*."

Ioan nodded sharply. "Then let us make haste."

Ioan set a brisk pace for the last leg of the journey, most of which they undertook on foot, leading their horses single file up narrow trails. The bulk of the party he broke up into groups of twos and threes, accompanied by one or two of his warriors, staggering their passage through some of the narrower areas and sending some by other routes entirely. Even so, they made excellent time up the last steep series of switchbacks, reaching the edge of the valley Ioan called his own with the sky only beginning to show signs of paling.

Looking down into the valley from the high ridge above it, Myca was quietly impressed. The "bastion," which his imagination had insisted would be a fortress, actually resembled more of a town, smaller than Alba Iulia, and contained entirely within the bounds of what appeared to be a low earth-and-stone wall. Roughly semicircular, it surrounded a terraced rise at the opposite edge of the valley, on which was constructed another series of walls—a series of palisades, more accurately, of rammed earth and stone topped in sharpened logs. Myca concentrated briefly, drawing on all the light available to him—starlight, moonlight, the lamps their party carried and the torches lit on the walls in the town below—and tried to see more detail as they descended the packed-earth road, leading their horses and following Ioan, who led the way.

"The rim of the valley is warded... by earth and fire, I think," Ilias murmured as they walked, looking about curiously. They were passing through an area of cultivation, vegetable plots for the most part. No large fields appeared immediately apparent, but Myca supposed they might always trade for sufficient grain.

Myca cast a glance about and, here and there, he caught sight of wooden plinths, carved and hung with charms of carved bone, wood, and metal. "The plinths are the wards? Or the anchors for the magic?"

"Yes. I saw some carved in the rocks along the road, as well, and there were two small ones hidden just off the road at the top of the rise." Myca watched his lover out of the corner of his eyes, and caught him, more than once, gazing fixedly at something Myca himself could not perceive. "I think the defenses around the rim are supposed to *protect* against fire. I did not see any signs of forest fire, but that does not mean that they were never nearly burned out of this place."

"The spirit-arts can accomplish that sort of defense?"

"If you entreat them properly, yes. Stone-spirits are a bastion against even skyfire, correctly instructed. I am certain that's a fire-break up there. And the plinths in the fields? Protection against foul weather and curses to blight the land, unless I miss my guess." Ilias rubbed his chin thoughtfully. "Well constructed, as well. But, then, I would expect at least that much from Lady Danika. She did not strike me as the sort to do things in half-measures."

They crossed the first of the walls, which was, as Myca had thought, constructed of a rammed-earth embankment four feet in height, topped in a mortared stone wall that stood another three feet above that. Beyond it, the town was silent and darkened, sleeping, and they passed through it quietly. Occasionally, Ilias gestured silently at something that caught his eye—the beaten-metal charms set into the rear of the wall, bits of carving on the lintels of doors—most of which seemed to have some kind of sorcerous significance. At the base of the terraces leading up to the far edge of the valley and the larger palisade, they were met by a collection of servants, who took the horses and baggage in hand, and they proceeded the rest of the way unencumbered.

Myca was beginning to suspect that Ioan had arranged this entire event for his benefit, and so he took copious mental notes, refusing to be intimidated but admitting to himself that the Hammer of the Tremere might not simply be all reputation. Skill was evident in the design and construction of this place and discipline was even more apparent among the men and women who occupied it. The palisade was guarded and patrolled, mostly by mortals, *szlachta* and revenants of martial disposition, Myca didn't doubt, but here and there he perceived the pale aura of a vampire, many of whom appeared to be prepared for immediate action, not simply command. The road wound up the side of the hill and, on each terrace, he caught glimpses of motion that suggested focused, organized activity. He did not see any dwelling places, per se, and that surprised him somewhat, until they reached the uppermost tier of the fortress.

Ioan's manse was built into the mountain itself, burrowed into the rise of the valley. From on high, Myca realized that the entire upper fortress was likely underground, and possibly accommodated far more people, and far more vampires, than he originally suspected. The visible portion of the manse itself was a series of low, domelike structures constructed of what appeared to be pressed earth and stone, rising out of the hill as though they had grown there instead of being built, with a small courtyard between them and the uppermost palisade. Torches flickered in the courtyard, and a pair of oil lamps lit the main door to the manse. Here, Ioan paused, removed his mask, and turned to face them. Myca was surprised: but for their differences in coloring, Ioan and Nikita of Sredetz could have been kin, graced as they were with the same sharpness of features, the same high cheekbones and angular shape to their eyes.

The Hammer of the Tremere bowed low, in formal greeting, and rose with a flourish of his pale hair. "I give you greetings, Myca Vykos syn Draconov, childe of Symeon, childe of Gesu, childe of the Dracon, most beloved of the Eldest. I give you greetings, Ilias cel Frumos, *koldun*-priest of Jarilo, childe of Dorinta, daughter of the gods. I welcome you in the name of my sire, Lukasz Brancoveanu, and the name of my house,"—the faintest possible trace of irony colored his tone—"and in my own name. Be named friend and welcome in my house, where no harm shall come to you and all of your wants shall be met, to seek your rest. This I swear by the holy names of Earth and Sky, and by the Waters of Life and Death."

"I am Myca Vykos syn Draconov, and I come to your house in the name of peace and friendship." Myca bowed deeply and rose after a respectful interval. "Your hospitality, my lord *voivode*, is as of the gods."

"I am Ilias cel Frumos, and I come to your house in the name of peace and friendship, and by the will of the gods of Earth and

Sky." Ilias bowed as well, and rose. "May their blessings never depart your house."

"I thank you, *koldun*, ambassador." Beyond Ioan's shoulder, the door to the manse opened, spilling a shaft of golden light across the courtyard. "Let us retire before the sun finds us here."

Myca could not help but notice as he passed that the door was more than a foot thick, and opened and locked by what appeared to be a fiendish mechanism of gears operated by some means beyond his perception. Ilias, however, was simultaneously startled and impressed, murmuring, "You know, there are some nights when all I can do is get them to do as I ask. Here? Shaped to will. I should probably be jealous."

"Lady Danika," Myca murmured in reply, "is indeed highly skilled, then."

"Not just Lady Danika," Ilias flicked a glance at their host's back, as he led them down the short hall, which rapidly turned into a staircase descending in a tight corkscrew. "Those charms he wears are spirit-bindings. The long one in the middle, the one that looks like a tiny flute? It is the mark of a master of the ways of air, and it has to be his own work, or no spirit would accept the binding of his will. So are the wind-flutes on the palisade walls." Thoughtfully, "I did not know that he was a *koldun*. He hides it well."

"A tactical advantage, no doubt."

"No doubt."

It struck Myca, as they descended, that Ioan's haven was as strange inside as it was on the out. It did, indeed, appear as though it had grown out of and under the mountain without any human interference whatsoever. The walls and stairs were entirely of smooth, polished stone unmarked by chisel. There were no sharp angles, no angles at all, in truth—only domed ceilings and supports that looked as though they had grown from the ceiling to the floor, and vice versa. The hall at the end of the stair was wide, and branched off into numerous side corridors, their floors flattened and scattered with finely ground sand to keep them dry, their ceilings arched, lit at intervals by recessed lamps. Myca glanced a question at Ilias and found him looking around, rapt with wonder, and received all the answer he needed. This place had been constructed with the aid of the spirits and it was likely they that gave it its unique and vaguely disturbing appearance. A female servant, dressed plainly in a long tunic and a hair-cloth, met them at the bottom of the stairs and bowed deeply, silently, in greeting.

Ioan nodded to her. "Please escort my lord *stapân* Vykos and my lord *koldun* Ilias to their chambers." He turned to face them again, and offered a shallow bow of his own. "Your needs will be met; you need only make your requests to the attendants awaiting you in your chambers. I ask that you forgive my abruptness. I have been in the field for fourteen nights and I must meet yet tonight with my lieutenants before I may address any other business. I shall call for you, ambassador, tomorrow evening. *Koldun*, I am certain that Lady Danika wishes to renew her acquaintance with you. For now, I bid you good evening and wish you good rest."

And, so saying, he left them to find their chambers.

Chapter Fourteen

"So," Ioan Brancoveanu said quietly, looking up from the stack of diplomatic correspondence he was perusing, "my beloved sire and his idiot brother are really going through the motions of making peace. I find myself not entirely surprised."

Myca inclined a brow questioningly. "You suspected it already, my lord *voivode*?"

"I suspected that my grandsire's current ambitions might drive them in that direction, whether they wished to go that way or not," Ioan replied, and began refolding documents and replacing them in the diplomatic courier's satchel they originally arrived in.

"Your illustrious grandsire, Noriz, is not actively involved in the negotiations, my lord *voivode*," Myca pointed out, with the faintest hint of wry amusement underlying his tone.

A snort. "Of course he isn't. Noriz has spent centuries cultivating a reputation for ravenous self-indulgence. He will not fritter that away on the off-chance he might seem effectual for a change."

Myca forced himself not to smile. "I had been warned, my lord, that you rarely mince words. What do you think of the peace proposal itself?"

"I think it has a snowball's chance in a bonfire of succeeding, ambassador, given the proclivity for petty treachery and personal sabotage present on both sides of the issue. I do not, however, think my opinion on that matter will be solicited by anyone but you, so I suggest you mark it well. This is going to end badly, and I predict it here and now." He kept only one document, the personal letter that Lukasz' ambassador to the court of Oradea had sent along. "That does not mean that I will not submit to my sire's request in this matter."

Myca was silent for a moment as he digested that, sorting and discarding conversational gambits as he considered. Ioan watched him, a faintly amused expression playing around the corners of his mouth.

"Surprised?" The Hammer of the Tremere finally asked.

"Yes," Myca admitted frankly. "I honestly thought you would require a significant amount of effort to convince."

"Diplomats." For an instant, he sounded very like his *veela* shield-maiden. "I have no love for my sire's idiot brother, ambassador, and, to be brutally frank, I have nearly as little regard for my sire. But it is beneath me to deliberately obstruct this process, no matter how little I believe it can succeed, when I might reap some benefit from it for my men and my allies. Does that satisfy you?"

"Partially. You do, of course, realize that the consequences of this matter will likely fall on your shoulders, whether it ends ill or well?" Myca watched closely; Ioan did not cultivate as expressionless a face as some in his position did, though he guarded his reactions well.

"I know it." Resignation, more than anything else, colored his tone. Resignation, and the faintest hint of bitterness. "Ambassador, I am not a fool, nor am I ignorant of matters taking place outside my domain, and outside the war. I know that Rustovitch is falling from grace, and that his allies are turning away from him. I have already received communications from two of them. I know that my grandsire, after centuries of wallowing in his own excesses, has suddenly rediscovered ambition." A pause, a smile so edged in anger it was difficult to look on. "As much as I would like to see Vladimir Rustovitch humbled, I find the idea of Noriz accomplishing that so completely repugnant that even I can scarcely give it words. By that same token, I cannot betray the blood that runs in my veins—Noriz is my grandsire, and Lukasz is my sire, and it was through them that I have become what I am now. I owe them honor, and service, and, in most things, obedience. I know what they want of me. They want me to take this… peace accord and turn it into the alliance that will break the Tremere, once and for all."

He rose, and paced. The room, which Myca supposed must be this strange place's version of a council chamber, was the largest he had seen in the underground portions of the bastion, long and roughly rectangular, though all the angles were softened into curves. The table occupied the approximate center and was surrounded by a collection of padded chairs and benches. A low fire burned behind a grate at the far end, keeping the room warm and dry despite the cool dampness below ground. Myca almost thought he could see grooves worn into the hard-packed dirt of the floor, where Ioan had walked this route before.

Myca watched, letting his vision blur and slip across the border between sight and vision, noticed the pensive cast to Ioan's colors. "You do not think such a thing is possible."

"No. You are not a fool either, ambassador, and I will do you the honor of not treating you like one." Ioan returned to his chair, but did not sit in it. "The war, at least as my sire and Rachlav and Noriz, and possibly even Rustovitch conceive it, has already been lost. It has been lost for decades. We have no chance whatsoever of exterminating the Tremere root and branch. They are too many now, and too entrenched, and if they are not beloved of our western cousins, they have at least made diplomatic inroads that we cannot easily devalue. Had we struck quickly, decisively, when they were weak and few and more vulnerable... perhaps then we could have destroyed them. But now? Now I think the best we can hope for is to make the price for remaining in our territory higher than they are willing to continue paying, and drive them out of our domains. My sources have suggested to me that they show a marked predilection for licking the boots of the Ventrue and the Toreador. Let them continue doing so if it brings them joy. We may yet be able to drive them to seek sanctuary in the west, and then we may close our ranks on one front instead of a multitude."

"Do you think such a thing can be accomplished?" Myca asked quietly. "They have clung to Ceoris—to the mountains of the south—in the face of everything that has come at them thus far. They have weathered both Vladimir Rustovitch and your own most determined efforts, have they not?"

"Anything may be accomplished with sufficient resources and a sufficiently well-developed plan of action, ambassador. I've had little to do for the last decade but attempt to husband those resources and think on that plan. I believe it can be done—not in one stroke, perhaps, and certainly not overnight, but it can be done. It is all in knowing—"

He broke off and looked up sharply, his nostrils flaring and his hand lifting to the necklace of bone charms he wore at his throat. Myca half-rose, a question on his lips. Even as he did so, the cause of his host's distraction became plain. A low, ululating wail echoed down the corridors of the subterranean bastion, beginning softly and rising to an almost agonizing pitch for sensitive Cainite ears—an alarm of some sort, Myca realized, even as he clapped his hands over his ears to block out the noise of it. Lukina brushed open the heavy woolen hanging separating the chamber from the hall and barked something at Ioan. Myca could not make out individual words but caught the gist: something was coming. Behind her, he caught glimpses of armed and armored figures hurrying through the halls. He sensed no panic but tasted a hint of fear in the air to go with a sudden jolt of nearly electric tension. Ioan caught his eye and he gingerly removed his hands from his ears, found the alarm had dropped from its earsplitting pitch to a low and continuous moan of agitation.

"Wait here, ambassador." The Hammer of the Tremere ducked beneath Lukina's arm, barking orders and demands for information to the men in the hall as he went.

Lukina let the hanging fall. Myca waited what he felt was an appropriate interval before peering into the hall and, upon determining the absence of any hurrying soldiers or permanently stationed door-guards, stepped out himself, looking about. Apprehensive though he was, and unsettled by the deep-throated moaning of the alarm, he was nonetheless also curious, and that curiosity was easily strong enough to overcome anything resembling fear. He retraced his route through the twisting, narrow corridors, having memorized as much of their layout and several navigation marks the previous evening, and reached the bottom of the corkscrew stair a moment later. The bottom of the staircase was unguarded, which pleased him. Unfortunately, despite the hint of fresh air that he found on the staircase itself, the door at the top was sealed and lacked anything resembling a handle or lever by which it might be opened by someone lacking command of the spirits of earth. He wondered how the ghouls and lesser Cainites managed it but found no obvious clues and, frustrated, he went back down, wondering if there was another way out.

"Myca!"

He turned, and found Ilias hurrying towards him down the corridor, visibly nervous and not troubling to hide his agitation. Following closely behind him was a tall, dark-haired woman in her middle years, her hair braided in a crown above the severe beauty of her face, clad in robes of russet wool and charms of bone and stone and twisted gold wire. From the girdle cinched about her waist hung three knives, beaten copper, iron, and what looked like stone or blackened bone. Her force of presence preceded her by the length of the corridor and Myca found himself bowing deeply to her before she had even come to a stop.

Ilias stepped into the circle of his arm, and he could feel his lover suppressing the urge to tremble, fighting the panic rising from within him, nearly overshadowing any other response. Myca rested his hand in the small of Ilias' back and drew him close, murmuring, "Did you not teach me yourself, my heart, that it is not shameful to fear when fearful things are happening all around you?"

Ilias closed his eyes and nodded, some of the tension leaching out of the set of his shoulders. A moment longer and he was capable of speech. "Forgive me, Myca, my lady... I was, for a moment, very disturbed."

The lady nodded fractionally and Myca, his hand still firmly in place, offered a faint smile. The corner of Ilias' mouth twitched wryly in response. "My lady, this is, I admit, not how I pictured this meeting occurring. My Lady *koldun* Danika Ruthven, it pleases me to introduce you to my Lord Myca Vykos syn Draconov. Lady Danika's greatness is such that my tongue is unworthy to tell it, and my Lord Myca's wisdom is valued even by his judicious sire."

Lady Danika's striking face relaxed momentarily in a smile. For an instant, she seemed nearly human and not the instrument of the gods. Myca could not imagine her ever laughing, regardless.

"You flatter me, priest of Jarilo." She turned her pale eyes on Myca then; he felt her assessing him, weighing him in a single glance, and when she was done he was thoroughly uncertain of whether she approved of what she saw. "Ambassador, your fame has preceded you, as well. My lord *voivode* has had much to say of you in the last several years."

Myca chose to take that as a compliment, and bowed from the neck. "My lady flatters me, as well. I am naught but a servant of my sire and my house."

"Of that I am quite certain." Lady Danika replied, dryly. "You were with my lord *voivode*, were you not?"

"Yes. Lukina came and collected him several minutes ago. I assume they went above ground." Lady Danika, Myca noticed, had the face of an experienced courtier, being almost as unreadable in her reactions as Symeon.

"I expected as much. Come with me. Quickly. We may be of some use above." Lady Danika brushed passed them and continued down the corridor. Myca and Ilias exchanged a glance and hurried after her, not particularly eager to be lost or left behind.

Lady Danika swept through a side door that led almost directly to a short, downward-slanting staircase, terminating in a roughly circular room into which half a dozen corridors ended. She chose one and strode down it fearlessly, despite the lack of lamps to illuminate it and despite the unpleasant sounds emanating from the far end. Myca and Ilias followed a few steps behind, with a bit more trepidation, and shortly the three emerged into a broad corridor, wider than any they had thus far encountered, broad enough for a dozen men to walk abreast up it, slanting gradually upward in a sort of ramp. Laboring to climb it were two enormous *vozhd*—creatures taller than a man on horseback, their flesh pallid and laced with thick blue veins where it peered through overlapping plates of bony gray armor—and their tenders. Each creature had four enormous, sinewy arms and a number of smaller, vestigial limbs, which they used to propel themselves along at a man's quick walking pace. The armor was pierced in places with heavy iron rings with thick chains attached, wrapped through the belts of the keepers, four to each *vozhd*, each warrior in *zulo* shape and carrying a long pike used to prod the *vozhd* along, a bundle of javelins hung across their backs. A half-dozen warriors came up the ramp behind them, all in varying states of midtransformation, limbs and skulls elongating, skins darkening and toughing into scale-like armor as they assumed their *zulo* war-shapes.

"Spear-throwers," Lady Danika explained shortly at their questioning glances. "Something is approaching by air, likely gargoyles. The spirits of air disapprove of something so earthy passing through their domain. That was the message we, the priest of Jarilo and I, heard when the general alarm sounded."

They waited until the *vozhd* completed their climb to the surface, the very face of the mountain rolling open with a horrendous echoing groan to allow them egress into the outer portions of the fortress, and then hurried out as well before the gap closed behind them. Outside, the sky was low, densely overcast, the moon little more than a silver blur behind the clouds, the air was thick with the scent of lightning strikes. A numinous blue-white radiance danced across the top of the palisades, illuminating the figures of men moving into position along the walkways, archers and spearmen, some of them in their bulkier, and physically stronger, *zulo* shapes. Lady Danika led them to one side of the palisade, where a stairway led upward to the walkways and observation platforms. On one of them stood Ioan, flanked at a respectful distance by Lukina and the small mountain that was Vlastimir Vlaszy.

Myca could easily see why his lieutenants kept their distance. Tiny blue-white arcs of lightning leapt from Ioan's body every few moments, danced along the charms braided into his hair, the bracelets around his wrists, answered by arcs flickering around a series of slender plinths placed at intervals along the palisades. With each arc, the scent of lightning intensified, until it made Myca's eyes water blood in response to the heaviness of the air. A savage wind was howling along the heights of the mountain, tearing new leaves from the trees, driving the clouds overhead into a tight, low-hanging circulation. In the distance, lightning arced from cloud to cloud, illuminating a cluster of dark shapes flying below the clouds, thunder echoing down the valleys and from peak to peak. Ilias clutched Myca's hand so tightly the bones ground together, and a sound of mingled pain and fear escaped his throat. Myca stole a glance and found his lover's face etched with a painful mixture of emotions, anger and hatred and a terrible grief. Myca closed his hand as best he could and offered all the comfort he was able through the bond they shared.

"My lord *voivode*." Lady Danika had reached the Hammer of the Tremere and attracted his attention. He glanced over his shoulder at her, nodding curtly in greeting—then he caught sight of Myca and Ilias over his shoulder, and his pale, storm-lit blue eyes narrowed a fraction in visible annoyance. The nimbus of unearthly radiance about him brightened for a moment, a curl of lightning licking out and leaving scorch marks on the palisade and observation platform around him. A tremendous sense of gathering power filled the air between them and Myca took a half step back, pulling Ilias behind him protectively. Ilias' hand knotted in the back of his dalmatic and they stood, pressed close together, a safe distance away.

"My Lady Danika, I am glad that you could join me so promptly." He greeted her cordially, and inclined his head slightly to Myca and Ilias, as well. "Ambassador, *koldun*, this should be educational for you." He gestured outward, pointing along the ridge of the mountains opposite their position. Almost on cue, the lightning lit the sky again, outlining the misshapen forms of the approaching gargoyle pack, too quickly for Myca to count precise numbers. An unpleasantly large number of the things, however, a fact he took in during that swift glance. "A dozen, likely a harassment flight—we have been expecting this much for weeks. Some Tremere weather-worker is manipulating the storm outside our little valley to drive them toward us with greater speed than they would otherwise be able to achieve. To get here, all they will have to do is glide on the storm-wind. They will lose that advantage when they cross the rim of the valley, where the winds become mine."

A high, thin shriek echoed down the valley. In it, Myca thought he detected an almost human note of frustration. A thin smile of satisfaction curled Ioan's mouth, and he turned to his enormous lieutenant. "Are the spear-throwers in position?"

"Yes, my lord *voivode*," Vlaszy replied.

"Excellent. Make certain that they are prepared to throw at my command." Ioan laid his hands on the top of the palisade wall, and Lady Danika stepped forward, past Lukina, and rested her hand on his. "Lukina, if you would be so good, make certain that no harm comes to the ambassador or the priest of Jarilo. I believe things are about to become rather... intense for them."

The sense of gathering power rose higher yet, lifting the hair on the back of Myca's neck and making Ilias shudder helplessly against his back, a low moan halfway between pleasure and anguish emerging from him. "Oh, Myca... if you could see it... if you could *feel* it..."

Ilias edged around him to his side and clung to him, trembling, all the pain and hate and grief erased from his face, his expression one of transcendent ecstasy, his eyes shining brilliant heaven-blue in sympathetic reaction to the magics being woven by Ioan and Danika. Myca could feel the intensity of Ilias' reaction stirring his own blood, rousing both his senses and his desire. His hunger was suddenly sharp, his fangs lengthening in his jaw swiftly enough that they scraped his own tongue, filling his mouth with the taste of his own blood. A force that was nearly electric leapt between the places their bodies touched. It was all Myca could do to control his sudden, violent need for his lover, the urge to push him up against the palisade wall and take him where they stood. Ilias was not helping on that score. His hands were everywhere, lips nuzzling Myca's shoulder through his clothing, his own fangs fully extended. Desperately, Myca pulled him close and held him tightly, shivers of magic-born lust shaking them both.

An earsplitting crack of thunder shook the ground beneath their feet, and the lightning rose around them like a shimmering blue-white curtain, striking from the earth into the low-hanging sky. Shrieks sounded from above as white-hot bolts found their targets, and a rain of dark ash fell across parts of the palisade wall. Archers fired almost directly upward, and they did not fire blindly. The sky above was filled with the rush of dark wings. Some of the creatures were massive, hugely muscled, the damage they were capable of doing brutally obvious. Others were long and slender, sinuous, cutting through the air to strike at the bastion's defenders like knives flung by the wind. Myca threw himself flat on the walkway and took Ilias down with him, half-covering his lover's body with his own as a hook-faced monstrosity sliced through the air where they had been standing, screeching as it went. An instant later, a hard-thrown javelin transfixed its misshapen skull, and Lukina was crouched above them, watching it fall.

"If you cannot fight," she snarled in Myca's face, *"get below!"*

Myca needed no further encouragement. He scrambled to his knees and from there to his feet, crouched below the level of the palisade wall, pulling Ilias with him. They fled down the staircase and found, at its base, an aperture piercing the mountain face. Myca shoved Ilias in ahead of him and threw a glance over his shoulder. The clouds above the fortress were numinous with the radiance of the lightning traps. Against the glare, gargoyles dove and killed, struck and were struck down, blood and ash showering from above. It was the most terrible thing he had seen since the death of Constantinople, and the most freakishly exhilarating. He turned and fled from the sight of it, his blood still pulsing in his head and his veins, afire with the power that had touched him and the desire that waited for him at the far end of the tunnel.

Chapter Fifteen

From the journals of Myca Vykos:

Six more attacks came and went before we departed from Ioan's bastion. Four of these came strictly by air, gargoyles bearing fire as a weapon, and two came from the ground, enormous wingless beasts that battered at the walls of the fortress and nearly brought them down in several places before being driven back. Each attack was repulsed, in most cases bloodily, by force of arms and sorcery. In each case, Ioan dealt more damage than his forces sustained, protected as they were by the strength of their fortifications and the preparedness ground into them by their commander. Ioan did not at any time, however, take the offensive, preferring to let the gargoyle legions of the Tremere break against him like the tide crashing against a great rock. A few weeks past midsummer, we withdrew from the bastion, Ioan leaving the extremely capable Lady Danika in command of the situation, supported by his left hand, the revenant warrior Vlastimir Vlaszy. We moved more quickly departing than we did coming in, using routes whose existence I had not even suspected while approaching, as speed was very much of the essence. A lull had come in the fighting, but such lulls rarely lasted long in the summer months when war could be made almost freely, unhindered by uncooperative mountain weather. We made Alba Iulia in less than a week, traveling by day in lightproof conveyance once we reached the lower hills.

When we paused briefly for supplies in Alba Iulia, I found a letter waiting for me from the Prince of Sredetz, Bela Rusenko, responding positively to my request to visit his court. Included was a brief discussion of the customs of his court—the rigorous formality of the Tzimisce did not pertain there, as the prince is a Cappadocian and a follower of the ways of desire. Those customs he kept were few and in no way onerous to his visitors, given the richness of his domain. He did, however, also advise us not to travel overland from Brasov to Sredetz, as there was strife among the Bulgar Tzimisce who dwelt to the north of the city, and he could not guarantee our safety if we approached through those domains. Our Bulgar cousins' pugnacity was not unknown to Ilias and me. We had spent many hours, safe within the lower halls of Ioan's bastion, discussing our routes of travel should the Prince of Sredetz extend us welcome. We had already decided, if such permission came, that we would travel by sea from the port of Constanta and sail to the Bulgar port of Varna, and travel overland to the capital from there.

I left Ilias in Alba Iulia with letters of credit and a generous supply of silver by which to arrange our travel from Brasov to Constanta, and proceeded to Oradea with Ioan and his retinue in tow. We arrived in the waning nights of high summer. The first harvest of ripe grain was being brought in as we crossed through the farmsteads bordering the Great Plain. Symeon, warned of our coming, greeted us gladly and feted Ioan like a prince for a week, apparently very much to the Hammer of the Tremere's bemusement. Before I departed Oradea, both parties signed and witnessed the long-debated peace agreement between Lukasz and Rachlav, Symeon had sent forth a call to the allied houses and warlords of the mountains to attend a gathering at Oradea (I was told this request originated with Ioan, who seemed intent on making the most of this opportunity that he could), and the trees highest on the mountains had already begun to turn with the first breath of autumn. When I reached Alba Iulia, I found that Ilias had not been idle in my absence. Not only were our travel arrangements made, but our escort of revenant bodyguards courtesy of my sire were assembled, his own attendants had completed the arrangements necessary in Brasov, and we would be departing from Constanta in six weeks aboard a merchant vessel carrying goods south and whose captain had agreed to take our entire entourage for an astonishingly good price. A letter also awaited me from Malachite, informing me of his intent to meet us in Brasov, having errands of his own to pursue prior to our departure. We did not manage to miss him, as he was very well informed of our movements. Fortunately, the autumn remained dry enough that we made good time reaching Brasov, traveling by both barge along the navigable waterways and by the unpaved traderoads. From there, we reached Constanta with whole nights to spare.

Ilias was, of course, enormously excited and completely intent on regarding the whole affair as the finest of adventures. He had never traveled on a large boat before, or across a body of water larger than a deep lake, and harassed nearly everyone he met, including myself, with questions about the sea. In fact, he had never actually seen the sea before, either, and could sit for hours watching the tide washing up on the moonlit shores around Constanta, completely rapt. He confessed to me that he thought the water spirits of lake and stream and river were much different from the spirits of the sea—even the river-spirits of the Danube and the Tisza, though they flood with great violence nearly every spring, were not so wild as the spirits of the open waves. I can only assume that he is correct in his assessment. Dwelling in the spirit-touched fortress of Ioan Brancoveanu for most of the summer left no sensitivity to their presence rubbed off on me, despite Ilias and Lady Danika both pointing out their workings to me. Perhaps it is a personal defect of some sort. If so, it is not a defect I currently have the time or inclination to fully address. Malachite kept much to himself during this time, his mood melancholic, and even Ilias could not draw him out, though he made the attempt. I thought perhaps that something he had learned on his "errand" had disturbed him in some way, but he refused to speak of it, and it was impossible to press him, as much as I wished to do so.

We sailed from Constanta with the dawn, Ilias and I resting together in our cabin, inside a thoroughly light-proofed chest-bed lined in heavy felt, with six inches of our grave-earth beneath us. We both took great pains to insure an adequate supply traveled with us, some pounds lining our sleeping chest and several more kept in oiled leather sacks, sewn shut, among the other pieces of baggage. Malachite chose to sleep in a separate, smaller compartment, traveling only with a single body-servant to tend to his needs, a man who had evidently been with him since his time in Ile de France. He persisted withdrawn and curt for the duration of the voyage, speaking to me only when it was unavoidable. I cannot say I found this decision on his part to be wholly disagreeable, as I found myself still entertaining the desire to twist his head off on occasion. The bodyguard slept on deck, with most of the ship's crew. Ilias' attendants shared the cabin with us, pretending with great verisimilitude to be the sons of a rich boyar traveling to Sredetz to winter with relatives. Most of them, having the hearty constitutions of revenants and ghouls, adapted to life aboard ship with little difficulty, only minor bouts of sickness and then mostly during rough seas marring the voyage for them. Ilias, on the other hand, suffered almost instantly, and constantly, from the moment we left port.

I personally did not think it possible for a Cainite to become seasick. Certainly, when I sailed from Constantinople I experienced some discomfort, but it was fleeting, and Symeon assured me that such discomfort was wholly natural and that he himself experienced it, as well. I felt it, as well, when we left Constanta, but it went away just as quickly. Ilias, on the other hand, felt it and kept feeling it, to the point that on some evenings (when we were at the furthest point from land in our journey, it seemed) he not only could not rise, he could not bring himself to feed, either. We emptied half his remaining supply of grave-earth over him, so that he might rest mostly buried, and this gave him some relief from the sickness. He told me that he felt as though the waters themselves were trying to rend the bond between himself and the earth-spirits, to drown him or cast him away, for water in many ways rejects the dead. As we drew closer to land, the illness abated somewhat, and he was able to walk the decks with me after dark, to admire the stars and the moon above the glass-smooth dark sea and to whisper to the wild spirits of the air above the water. He apologized, more than once, for being a burden to me, and I had to hush that foolishness quite vigorously.

We made port in a little less than a month, the worst of the autumn storms holding off until after we arrived. The journey across the southern reaches of Bulgaria in the autumn rains was more pleasant than I thought it would be, though rather slow going. We arrived in Sredetz three weeks after we made shore.

Sredetz reminded Myca of a smaller, humbler, more thoroughly Slavic imitation of Constantinople, an opinion he kept firmly to himself. The local Cainites, those that had survived through a half-dozen changes of rulership and upheavals both great and small, were a proud and somewhat insular lot, as quick as a Tzimisce warlord looking for a reason to fight when it came to taking offense, capable of extracting insult from even the blandest remarks when it suited them to do so. Myca learned this early on, and learned to tread and speak softly around those with the quickest tempers. His Byzantine "origins" were not necessarily a mark in his favor here, at least among those who carried grudges left over from their mortal days, and lingering resentment against the "Byzantine yoke" hid in the oddest places. Ilias had more fortune when dealing with the local Cainites, having an almost magical knack for loosening tongues and soothing hard feelings. It did not hurt his position at all that a substantial number of the city's residents followed the same moral paths as he and his lover, and they ungrudgingly acknowledged Ilias as priest and teacher of the ways of desire, and, somewhat more grudgingly, Myca as his apprentice on that way. Malachite dealt with the situation by making himself invisible, even to Myca and Ilias, who had difficulty keeping track of his activities on a night-to-night basis. He was, evidently, going out of his way to avoid contact with most of the high-blooded Cainite residents of Sredetz, seeking converse with others of his own kind, disappearing for whole weeks at a stretch, apparently traveling about the region as best he could.

Bela Rusenko, the prince, was a walker of the paths of desire himself, but a particularly eccentric species thereof, a reclusive and unsocial scholar who rarely interacted with either the residents of his city or the visitors that he periodically received. He held court infrequently, accepted guests with little fanfare, and delegated the majority of the social tasks of his position to his childe, the Lord Ladislav. Ladislav followed the same moral codes as Rusenko, but unlike his sire, was relatively gregarious and substantially more approachable. He conducted most of the night-to-night business of the domain with the aid of his childe, the Lady Erika. Both proved themselves invaluable to Myca during the early stages of the investigation in Sredetz, offering advice and assistance. Myca was certain he was incurring a massive debt to both of them, but hardly cared. Neither had been resident in Sredetz during Nikita's brief reign there as heretical bishop. Neither, for that matter, had Bela Rusenko himself. They did, however, know who among the current residents of the city and who among the locals in the countryside had been present during those years, and who might have reason to know Nikita somewhat personally.

Ladislav also answered Myca's request to take possession of Nikita's haven, which, they discovered, had sat empty but well tended since the Archbishop of Nod's departure on his tour of the heretical dominions. Nikita had, apparently, left behind no ghouls and no childer, which was itself unusual. Most Tzimisce who wished to leave their personal domains secure behind them made extensive use of both. The caretaker of Nikita's house was a revenant, as were the man's wife and three sons, but they were also either appallingly ignorant of the power running in their veins, or else deliberately tampered with in such a way as to render them ignorant. Their loyalty to Nikita was absolute, ground into them with such permanence that even the harshest questioning could not dilute or break it. All five now dwelt in a room in the basement and provided most of the sustenance for the Cainites of the household, being useless for anything else, as they would not speak of their previous master and could not be trusted.

Nikita's house lay in the oldest part of the city, the section once known as Serdica by the tribe that originally dwelt there, and as Triaditsa by the Romans, where most of the wealthiest citizens still dwelt. A mock Roman villa of two stories with numerous pseudo-Byzantine architectural embellishments, it was more than sufficient for Myca's purposes, and Ladislav was quite willing to let him have uncontested use of it. None of the locals wanted it, seeming to believe the place of ill aspect, considering the fates that had befallen its last two owners: the former Prince Basilio, driven into exile, and the Archbishop of Nod, apparently vanished off the face of the earth. Myca spent most of the late autumn and early winter tearing the place apart, while Ilias circulated among the locals, collecting gossip and engaging in subtle interrogations. Periodically, Malachite himself would appear at the villa, bearing news and rumors culled from the gutters, and the results of his interrogations of the region's low-blooded heretics. No new leader had arisen to replace Nikita. There did not appear to be sufficient organization intact, even here in the heartland of the Cainite Heresy, for such a political act to occur. The Nosferatu, whose detestation of the Cainite Heresy was both personal and deeply ingrained, did not bother to hide his satisfaction with that development. He did not, however, have any more success than Myca or Ilias in uncovering any details of Nikita's origin.

The villa's single large storage room was crammed to the rafters with what appeared to be the accumulated detritus of at least a century of heretical religious endeavor. Nikita was, evidently, an obsessive collector of potentially historically significant minutiae and never threw anything away, no matter how ancient, virtually illegible, or patently insane it might be. Six crates contained decades of neatly temporally organized correspondence alone, while another dozen contained documents of varying ages and degrees of religious and secular significance. Despite himself, Myca was impressed by the thoroughness and the single-minded intensity of the effort that had gone into creating this edifice of unclean knowledge. He began ripping it apart, looking for some significant personal correspondence, some details by which Nikita himself would become known or by which he would reveal himself. Ilias did the same among the city's residents, circulating among them with inimitable charm and grace, working on even the most standoffish to the most hostile. No small number of the Tzimisce dwelling within riding distance of the city were bitter that they had failed to seize the rulership of the city when the chance lay in their hands.

During the long slide into the deepest parts of the winter, Myca learned more than he wanted to know about the inner workings of the Cainite Heresy, the petty grabs for power, the rancor and divisiveness at its highest levels, and the almost universal terror that many of its bishops and lesser functionaries held for the previous Archbishop of Nod, Narses of Venice. Narses' fanatical loathing of Constantinople and all that it stood for had helped lead the Queen of Cities to its own destruction but, in the end, Narses' hatred had consumed him, as well, and led to Nikita's rise to power. Much of the correspondence he found dealt with the events immediately preceding Narses' fall from grace with the Crimson Curia and immediately following Nikita's assumption of the Archbishopric of Nod. There was nothing, absolutely nothing, that pertained to the time during which Nikita successfully plotted and executed his coup against the demented Lasombra elder. Similarly, Ilias discovered much in the way of anecdote and gossip, but little in the way of hard information. Nikita, much like Bela Rusenko, had not been an overly social individual, except when engaging in the rites of his faith. He could be a fiery and charismatic speaker when he chose to be, but he did not engage in meaningless social pleasantries, and apparently saw no need to do so. None of the current residents of the city knew him well. In fact, he appeared to discourage any such effort. Even those who still maintained some devotion to the heretical faith, few though they were, did not consider him so much a shepherd as a distant and unattainable ideal. When pushed, Ilias caught a hint of glassiness about many of the Archbishop's former followers, a vagueness that appeared among them so regularly as to be uniform. Ilias suspected their memories might have been tampered with, and said as much to Myca as the year waned and no new leads showed themselves.

Nikita, even in his absence, guarded his secrets well.

Myca laid down his pen and raised his eyes from the parchment over which he labored, transcribing several pages of loose notes into permanent entries in his personal journal. The candle was burning low in its holder, but he felt no inclination to change it and continue writing. He was seized, in spirit, with a great wintry lassitude, the desire to curl in his earth-lined, fur-covered bed for the rest of the night and through the next day. Instead, with a monumental act of will, he rose from his comfortably cushioned writing chair and crossed the office to the high window slit, thumbing open the slats on the shutters and letting the cold, damp night air flow over him. It was, he thought, snowing again. The breeze tasted of ice and penetrated even his thick, fur-lined winter garments. He tucked his hands into his sleeves and closed his eyes, letting the cold wrap around him.

A door opened, down on the first floor of Nikita's spacious city haven, voices and footsteps echoing up to him; they did not motivate him to move, or to investigate. He recognized Nicolaus, chattering excitedly, and the lower, deeper voice of Sergiusz making the occasional reply. Ilias' tread on the stairs was soft and unmistakable. He opened his eyes as his lover entered with the most perfunctory of knocks, red-golden hair and thick dark furs still glistening with droplets of half-melted snow.

"Your eyes are over-bright," Ilias informed him, by way of greeting, and crossed the room to envelop him in a cool, evergreen-scented embrace.

Myca rested his head comfortably on the marten-covered shoulder of Ilias' winter cloak. "I should have gone with you."

"Yes, you should have. You would have enjoyed yourself." There was no censure in Ilias' tone. His hand reached beneath the loose spill of Myca's hair to rest on the back of his neck, caressing gently. "Lord Ladislav hopes the investigation goes well."

Myca allowed his lover's skillful hands to do as they willed. "Lord Ladislav is kind to say such things."

A chuckle, directly beneath his ear. "I think Lord Ladislav was hoping to see more of you at the *Saturnalia*—he has inquired after you several times, since he saw you at the baths that night."

Myca made a noncommittal noise in his throat and draped his arms around Ilias' waist. "I was covered in dust and looked like a drowned rat."

"Perhaps he favors that look for the touch of the exotic it brings to the table." Ilias was enjoying teasing him far too much. Myca made a mental note to take vengeance as seemed appropriate later. "He has also suggested, again, that we might write to the Lord Basilio, who may be able to assist us in this matter. I think he just wants to make certain we stay through the summer. He asked if I would preside at the Aphrodisiac, since we are certainly not going anywhere until the spring, at least."

Myca looked down into Ilias' cold-whitened face, smiling impishly up at him. "We cannot refuse that honor, then."

"I was hoping that you would say that. We have not attended a true Aphrodisiac since your first—I would like to see how the customs are kept here, where the court is mostly our own kind." Ilias' hand slid around and caressed the curve of his throat. "And we have shamefully neglected your spiritual needs since this affair started." He cast a pale-eyed glance at the stacks of ledgers, parchment, and bound stacks of correspondence piled around what had been Nikita's writing desk. "Come with me to the *Saturnalia* tomorrow night. I saved a *sigillaria* for you to wear, and no one will care that you missed the first night. You have worked hard enough for now."

"I almost think you are right." Myca ruefully followed the direction of his glance around the room. "There is a decade's worth of sorting alone, and a week…"

"A week will not harm the investigation." Ilias bent and kissed him with ice-cold lips. "Of course, I'm right. Say you will attend."

"I will attend." Myca surrendered, recognizing his own lack of desire to fight. "I suppose you have an idea what sort of costume I will wear during the masquerade."

"Well, yes." Ilias admitted shamelessly, his smile growing even more impish.

Myca inclined an eyebrow. "Should I be *afraid* of this idea?"

"We do not fear the unknown, my flower. We embrace it and grow strong from the learning."

"Very afraid, then."

Ilias laughed, and tugged Myca along with him downstairs.

Chapter Sixteen

Myca took Lord Ladislav's advice, and wrote to the former Prince of Sredetz, Basilio, in exile in Iberia among his Lasombra kinsmen. He wrote three copies of the letter and sent them out by three different routes, one by ship and two by land, hopeful that at least one would reach its destination. Foul weather continued to fall on Sredetz, funneled down the valley in which it lay, keeping most of the city's residents haven-bound and searching for means of killing the tedium. Even Malachite returned from his restless wanderings and took up residence in the room provided for him. He asked for, and received, permission to assist in reviewing Nikita's documents and, as Myca was thoroughly involved with the correspondence, he took over the task of combing through the boxes of heretical texts and polemics for any information of worth. Myca addressed the problem of mind-crushing winter doldrums by burying himself in Nikita's papers for whole nights at a stretch, struggling to extract more information than the words alone contained. Like the letters that had come to him from Lady Rosamund, most of the correspondence and sundry other documents had somehow been scrubbed clean of lingering psychic traces. Only the palest ghosts of old recollections clung to them, attached mostly to letters originating decades before the present, none of which seemed to feature Nikita himself. This hinted at a disturbingly great degree of well-hidden power residing in the Archbishop of Nod, confirming the impression that both Myca and Ilias had received, but otherwise not adding anything new to their store of information.

Nikita's writings gave the impression of a man made of equal parts sincere and deeply held faith and quietly burning ambition. Again, this was not a surprise to Myca, who doubted on principle that anyone lacking ambition would bother to claw his way to the top of even a heretical religious hierarchy, no matter how deeply faithful he might be. It also did not entirely surprise him that many members of the Crimson Curia—the more truly devout members—had regarded Narses of Venice as severely lacking in his faith, and had, evidently, been quietly working for some decades prior even to the sack of Constantinople to place Nikita on the Archbishop's throne. Narses was a bit too naked in his secular obsessions, it seemed, for even the only quasi-righteous Crimson Curia to continue overlooking those flaws forever. Nikita, on the other hand, projected the correct blending of genuine devotion to the doctrines of the Cainite Heresy and a finely honed awareness of the secular challenges facing the Crimson Curia. Evident in both the text and subtext of the letters was that many senior leaders of the Heresy held Nikita to be almost the perfect priest-statesman and an ideal proponent for their cause.

Myca wondered what had happened during Nikita's tour of Europe—and the apparently disastrous series of "lectures" in Paris—to rob Nikita of his eloquence, his ability to sway the hearts and minds of others. He was certainly articulate in writing, and if Ilias' information from Nikita's former flock was true, the man could most certainly speak with conviction and skill. Myca found himself simultaneously frustrated and intrigued by a mystery that grew more obtuse with every clue he uncovered.

Myca also found himself being dragged outside more often than nearly any other Cainite in Sredetz, very much to his chagrin. Ilias was undaunted by the weather and was only kept inside by the fiercest winds and the deepest snows. Myca knew this insistence that they not hole up all winter like bears in a cave was born at least partially of pure contrariness, since Ilias detested being cold almost more than anything else in the world, and partially on genuine instinct. Nikita's earth had shown Ilias a vision of his homeland deep in the grip of winter, and Sredetz was now most assuredly caught in the talons of some unpleasant deity of frost. On the nights that Myca spent puzzling over Nikita's correspondence, Ilias was often abroad in the cold, prowling the edges of the city and, in some cases, wandering the forests with one of his attendants (usually Sergiusz, who withstood the cold better), a bone flute and a bag of blooded salt to tempt the spirits, and a heavy oiled leather tent to sleep in should they not make it back before dawn. Occasionally Myca accompanied him on these trips, if for no reason other than to reduce his anxiety for the safety of his lover, especially given Ilias' propensity for wandering about barefoot and semi-nude. After several weeks, Ilias felt secure enough in his judgment to tell Myca that he felt Sredetz was not truly Nikita's homeland. The spirits were too different from those clinging to the Archbishop of Nod's grave-earth, the mountains were not shaped correctly... the land itself was simply *wrong*.

Ilias sensed a darkness hiding in Sredetz that was far deeper than Nikita's own and, despite delicate questioning from Myca, on that topic he would speak no more.

The winter wore on. Ilias, satisfied with his investigation and unwilling to provoke the spirits with any further impertinences on his own part, was more inclined to remain closer to home, if not strictly inside. Nikita's house was within walking distance of the old Roman baths, of which Ilias made regular use, as they were also a favored gathering place for winter-crazed sensualists itching for the arrival of spring. Myca periodically permitted Ilias to drag him along and endeavored to enjoy himself as best he could. He had never quite shed his lingering dislike of over-intimacy with strangers, but he could control it when the situation warranted. In this fashion he came to know Lord Ladislav quite well, and concurred with Ilias' assessment that he wished them to linger in Sredetz at least through the summer. Ladislav radiated disciplined, focused desire. Myca could see it in him when their eyes met, or they lounged together in one of the larger thermal pools at the baths, and never ceased to find it both puzzling and flattering. It was generally on those nights that he and Ilias went home and loved each other thoroughly until the sunrise. Holding his lover in his arms, hearing him cry out and beg for more, allowing Ilias to make him beg, made Myca feel slightly more real as an object of desire.

"Only *you* would be confused by the idea of someone wanting you, Myca," Ilias opined, not for the first time, as they lay tangled together in Nikita's spacious bed, pleasure still pulsing gently between them.

Myca rested his cheek against Ilias' curls, spread on the pillows beneath them. "I am not half as beautiful, or as desirable, as you, my heart. Were I Ladislav…"

"Flatterer." Myca felt, rather than saw, Ilias' quick, bright smile. "If Ladislav wants a pretty golden creature, he has his childe. You draw him with more than your flesh, my flower. He has, I think, looked on your mind and soul, and he wants you for what he sees there, as much as for your blood and your body."

Myca shivered. "Ilias…"

"Myca." A small, strong hand rested on the flat planes of his belly, stroked a soothing circle. "I will be presiding at the Aphrodisiac this year, here in this city… it will be my duty, and my honor, to initiate those who come to me into the ways of desire, as I showed you the way. I know that you hold fear in your heart, yet, and this is not a wrong thing, for you are growing past those fears—the scars on your heart, the things that haunt you. You cannot expect to shed those things overnight. Even I am sometimes frightened by the strength of my own desires—I am sometimes even frightened by the strength of my love for you—but these fears and these desires are things we must face, must taste of and understand, make our own."

"I… do. You know that I do." With a convulsive movement, Myca drew his lover closer against him, more fully into his arms. "I… do not know why I cannot say the words, but I…"

"I know." Gently. Cool lips pressed a kiss to the hollow of Myca's throat. "You are not less than me, Myca. You are not less worthy of love, not less worthy of desire. In many ways, you are greater than I can hope to be, and it honors me to aid you in finding the greatness within yourself, the person you can truly be. I am honored… by your love." Myca made a small sound in the back of his throat, and even he did not know if it was a sound of pain or joy. "This spring, you will show who and what you can be, and find your joy on the paths of desire. I promise you, you have nothing to fear."

Chapter Seventeen

Spring reddened the trees with sap, and then frosted them green with emerging buds. The snows melted and raised streams flowing down the mountains, and the ground began to thaw at last. Malachite regarded the change of seasons with seeming indifference, now deeply enmeshed in the process of sorting and translating heretical religious documents, combing through them for clues. It was he who discovered that the Crimson Curia first knew Nikita through a polemic of his own writing, in which he intelligently and passionately expounded at length on several problematic issues of doctrine. He had been a minor functionary in the service to the bishop of Varna, and evidently had the good fortune to exceed his superior in many ways. He was awarded a bishopric of his own, based in Sredetz, and eventually eclipsed his former prelate in every way, climbing in subtle power and influence within the Cainite Heresy from that point forward. Myca was ungrudgingly impressed with Malachite's discovery and managed to corroborate it from the text of various letters, whose oblique references to Nikita's allegedly humble origins within the Cainite Heresy now made considerably more sense. No new information, however, came to light about his actual origins. Letters of inquiry Myca had sent out in the fall slowly began to yield dividends now that spring had come. No Tzimisce lord or lineage within the area of Bulgaria claimed Nikita as its scion, or even its black sheep, a decidedly great surprise. It was Myca's experience that the only clan of high-blooded vampires more lineage obsessed than his own were the Ventrue, and even the Ventrue claimed their disgraces. Nikita, given the stature he had achieved within the

Cainite Heresy, could not strictly be termed a disgrace or an embarrassment. Even if the man's sire profoundly detested him, he would still be claimed, for the Tzimisce rarely disowned their childer outright.

Myca spent the nights leading up to the Aphrodisiac writing a second series of delicate interrogatives to the local Tzimisce lords who seemed least likely to take mortal offense at the presumption, waiting impatiently for one of his messengers to return from Iberia, and disciplining his nerves. And he was far more nervous than he liked. It had taken Ilias a great deal of concentrated effort to bring him to the point where he could tolerate casual physical contact without responding with violence or flight. He had survived the first test of those efforts during his first—and, to date, his only—Aphrodisiac, the night he was formally initiated into the practice of his faith by his lover and mentor, the witch-priest. He had not been put to a serious test since then, as the opportunities to do so had been few and far between among the various diplomatic tasks his sire had sent him on. He was not entirely certain he was prepared for a serious test of himself *now*—a fact he confided only to his journal, as he did not wish to trouble Ilias and could not imagine confiding in Malachite or any of the servants. A part of him quailed at the thought of walking into the gathering and finding himself surrounded by temptations for all of his senses, and another vampire who desired him. He was afraid of what would come of those temptations and those desires, and could not say why.

Ilias spent most of the nights leading up to the Aphrodisiac at the ritual's chosen site, making certain all of the last minute details were arranged as they should be, returning to the villa only to sleep. During those brief times together before sunrise and just after sunset, he did his best to soothe Myca's fears, to which he could not be ignorant; the strength of the bond between them was too great. On the night before the Aphrodisiac officially began, Ilias and his servants did not return home at all: all three were sheltering with Lord Ladislav for the day, as they would need to be in place once the rite began. Myca slept poorly that day, never fully falling into true rest, tossing and turning in the comfort of his bed. He rose almost before the sun had fully set, limbs heavy with weariness, thoughts swimming with anxiety. He almost decided not to go, but found upon entering the study and surveying masses of Nikita's correspondence and the journals containing months of effort, that he had no taste for burying himself in work, either. In the downstairs room that Malachite claimed for his own, he knew the Rock of Constantinople was hard at work. He could nearly feel the self-righteous disapproval radiating through the floor. The Nosferatu had said nothing—he did not need to. His cool condemnation of Ilias was written in his behavior, the manner in which he ignored any attempts by the witch-priest to engage him in civil conversation, the brusqueness that characterized their every necessary interaction. Ilias tolerated it, far better than Myca would have, in his place. He knew that Malachite's silent condemnation would fall on him, as well, should he choose to go out tonight.

Myca realized that he was making excuses to himself, and quietly went back into his bedchamber to change his clothing and wash his face and hands. Outside, filtering through the window shutters in the next room, he caught the hint of music and voices. The mortals of Sredetz, much like the Cainites, celebrated the coming of spring. Taking down his cloak, he crept down the stairs and out the door. On the muddy streets, a procession was in progress, groups of mortals carrying torches and enclosed candle-lamps, singing and laughing among themselves. Myca waited in his door for the majority of the procession to pass, then followed it down the puddle-strewn road. These people, he knew, were wealthy residents of old Sredetz, returning home from the mortal celebrations that took place beneath the brilliance of the sun, in the fields and forests outside the city. The Cainite Aphrodisiac celebration was taking place within the city itself, among the cluster of bathhouses in the center of the old city and the buildings surrounding it, many of which were the havens of the city's wealthiest Cainites. The first and largest of those bathhouses, the House of the Eagle, and its surrounding gardens were the center of the Aphrodisiac celebration.

Myca found the path leading to the House of the Eagle well lit with enclosed lamps rather than torches, the doors opened but guarded against entry by the city's mortal residents. The house's enormous proprietor ushered him in and gave him immediately to the care of two young women, clad in undecorated white tunics, who guided him into one of the private bath chambers, then obediently left him alone. A white tunic, its design having more in common with the loose drape of a truly Roman garment than any modern article of clothing, was left for him, along with freshly warmed towels. He shed his dalmatic and hose, and slipped into the warm, scented waters of the bath. He took a deep breath to sample the scent of the perfumed water and realized, with a bit of bemusement, that it was linden blossom, then dunked his head beneath the water. He drew in a deep breath of water, letting the sweetness of the perfume permeate his flesh from within as well as without, exhaled, and rose to soak for a long moment. His stomach was still tied in knots of nervousness and near dismay, but the warmth of the water and the silence of the building soothed him somewhat. He rose from the bath more at ease, and toweled himself dry, wrapping in the loose tunic, which hung to his ankles. In the hall, he found one of the servants waiting for him, a young woman whose loose brown hair hung past her waist and voluptuous curves invited caressing hands, who bowed low to him and guided him through the bathhouse's twisting halls to the rear of the building. Here, rooms had been prepared and a rear porch opened onto the gardens, where musicians were playing and the celebrants were milling about, socializing and celebrating with acts of passion and pleasure.

Soft moans and cries filled the night, a counterpoint to the low murmur of conversation and the music. In secluded corners of the garden the Cainites of Sredetz celebrated the return of spring, sporting among themselves and with mortals provided for their amusement. Myca stepped down off the porch and walked among the garden paths, searching for something to draw his attention and his appetites, something that was not the linden-perfumed arms of his lover. It occurred to him, with a bit of surprise, that the emotions he felt were not wholly nervous any longer, but tinged with jealousy. Somewhere in this garden of delights, Ilias was doing his duty as Sinner and priest, and that duty was to pleasure the new initiates to the ways of desire, to welcome them to the service of their own wants. The idea of anyone else lying in the arms of his lover, enjoying the pleasures of his body and imagination, gnawed at him more than he wished to admit, roused the Beast within him. He walked to control his churning emotions, and to distract the monster in his breast with sights to entertain and entice it.

Those sights were many. In a wide, well-lit expanse of grass, to the music of flute and tambour, half a dozen young women were dancing for the appreciation of a small audience both human and Cainite. Few of the young women wore more than the briefest of diaphanous scarves about their hips and the occasional bit of jewelry or paint to enhance their charms. Their brown skins glistened with perfumed oil and the nipples of their uncovered breasts were daubed with rouge. Their dance was clearly an offering that the audience was meant to accept. In the darkened alcoves at the edges of the open space, Myca caught sight of couples and groups engaged in a more primal dance, the air filled with the tang of sweat and perfume, musk and blood. To his surprise, one of the dancers threw her scarf teasingly around his neck and tried to draw him away with her. Within him, his Beast growled and surged, roused by the sweet scent of her, and he followed into the alcove she chose. Her breasts were firm in his hands, her nipples springing fully erect at the cool brush of his thumbs as he smeared the rouge she wore there. Pressed close against her, he could smell the use she had already been put to, reached down and found her moist yet with the lust of the lover she had just served. A slow caress of his fingers had her whimpering softly and grinding herself against him. Her pupils were hugely enlarged and he tasted something sweet on her tongue when he kissed her, something vaguely familiar, and then the taste of her blood was overwhelming all else, hot and smoky with her own lust, her own pleasure. He drank deeply of her and left her in the alcove when he was done, half-senseless with ecstasy and blood-loss.

She had, in fact, consumed something familiar, the sweet aftertaste lying yet on his own tongue as its effects washed through his body. He felt all of his senses sharpening and refining, growing exquisitely more sensitive. Soon, even the soft fabric of his tunic was too rough to lay directly against his over-sensitive skin. He peeled it off and tossed it over a hewn marble bench where, he noticed with some amusement, a number of other tunics already lay discarded. In the small clearing beyond it, a group of Cainites watched and talked among themselves as their servants had their pleasure of a young woman, bound at the wrists, weeping and begging, her hair shorn at a novice's length and her pale thighs smeared with her virgin's blood. Something about the sight struck him and he turned away, simultaneously aroused and revolted, hurrying away with the image of her tear-streaked face hanging before his eyes. It was washed away soon enough—pale arms beckoned him from darkened alcoves, half-familiar voices called his name, here and there he thought he caught sight of a face he recognized. Ilias was not among them, but then, it was unlikely that he would be there. The initiation was a private event, a sensual communion, and Ilias would not likely consent to sharing such a sacred act for the titillation of others. He did not join any of them, but walked on, aroused within himself but unable to find the thing that would satisfy him, senses burning with the need for sensual release. Eventually, he found an empty alcove of his own, grassy and shrouded in vines and hedges already thick with leaves, and lay back in the grass to let himself enjoy the cool of the evening against his heated flesh.

Overhead, the sky was starry and the moon half full, washing the sky with its silvery radiance, a shaft of cool light falling over him where he lay. Beneath him, the ground was cool and slightly damp with dew. He though he could feel each individual blade of grass where it touched his flesh, his skin was that sensitive. Here, at least, the night was almost wholly quiet, the music and conversation of others muffled by distance and dense foliage. He allowed himself to enjoy it, closing his eyes and breathing deeply of the peace. Gradually, he realized that he was not alone.

Myca opened his eyes, and found Lord Ladislav standing in the entrance to the alcove, watching him silently. For a long moment, Myca said and did nothing, and neither did Ladislav, both simply gazing at one another. In the moonlight, he seemed pale and perfect, the corpse-white skin of his Cappadocian heritage a blessing rather than a curse, the cool light smoothing away the lines around his eyes, around his mouth. He still wore his tunic, Myca noted, and it was pristine, unstained by another's blood. His dark eyes burned in their shadowed sockets with a hunger that Myca did not need to see in order to perceive.

Slowly, Myca sat up.

Ladislav stripped off his tunic, hung it wordlessly over the arch of the alcove's entrance, and approached, kneeling at Myca's side. At some level, Myca was entirely aware that, were he alive yet, his blood would be thundering in his temples and his breath would be echoing in his ears, his manhood an aching hot weight between his thighs. He was that fully aroused now, in the way that only a Cainite could be aroused, his senses sharpened enough to see every detail of his companion's expression, to feel the naked want vibrating the air between them, to smell the blood beneath their skin and taste the hunger heating it already. He wanted to feel Ladislav's hands on him, caressing pure sensation untainted by any human drives into his flesh. He wanted to taste of Ladislav's skin and drive his fangs past its pale surface to draw out a draught of raw passion, desire in its purest form.

No words passed between them. Ladislav tangled his long, pale hands in Myca's hair, and the kiss bore them both to the ground, tongues entwined, fangs unsheathed, drawing blood already. Pressed belly to belly they struggled, legs tangling and arms twining, Ladislav succeeding in pinning down one of Myca's wrists. Myca stroked his free hand down Ladislav's spine and found his skin to be unusually soft, supple with oil, difficult to gain purchase on. He dug in with his nails, raked them down Ladislav's spine, drew blood. Ladislav broke the kiss with a groan of pleasure, his back arching beneath that hand, inviting him to continue. Myca worked his other arm free and touched every part of Ladislav's body that he could reach, stoking the desire between them higher. Blood from the furrows he raked down Ladislav's back flowed over his sides, across Myca's belly and loins, salty-sweet and coppery in scent.

A low sound escaped his companion's throat and it occurred to Myca that Ladislav might not be wholly accustomed to being touched in the way that Ilias had taught him, the way that made the flesh remember what it was to live and lie in the arms of a lover. Ladislav shuddered beneath his hands, shuddered as though he were being wracked by bliss, and Myca continued his ministrations until, with a cry, his companion caught his wrists and bore him down again. Ladislav's knee parted his thighs. His hands gripped Myca's hips, ungently. Then Ladislav was inside him, and Myca could do nothing but moan and beg himself. He threw back his head and cried out, his back arching. Ladislav's mouth found his throat, and the ecstasy welled up from the places their bodies joined to obliterate all else.

Golden light enveloped and filled him with a pleasure such as he had never known before and feared that he might never know again. They moved together, sensually entwined, bodies refusing to be parted for more than a few seconds. He cried out softly as his lover took him even more deeply, his back arching against the bed of silk in which they lay, the tendons in his neck drawing taut, eyes squeezing closed against tears of perfect joy. Cool lips pressed a kiss to the hollow of his throat and a sigh escaped his lips, his lover's name...

Myca woke suddenly, completely, sitting bolt upright in the darkness of the room he had slept in, head spinning with disorientation, fear and horror clawing at the inside of his chest. For an instant, panic ruled him unalloyed by any saner emotions, and it was all he could do not to fling himself from the bed and batter at the walls, shrieking and wailing. His Beast was fully awake and as fear-ridden as he. It fought against his every attempt to control it until he did as it wished, and clawed his way to the edge of the familiar, comfortable bed, spilling himself to the wooden floor. Splinters gouged his palms and he lashed out unthinkingly. His fist encountered the slender legs of a table and smashed one to kindling, sending its contents to the floor with a crash of breaking glass and pottery. Deliberately, he slammed his open palm down on a thick shard that fell nearly atop his hand. It pierced his skin and dug deeply into the flesh beneath, pain and blood-scent lending him the focus necessary to beat back mindless fear. He sat on the floor, naked and shuddering in near-frenzied reaction, picking pieces of a broken pottery bowl out of his hand and licking away his own blood, strenuously trying to force his mind to function.

His memory was blurred. The previous evening was little more than a hazy mass of dim images and sharply engraved sensations. Slowly, he remembered, remembered Ladislav and the alcove, and how they had slaked their hungers until the stars began to fade before the sunrise. His flesh still burned with the memory of lust and...

The dream.

He remembered the dream. It shocked him, for he rarely remembered the details of his dreams, only the pain and disquiet they left behind. Now... now he recalled it all. It was almost too real to be a dream, the strength of it, the way it lingered now in his mind like a thing of beauty he had feared lost forever. It felt, and it shook him to the core to admit it, like a memory. The golden light in the shape of a glorious man, shining from within as though lit by the sun's own light, a light that filled every inch of the city that was his dream and graced all whom it touched. The caresses... the caresses and the ecstatic pleasure they brought, a pleasure that was more than the satisfaction of base lust, a rapture that claimed him in his entirety, mind, body, and soul, that made him tremble even now with the intensity of it. The words of love whispered between them, the name of the lover in his dream still shaping his lips.

Michael.

Chapter Eighteen

Myca said nothing to Ilias of his dream, and they spoke little of the night of the Aphrodisiac itself. Ilias kept the secrets entrusted to him well, and, in truth, Myca had no desire to pry. He and Lord Ladislav saw each other regularly, the atmosphere between them no longer charged with unspoken desire but warmed instead by the memory of what they had shared. Myca did not seek Ladislav's bed again, nor did Ladislav press the issue. Both were content in the knowledge that they could if they wished to, and left it at that. Likewise Ilias, if he sensed the secrecy laying in his lover's thoughts, did not inquire or pry into its cause. Myca thought that his lover trusted him enough to let him speak in his own time, and he appreciated that more than words could say.

Ilias, in fact, seemed to be productively employing himself ignoring Malachite's general disapproval of the depraved existence he led, and spent most of the early summer attempting to draw the Rock of Constantinople out and soften his attitude. His charm was, evidently, up to the task. Malachite became much less disagreeable, brusque changing to oddly gruff when dealing with the witch-priest, their conversations taking on a more natural cadence even in Myca's ears. Ilias induced Malachite to ask to review Nikita's letters, now that he had finished his perusal of Nikita's library of heretical literature. Nikita, Malachite reported grudgingly, was quite a prolific writer, literate and intelligent, his commentaries on the fine points of heretical doctrine actually approaching the logical. Myca gave Malachite access to Nikita's letters and his own notes without argument. Reviewing them would give Malachite something productive to do, which was more than Myca could say for himself. He was nearly at his temper's end with literary-minded heretics who never said anything of consequence about themselves, and waiting for a letter from Basilio to arrive. For his own part, he distracted himself by entertaining diplomatic overtures from various Bulgar Tzimisce. Most amounted to a hope that the Obertus Order and the Draconian Tzimisce would lend their influence to the effort to oust Bela Rusenko from Sredetz and place a more appropriate ruler on his throne. Myca collected their requests, which he forwarded to Symeon with a letter outlining his progress to date, but otherwise made no promises.

In such ways did the bulk of the summer pass. No letter arrived from Basilio, and they found themselves entertaining the prospect of spending another fruitless winter in Sredetz, a possibility none of them particularly looked forward to, each for his own reasons.

"We should, I think, leave for home now, while the roads are still clear enough to travel and before the worst of the autumn rains settle in," Myca announced thoughtfully, one night as they sat together in the villa's small garden, enjoying the warm breeze flowing down off the mountains. Nicolaus had bent his efforts to bringing the garden back to life, watering and weeding it, encouraging healthy new growth. The results sweetly perfumed the air along with the beeswax candles lighting the small table where they sat. "I have already spoken of it to *stapân* Boleslaus and *stapân* Vladya—they have told me that they will allow us free passage through their domains and host us, as well, should we desire their hospitality. I can write my colleague Velya from their domains, and I am certain that he, too, would accommodate us in this."

"You have given up hope of receiving word from Basilio, then?" Malachite asked, his voice grave.

"Nearly." Myca cast a glance at Ilias, who was looking fixedly out into the darkened garden beyond their warm circle of light. "My heart?"

Ilias came back to himself with a start. "I heard you speaking of Basilio…?"

"Yes." Myca wondered at his lover's distraction, but decided not to inquire of its cause in front of Malachite. "What do you think?"

"I think Basilio can write us in Brasov as easily as Sredetz, or we could write him again, if you wish." Ilias replied, frankly. "It may not be worth the effort—he may be ash, or he may be in torpor, or any number of other things could prevent him from replying to your letters. He could have no interest in helping us, for this place cannot but return painful memories to him. We have other avenues we may explore to uncover Nikita's lineage, which do not rely upon any information he might provide, after all."

"Other avenues...?" Malachite echoed, his expression, as always, unreadable.

"Damek Ruthven." Ilias answered with a nod, his eyes flicking suddenly off to one side, distracted. He said no more.

Myca filled in the rest for him. "Damek Ruthven is one of the most renowned genealogists and scholars of the history of our clan. If anyone knows, or can discover, which branch of the lineages Nikita of Sredetz springs from, it would be he."

"Have you given any more thought to the theory I proposed in that regard, my Lord Vykos?" Malachite asked, with an odd formality, his hand stealing toward the breast of his tunic and withdrawing from its folds a small object wrapped in a silken cloth.

Myca stiffened. "No. Nothing we have uncovered thus far has given any evidence that Nikita is a descendant of the Dracon."

"Nor has anything we found disproved that possibility," Malachite countered, laying the object he had drawn forth on the table, and folding open its wrappings, revealing a small, cracked tile. Myca knew what it was, and glanced away, his hands curling into fists against his thighs, fighting against the sudden, violent urge to take the thing up and finish smashing it.

Ilias, on the other hand, rose to get a better look. "May I...?" At Malachite's nod, he lifted the painted tile out of its silken nest and examined it closely in the candlelight. "This is his true face? The Dracon?"

"His true face? I do not know. It is the face that I knew him by, and the face that I will recognize him by, should we ever meet again." Malachite's voice was soft, and slightly wistful. If his face could show a true expression, Myca knew that it would be reverent, and he had to force down a renewed surge of temper at that realization.

"It is not, however, Nikita's face," Myca interrupted coolly. "I shall write Damek Ruthven from here, and beg him to send any response to our house in Brasov. I suggest we give Basilio until the end of this month to reply and, in the meantime, we make our preparations for departure. Are we agreed?"

After a moment more of contemplating the icon, Ilias laid it back in its wrappings and nodded slightly in agreement. Malachite, perhaps recognizing himself outnumbered, nodded as well.

Basilio's letter arrived as they were finalizing their travel preparations, in the travel-worn hands of the guardsman who originally carried Myca's inquiry. Myca, breaking the seal with trembling fingers, found it to be quite satisfyingly thick, given the amount of time it had taken to reach him. In it, Basilio admitted to knowing Nikita when he was a minor priest in the service of the bishop of Varna, and even of being aware that Nikita was a Tzimisce. Nikita himself did not appear to make much of the issue, nor did he abide by most of the common Tzimisce naming customs. He did not give his lineage when introducing himself, nor did he claim the identity of his sire, preferring to rely upon the patronage of his superior to ease the way in social situations. Basilio recalled him as reserved, unless a matter that particularly roused his passions was an issue of discussion. In those cases, he would often speak with great eloquence. All of this confirmed what they already knew, and Myca handed those pages to the eagerly waiting Malachite and Ilias with slowly mounting impatience. If that was all Basilio could tell them, he was prepared to be extremely disappointed.

The opening paragraph of the last page, however, considerably amended his feelings in that regard.

"When I owned the villa in which Nikita dwelt, and in which you *currently reside, there was one large room on the first floor given over to storage of various items, which Nikita clearly put to that use, as well. There is, however, a second, smaller storage space in the upstairs office, which I personally used to store correspondence of a delicate or private nature. It is inset in the bottom of the cabinet-chest used to store writing materials, which you described to me as yet being in the place I originally left it. The floor beneath the cabinet-chest is false, though cunningly made to resemble the floor otherwise. The space beneath is large enough to hold a small correspondence chest or, perhaps, several smaller items."*

There was more, but Myca hardly cared. He shoved the last page of the letter into Ilias' hands and hurried to the storage cabinet, long since divested of any writing materials, tearing open the door. An exclamation of mingled surprise and dismay escaped Malachite as he knelt in front of it, feeling along the edges of the floor inside the chest, searching. His fingers came down on a slightly raised segment, and he pressed down hard on it. The pressure-switch triggered, and the entire piece of the false floor came loose from its moorings. Hands trembling with excitement, he pulled it out and laid it aside, feeling about in the space beneath, and encountered a small wooden box. He lifted it out with care, using its handles, and set it down on the floor before them. A series of three metal plates were inset on the lid, marked around the edge with symbols, and Myca whispered, "It is the same sort of lock that Nikita used on the correspondence chest the knights found in the monastery."

"Can you open it again?" Ilias asked, fetching another candle.

"Give me a moment."

Myca worked silently. The original lock was as much a puzzle as anything else, predicated on the ability to recognize a pattern, and this was no different. Within the hour, the tumblers clicked into place and the cunning mechanism opened, revealing three small folios bound in leather, the pages of the finest and thinnest vellum. Each took a book and, with a certain air of ceremony, opened it.

"I do not recognize the language." Malachite admitted it

first. "It... is not Greek."

Myca struggled for a moment with his pride, then nodded shallowly in agreement. "Neither do I. Nor is the alphabet familiar—the letters are not Greek or Cyrillic. Nor Latin. Ilias?"

"It... almost reminds me of the tongue that my sire taught me to use..." Ilias paused and looked up from his folio. "It almost resembles the spirit-tongue—the language used to evoke them in word, spoken and written. The letters are similar, see?" He pointed out a line on the page he had opened to. "I would swear that is the letter for 'fire'... but it is not quite the same."

"Is it the same hand," Malachite asked suddenly, "as the one that wrote Nikita's letters and other documents?"

Nicolaus was hurriedly summoned and sent back downstairs to retrieve one of Nikita's writing chests, and Myca's, as well. A quick comparison showed them that the hand that wrote Nikita's letters was different from the writer of these journals, and Myca compared the books against Basilio's letter as well. There were no similarities.

"Though Basilio may have used a scribe," Myca admitted.

"Yes, but he also said that he took all of the private documents he had stored there when he went into exile." Ilias pointed out, exchanging a glance with Malachite. "What reason would he have to lie on that matter?"

A dozen reasons leapt immediately to mind, but Myca also found sufficient reason to reject them all. "These must belong to Nikita, then, and he did not wish them to be found. He did not care about the correspondence and the other documents downstairs. Had he, he would have left it carefully guarded, or would have stored it elsewhere or destroyed it."

"He probably expected to return." Malachite pointed out.

"Perhaps." Myca closed his book, and replaced it in the chest. Malachite and Ilias handed back theirs, as well, and Myca closed the lid, spinning the lock back into place. "Ilias, could Nikita be a *koldun*—a *koldun* like Ioan, who conceals his true power for some advantage greater than the honor it would bring to his name?"

Ilias did not look at all startled by that question. "I thought that it might be so, but I had no proof, and could find none in any of my own investigations. But since this place is not truly Nikita's home, that proof would not lie here at all, particularly if he were trying to conceal the truth of himself. This place has no strong spirits bound to it, after all, and no signs of any great magic lingering around it."

Myca nodded and rose, the chest held carefully between his hands. "I think I wish to consult with someone wiser than us all in that regard. I believe that we shall, indeed, pay a call on my friend Velya."

Interlude

*I*did not hate Antonius as much as he hated me.
    I tell myself this every night when I wake and, for a short time at least, I can make myself believe it, and the ache of his absence eases.
    I did not want to kill Antonius. Had I thought for a moment that there could ever be peace between us, I would have stayed my hand and persuaded Michael to mercy, as well.
    I tell myself this every morning before I sleep, but it does me little good. Regret is a pernicious emotion. I almost envy those who can excise it from their hearts and suffer not from those things they must do to survive. And I know that it was survival—my own survival, the survival of my childer, the survival of all that I built in Constantinople—that was at stake when we chose to destroy Antonius. I know this, and it does not help. The knowledge that Antonius would have destroyed me, destroyed the Dream to deny me, had we not destroyed him first is not a soothing balm upon my grief.
    Odio et amo: quare id faciam, fortasse requiris. Nescio, sed fieri sentio et excrucior. A Roman poet whose work Antonius despised wrote those words. 'I love and I hate. You ask me why this is so; I do not know, but I feel it, and it torments me.' The essence of the bond between us, though I know why I loved him and hated him. He was the incarnation of something that did not exist within myself—solidity, permanence, unyielding, unbending, the bedrock foundation, the strength of mountains. I was drawn to that strength. I wanted to feel it, folded around me like guardian wings, held before me like a shield between myself and the world, wound through me, protecting me from the weaknesses of my own flesh and spirit. By that same token, he

was also something that I despised, not only solid but hard, uncompassionate, not only unyielding but unchanging, the enemy of change, who preferred stasis except when violent change served him better. Not only strong, but vicious in his strength, cruel when his protection was rejected, or not wanted. He would have smothered me in his strength, had I surrendered completely to the hold he had upon my soul. He would have remade me in his own image, and I cannot even say that I would have fought him with all my strength. Change is, after all, my nature, my deepest failing, and to please him, to know that he was pleased with me, I might very well have surrendered all I am to his desire.

The history of Constantinople and of the Dream that we built together claims that we were lovers, we three, but that is not wholly true. Michael was the center of gravity around which both Antonius and I turned, the object of both our affections, very much to his own delight. Michael loved Antonius. They were lovers for centuries before my angel and I ever met, and the bonds between them were deep. Michael loved me, and to this night I do not know, even for my own peace, why he chose me. A part of me thinks that he decided to love me solely to craft a balance to Antonius within his own being—order, of course, requiring chaos to be complete, and Michael always being exquisitely aware of the aesthetic pleasures to be found in such a union of polar opposites. Antonius, I think, did not perceive the matter in quite that light. I do not doubt his rage, the hurt and betrayal of a man who had found his happiness in the arms of a perfect love, only to have that love offer himself to another. Antonius never forgave me for the part of Michael's heart that I possessed, no matter how small that part might have been, and he was never the lover to me that others have romantically thought him to be.

Except once.

Once, and only once, did he touch me as a lover, and that night is branded into my soul as though by fire. I knew, when Antonius unleashed his image-breakers, his Iconoclasts, on the Empire that it was not the icons, nor the power of the monasteries, nor the ancient tradition of the blood-cults that he truly wished to break, but me. It was me that he wished to see shattered at his feet, me whose bones he wished to feel break beneath his hands, me whose blood he wish to see flow and whose flesh he wished to see burnt to ash. Antonius never loved me, but I knew then that his hatred of me had overwhelmed his love of Michael and his love of the Dream. I knew... and I knew that if I did nothing, if I made no gesture, that he would destroy all he had helped build rather than suffer me to live at peace within it.

For three nights, I went to his haven, and craved entry. For three nights, he refused to see me. On the fourth night, I did not ask the permission of his guardians but walked past them, and commanded them to hold their places. I found him in his study, his very proper Roman study, screened off from the rest of his haven, its walls painted with a murals of Michael—Michael as he showed himself in Rome, clad in robes of white and gold, Michael as he showed himself in Constantinople, all gleaming golden flesh and snow-pale wings. He was alone, and I closed the screen behind me, that we might speak privately. We did not speak. We argued. I cannot, in fact, remember a time when a conversation between us did not devolve into an argument, and this was no exception. I do not remember the words we spoke to one another, but they were cruel, and most of them were true.

He struck me, harder than I have ever been struck before, by anything or anyone, and in that I include my sire, who was not above physical violence when properly enraged. I fell back against the painted wall, stunned, my head reeling and the taste of my own blood filling my mouth. When my vision cleared, Antonius stood less than an arm's length from me. He looked appalled, possibly even with himself, and was staring at his hand, my blood smeared across his knuckles. I recall being surprised that his hands were shaking so violently. His face was marble-white and his pale eyes were wild with emotion, his mouth held in a trembling line and the nostrils of his fine, sharp nose flaring. He lifted his hand to his lips, and licked my blood away. I was transfixed, watching the tip of his tongue moving across his own skin. A tremor ran through us both, and then he was on me, his hands striking me across the face, battering me to my knees with his strength, bearing me to the floor. He crushed both my wrists and tore my hair forcing my *head back. He licked the blood from my face, from my lips, ripped the silks from my body.*

He took me there on the floor, and I wanted it, I wanted him, I wanted him to claim me at last, by force if he needed it that way, to give us both what we had desired, and denied ourselves, for so long. His eyes were hot with mingled lust and loathing, I could feel his raw and naked want, his hatred and his desire, in every touch. He pleasured me so completely that I could have died that night and felt my existence complete; I surrendered myself to him utterly, let him pour himself inside me and twist the whole of my being to suit his needs, gave all that I was capable of giving. At the height of it, at the instant when our souls and flesh became molten and blended wholly with one another, as the ecstasy of our union sang through us, I cried aloud my love for him, and knew that it was true.

It did not matter.

I did not hate Antonius as greatly as he hated me, and Antonius did not love me, at all, before that night or after it, even as he held me sobbing in his arms, even as I understood how Michael felt when they lay together.

I love him. I will always love him. I loved him as he crumbled to dust, and I will love him until the world itself follows him into darkness. Perhaps, one night, I will follow him, will be permitted to follow him, and know peace from the grief that has lived in my heart, in the deepest places of my soul, since the morning he met his death.

I should not have let it happen.

Part Three

Dragon's Breath

"Omnia mutantur, nos et mutantur in illis."
(All things are subject to change, and we change them.)
—Anonymous

Chapter Nineteen

From the journals of Myca Vykos:

*T*he summer lingered long that year. Though the trees slowly changed their colors and just as slowly fell, the rains did not, nor did the frosts come to chill us while we were on the road. Looking back, I see that I noted the unusual weather in my journal, but gave it no other thought, for Ilias did not seem overly disturbed by it, at least not at the start. Drought is natural, after all, and we had had many hard, wet autumns and winters of late; I think he was grateful not to travel soaked to the skin. We slowed most when guesting with our Bulgar cousins, those who wished to curry favor with my sire and me and achieve our aid in their schemes. These Bulgars were evidently willing to swallow their distaste for Byzantines and insisted on the observation of all the formalities, the giving of gifts as a sign of good will between all parties, the blood-feasts of greeting and parting. If nothing else, we were fed well on the blood of slaves purchased in the markets of Sredetz that autumn as we made our way steadily northward.

We reached the border of Velya's domain as the last of the leaves fell. There we met the captain of his ghoul-protectors, a Bratovitch bred for at least a little intellect as well as massive size, and a large contingent of guards to guide us to his house....

Velya the Flayer greeted his guests in the dooryard of his manse, which did not surprise Myca at all. On their last meeting, Velya had clad himself also in the traditions of the clan, playing the gracious and urbane host to the hilt and beyond.

There was no reason to doubt that, given the chance, he would not do so again. Velya stood on the shallow stair leading to the door of his house as they rode into the dooryard, accompanied by two contingents of guards and a string of servants leading the baggage animals, surveying them with the sort of majestically paternal air that only he could produce properly, a faintly fond smile playing about the corners of his perfect mouth. And Velya was, indeed, perfect. He wore white, a long dalmatic that shimmered with subtle embroidery at neck and hems over equally snowy hose, his impeccably groomed hair falling to his waist in silver ringlets, his face a mask of hawklike patrician elegance. When he raised his hands in the traditional gesture of greeting, his long, sculptor's hands glittered with fine silver rings.

"I give you greetings, my most honored guests, and welcome to my house. I give you welcome, my cousin Myca Vykos syn Draconov. I give you welcome, my old friend Ilias cel Frumos, beloved of the gods. I give you welcome, my Lord Malachite, the Rock of Constantinople." He bowed, the torches sprinkled about the dooryard scattering reflections from his pale hair and the silver embroidery on his tunic. "Within my walls will you find safety and comfort for so long as you abide with me, this I swear by Earth and Sky, and the Waters of Life and Death. Come..." He rose, his face relaxing in a genial smile. "You have traveled far and I see the weariness on you."

Servants came and took their horses, the men of the guard being led away to their own quarters to take a meal and their rest. Myca dismounted slowly, and last, as Ilias and Malachite gathered themselves behind him, waiting for him to make the ritual response to Velya's greeting. Myca was abruptly sick of tradition and felt his Beast roil, angrily, hungry for blood instead of endless words. He made his most courtly bow to the oldest of his friends and colleagues among the clan and murmured softly, "I give you greetings, my cousin Velya, and accept your gracious hospitality, for which your house is well known."

Velya stretched out a hand to him, which Myca accepted, allowing himself to be drawn up the steps. "Come—I was not speaking poetically when I see that you are all weary. A bath awaits you, and a meal. We will speak of what brought you to me later."

Velya's house was neither Byzantine nor anything resembling Roman in its construction. It was low to the ground, one story tall, and did not rise above the lowest branches of the surrounding trees, blending instead among them. Its largest rooms were round more than any other shape, its halls short, its walls and ceiling and floor carefully shaped, sanded, and fitted wood. There was no paint, no stone except around the fireplaces, and no mosaic or other ostentatious ornamentation. Parts of the walls and many of the ceiling support columns were carved in elaborate and fanciful designs, and many were hung with long, woven panels of woolen cloth to keep out the damp. There were no doors, only more fabric hangings, except in the long rectangular bathhouse, to help keep in the heat.

Malachite, perhaps predictably, refused the use of the bath and sauna, instead asking to be escorted to his chamber to refresh himself privately. Nothing, however, could have kept Ilias from the presence of hot water and Myca allowed himself to be drawn along without much struggle. The hot water refreshed him, Ilias tended to his needs rather than the bath servants, and the guest-garments that Velya provided were smooth wine-colored silk embroidered in gold and garnets, a treat to his senses after months of wool and fur. The attendants guided them to the main hall when they were finished and there they found Velya and Malachite already seated in a nest of floor cushions and thickly woven rugs, making polite conversation. Myca was privately convinced that Velya could make polite conversation with anyone, and was faintly amused to see that theory borne out on the somewhat bemused-looking Rock of Constantinople. Malachite had chosen to conceal his true face behind another illusion for the evening, a weathered, middle-aged man, and was responding to questions and idle banter with the air of a man wondering what he'd gotten himself into. Myca entirely understood—Velya was almost disturbingly easy to talk to when he was exerting himself to be social.

"Ah, there you are," Velya rose to greet them, and motioned

for them to choose the places they most liked, "I was just telling Lord Malachite that, in your absence, your sire has become a man of much industry."

"Oh?" Myca inclined a brow, and settled himself amid a nest of riotously colorful pillows, Ilias sinking down beside him and tugging a fur over his legs to keep the warmth of the bath. "It seemed that might be the case as we were departing, I will admit."

Velya reseated himself, reclining comfortably against a piece of furniture Myca initially took for wood in the soft lighting but realized, when it moaned softly, was actually a rather erotic sculpture involving at least two ghouls. He resisted with all his might the urge to shoot a glance at Malachite.

"Yes. He has, evidently, been engaged on two diplomatic fronts—with Jürgen of Magdeburg and our friend Noriz' vile little brood, if not Noriz himself. It has been most amusing to watch from a safe distance." Velya's eyes glittered with an emotion halfway between amusement and malice. "The warlord appears to be finding your sire not particularly easy to deal with, now that he has obtained the aid of *allies* more useful than Vladimir Rustovitch. I do not expect the pact you spent so much blood on to survive another year and while I grieve for the effort you put into it, the politics of the situation are shifting."

"I thought they would," Myca admitted, coolly. "Jürgen of Magdeburg is accustomed to dictating terms, not being dictated to, and I doubt he thought he would see any consequences from his actions. What does Rustovitch do, while my sire is at work?"

"Still brooding in his tent, in an even fouler temper than he was before." Velya laced his fingers together, his mouth set in the thinnest of smiles. "I believe that even Radu—poor, faithful Radu—is getting weary of his everlasting sulk. It has, evidently, gotten worse of late, and we can blame your sire for that, as well."

"When we were leaving, Ioan Brancoveanu had just asked my sire to call together an assembly of the *voivodes*, the leaders of the largest war-bands. I admit I did not think that Rustovitch would attend…?" Myca inclined a brow questioningly.

"If he did, no word of it reached me. Rumor suggests,

however, that under pressure from the inestimable Radu, Rustovitch permitted those *voivodes* allied under him to attend as they willed and he was most displeased by the large number that so willed." Velya did not sound entirely gleeful—his personal dignity was too great for that—but his tone made it clear that he thought this humiliation no less than Rustovitch's just desserts. "Ioan Brancoveanu's forces were swelled quite profitably, and with allies more trustworthy than his own kin."

Ilias shifted slightly at Myca's side, and he glanced down at his lover, finding him, as he often was of late, abstracted in expression, gazing at a point in the middle distance. Myca frowned and slipped an arm about him. Ilias came back to himself with a small start, and smiled reassuringly.

"Ioan is better placed than he was before then?" Ilias asked, proving that he hadn't been entirely absent during the conversation.

"Yes. Ceoris is encircled, and has been since late this summer. He hopes to choke them into submission over this winter, and he may just. The Tremere themselves scorched their own earth closest to the fortress years ago, and unless they are replenishing their supplies from their heathen sorceries..."

"They may have such sources," Myca opined, without elaboration.

"Perhaps. Or they may be trapped in their own tomb with half the *voivodes* in the east gathered about them, feeding on their herds and reducing their outer works to smoking rubble. Time will tell."

"The gargoyles..." Malachite suggested quietly.

"Neutralized, at least for the time being, I am told. The winged ones, at least. Lady Danika has been, shall we say, advancing certain aspects of the *koldun*'s art in intriguing directions of late. A cordon, of some kind, to contain the things, and hold them at a safe distance from the besieging forces." Velya shrugged slightly, though Myca could sense the depth of his interest, and Ilias' curiosity sharpening, as well. "My information on that matter is not as complete as it could be, though one of my grandchilder regularly writes me from the camp where she resides."

"Ilyana? I always knew she would make a warrior," Ilias asked, leaning forward slightly.

"The very same. She begged my permission to run off to war as soon as the chance came to her," Velya looked and sounded half-bemused, half-regretful. "She trotted off to join two of her cousins with a war-band from Ruthenia. I made her promise to indulge my old man's fancies and write me so I would know she was not ashes in the wind."

"Speaking of cousins, my friend," Myca cleared his throat slightly. "That is at least part of what brings us to you tonight. If we may…?"

A soft chime sounded, from somewhere beyond the hanging-covered doors, and a procession of servants entered, bearing bloodletting tools and goblets.

"No, we may not." Velya smiled faintly. "Now that I have you in my house, dear cousin, I am going to force you to submit to my old man's fancies, as well, and leave the business of what brought you here for tomorrow night. Tonight, we will dine, and tell one another stories, and remind ourselves that our existences are not wholly made up of politics and war."

Myca nodded shallowly, seeing no graceful way to disagree.

He lay still, unmoving, and in truth he was not certain that he was able to move. His body felt heavy, inert, almost as though there were a stake through his heart. His thoughts felt strangely disconnected from it, and sensation came to him as though from a great distance. He could not open his eyes. A part of him wanted to shriek and writhe, but he was incapable of doing so, incapable even of mustering all the emotional responses that would have gone into such a display. His mind was curiously empty of coherent chains of thought and he discovered in himself a great difficulty when he tried to concentrate on any of the meandering fragments of ideas wandering through his skull.

He was cold. The air against his—bare?—skin held an unpleasant damp chill. He lay flat on what felt like a slab of marble, spread with the thinnest of coverings, doing nothing to prevent the cold from invading his flesh. From a great distance, he heard footsteps—two pairs? One?

He could not tell—then a door opening and closing, a bolt sliding into place, iron grating on stone. Light spread across his eyelids, staining his field of vision briefly crimson, as the lamp that was its source came to rest nearby. Quiet footfalls—one pair, he could now tell. A hand, cool even to his contact-chilled flesh, rested on his brow and laid there for a moment. Once again, his body resisted any effort to open his eyes, even as a second hand joined the first and began stroking gently over the contours of his face.

Through the disconnection between his mind and his body, Myca felt himself beginning to change. His skin split and his flesh parted, the bones beneath reshaping themselves under the careful touch of his captor, who caressed the shape he desired from Myca's flesh with the precision and skill of a master sculptor. Gradually, the slope of his brow changed, the shape of his eye-sockets and the width of his nose, the angle of his cheekbones, the contour and sharpness of his jaw, even his teeth. There was, naturally, a great deal of pain, against which he could not even cry out. His throat refused to tense, his lungs refused to draw air.

It seemed to go on forever, Myca aware and powerless to resist his captor's hands, the reshaping of his entire form. Inside himself, he wept and raged, his Beast wholly roused by the agony of his body as his bones and flesh and skin were stretched and twisted and reformed, by the anguish of his helplessness in the face of such an absolute violation of body and self. No amount of Beast-rage or fiercely focused will made it stop, or affected the slightest reversal of the changes in his form. At the last, his captor laced long hands through his hair and drew out its length, spilling it across his throat and breast, nearly to the knees, in a perfectly straight curtain, draping it over him like a garment.

The door opened again, and a single set of footsteps approached. A voice he did not know spoke. "Is it done?"

"Yes. The next part is yours, Gregorius."

Myca's heart froze and shattered, for that voice he knew as well as he knew his own. That voice greeted him as he clawed his way from his ritual grave deep in the mountains of his homeland. That voice spoke to him when he rose each night, and before he sought his rest each morning. That voice was the very last he expected to hear.

Myca woke, a shriek lurking somewhere in the back of his throat, shuddering uncontrollably within himself and still unable to move. The sun had not yet set, and his body was as still and immobile as a statue, a forced immobility that sent his Beast ravening against the confinement. He let it rage itself into exhaustion, having no will to resist it, his emotions raw enough that he had no desire to try to rein them in, thick, cold tears pouring down his cheeks, across the tight seam of his mouth. He wanted to sob, but could not force himself to breathe, even as the feeling returned to his limbs, the weight of daylight fatigue lifting from him. Snuggled close against his back, one arm flung about his waist, Ilias slept on. Moving slowly, for slow motion was all he could manage with the sun still above the horizon, Myca lifted that arm away and sat up carefully. In the corner, one of Velya's excellent servants, trained to respond to the slightest motion, rose quickly and attended to him.

"Hot water, and a cloth. Now." It took all the concentration he could muster to manage the words, clinging fiercely to the edge of the bed, refusing to fall back to sleep.

The servant returned a moment later with another of its cowled, sexless kind, bearing a lit lamp as well as a basin, a pitcher of hot water, and several cloths. He made use of all of these, bathing his face and neck, shuddering even to touch himself. The second of the two servants offered its neck and wrists, which he refused with a stomach-churning jolt of near-revulsion, and commanded it to seek out its master and crave an audience as soon as could be arranged. As Ilias began to stir, he left the bedchamber for the small study they had been afforded and found the box containing the three journals. In the hall, he met the returning servant, who informed him that the master would see him immediately.

Velya's private chambers were in the same wing of his sprawling haven as the guest quarters and so they did not have far to walk, for which Myca was grateful. His concentration was in pieces and his temper was on edge. He feared if he had to speak with or even see more than the bare minimum of others, he might snap, and lash out violently. He had no desire to give that insult to Velya, who had been his confidante and nearly his friend for longer than anyone else within the clan. It nonetheless nettled him considerably to enter Velya's private chambers and discover that the man rose looking as pristine as God's own angels, draped in white, his silver hair an artfully disarranged spill of curls across his shoulders.

Myca throttled an unworthily snide remark and bowed deeply in greeting, the box held close against his middle. "My lord, I apologize for the preemptory nature of my request, and I thank you greatly for answering it nonetheless."

"Oh, 'my lord,' is it?" Velya's tone was richly, deeply amused. "For the love of Earth and Sky, Myca, come in and sit down. You look like you just clawed your way out of your grave again. Have you eaten?"

"No, my—" He paused, rose from his bow, and at Velya's gesture joined him in the nest of pillows and furs in which the Flayer reclined with no fewer than three servants, from whom he was dining. "Velya, I *am* sorry. I slept... very poorly. I think it is my spirit's way of telling me I have been away from home quite long enough."

"It is possible." Velya eyed him closely, and gestured for one of the servants to attend him. "You do not look yourself, and you have spent more time traveling in the last handful of years than any other of our blood that I know. It would not surprise me if that has finally begun to affect you."

A little thrill of mingled fear and anguish rippled through him at those words, and he had to force himself to drink shallowly of the servant's wrist, swallowing against the urge of his throat to close, the desire of his flesh to feel no contact with another. "It would not surprise me, either. Ilias lectures constantly but... there are some things that I feel that I must do. We were in Sredetz on just such a... mission."

"I see." Velya waved the servants hovering over him away, steepling his long-fingered hands before his breast. "Tell me."

Myca did so, telling him the entire story from Nikita's unexpected delivery to the largely unrewarding trip to Sredetz to investigate the Archbishop of Nod's background. "The only substantive evidence we found was an absence of any connection between Nikita and Vladimir Rustovitch. There was no correspondence between them and, as far as I could determine, Nikita had no interest in converting Rustovitch to his cause.... And we found these journals." Myca worked the locks on the correspondence chest and opened it, removing the first of the journals and handing it across to Velya, whose brows inclined in obvious interest. "The journals, like the letters, have no impressions clinging to them. Before I encountered it here, I did not think such a thing was possible, but you hold the evidence in your hands. They are written in a tongue that none of us can read. Even the alphabet is not familiar, though Ilias says it reminds him of the koldunic spirit-speech."

Velya opened the leather cover of the journal with care and examined the first several pages in meditative silence. Finally, he murmured, "Ilias is correct. The form is very similar, but... different somehow. If you wish, I will examine these more closely.... I may have some resource in my own library that will allow me to translate them."

Myca fought down an urge—a wordless, powerful urge, too strong for any rational, thoughtful impulse—to automatically deny that request, not wishing to let those journals leave his hands. He swallowed it with difficulty, and nodded shallowly. "I have little to offer you in recompense for this generosity, Velya, but I nonetheless am grateful for your largesse in this matter. I feel strongly that these books may hold the key to Nikita's mystery. If you help me unravel that, I would be forever in your debt."

"Let there be no talk of debt between us, Myca. You came to me once craving knowledge and advice, and it pleased me then to teach you what little I could. It pleases me still to know that you were as apt as any pupil I have ever instructed, and to see what you have made of yourself since you came among your true people." Velya closed the book and set it back in the correspondence box. "The love and friendship I bear you has survived the years, and if you wish to speak of compensation, repay me by writing me and visiting me more often. There are few enough among our kind whom I chose to tolerate, and even fewer whom I find more than tolerable. You are one of those. Let us be again as close as we were when it took months for our letters to reach each other."

Myca lowered his eyes and bowed from the shoulders. "You honor me."

A chuckle. "And still so serious. I had hoped that young Ilias would cure you of that. Come, I am certain the good priest of Jarilo has risen and seeks after you even now. Best not to keep him waiting."

Chapter Twenty

Myca was not of a humor that made him accept the second-guessing of his decisions gracefully. When Malachite and Ilias both questioned the wisdom of leaving the journals in Velya's care, each with his own argument against that course of action, Myca snarled at them and ordered the servants to immediately prepare for their departure. Malachite, predictably enough, withdrew into a stiff and disapproving silence as he prepared his own baggage. Ilias, who had become accustomed to occasionally being snarled at over the years, merely observed mildly that it would be pleasant to sleep in their own bed again, and then wisely let the matter lie. They departed Velya's house on the first truly cold night of the autumn thus far, and made good time in the cold, dry weather that followed. The forests and mountains, Myca noted when he bothered to pay attention to the landscape, were sere with drought, the rills and streams running low, the hard-packed roads clearly little touched by rain. Ilias noted it as well and spent much of his time bespeaking the spirits from the saddle, murmuring to himself in the lilting tongue used only by the *koldun*. Malachite kept to himself and Myca wasted little thought or energy worrying about what the Rock of Constantinople might be planning within his tenacious silence.

By day, Myca dreamed strange and disturbing dreams, which he recalled in increasingly vivid fragments. The supply of his grave-earth, he could not help but notice, was dwindling rapidly now, crumbling away to gray powder as its spiritual strength fled it. Ilias was in similar straights, but Ilias was also not dreaming terrible dreams. Instead, he was besought by agitated spirits, in a state of almost constant distraction. Myca dearly wished to speak to his lover about his own agitation of spirit, but held himself back, partly out of fear, partly out of self-disgust, and mostly out of pride. A part of him refused to admit even the possibility that there was something within himself that he might not be strong enough to face on his own, despite the abundant examples he knew of to the contrary and Ilias' own teaching on that topic. It was a folly, he knew, but at least it was a folly of his own choosing, and he kept his peace—and his lack of peace—very much to himself.

They arrived at the monastery late in the autumn, with Christ-Mass approaching and still no snow to speak of on the ground, except at the highest elevations. Returning home, for all of them, even Malachite, was like slipping into a hot bath after a raw day, stepping into comfortably well-worn shoes and clothing, walking into an embrace of pure consolation. Their rooms were prepared, cleaned and aired, smelling gently of lemon oil and the freshly turned earth filling their bed. Malachite's guest room, having no such need, was instead decorated with pine branches that filled the air with their resinous scent. The servants nearly mobbed Ilias, so glad were they to see him again, and in the confusion of hauling everything they'd carted along with them and acquired since their departure, Myca managed to creep off and take a quiet report from Father Aron who, his frailty notwithstanding, had managed to weather the passage of time quite well. More than a year's worth of backed-up correspondence—from his sire, from several other Obertus monasteries, from half a hundred spies and partisans scattered from one end of the East to the other—waited for him in his office, and he was privately glad that he had something to concentrate on beyond his own woes again. It took him two weeks to find the bottom of his desk again, and during that time he completely ignored anything else in favor of that activity. He sent letters *en masse* since the weather seemed to be perversely intent on cooperating with his desires. One of the first to go out was the letter that Velya had handed to him before their departure, sealed in the Flayer's arms and intended for the hand of Damek Ruthven. Myca wrote to that worthy, as well, and sent two letters for every one he had received from his sire, reporting in detail on his current investigative progress and the information pouring into him from his other sources regarding the activities of the Black Cross, at least some of which he was certain Symeon already possessed. It was pleasant, he decided, to immerse himself in a completely intellectual activity after the sensual excesses of the previous year.

Ilias gracefully took up the task of playing host to Malachite again, in addition to the long-delayed resumption of his duties as resident ghoul-master and priest of Jarilo to the surrounding community. Myca, distracted and still dreaming dark dreams, completely failed to notice when their relationship passed the point of cautious tolerance into something approaching genuine amity.

The spirits were agitated. Ilias did not find this to be wholly unusual. Spirits, like people, could become irritable, sullen, and withdrawn for no discernibly good reason. Ilias knew precisely why Myca had turned irritable and sullenly withdrawn without having to ask. He was dreaming again, and more frequently, as well. The painful echoes of those dreams disturbed the bond between them and lingered in Ilias' mind long after he woke, a shadow that he could neither banish nor wholly understand by himself. Myca was not approachable on the issue, at least not yet, and Ilias hesitated to force it before his lover was mentally prepared to confront it. He turned his attention instead to the spirits, whose distress was at least a distracting mystery he could investigate with the tools at his own command.

If nothing else, dwelling in the house of Ioan Brancoveanu and Danika Ruthven for a season had taught him how to make the simplest of the windflutes, and it was to that task he attended during the two weeks Myca spent buried in the duties of his office. Often, Ilias sat in the oriel room next to a brazier, working the long slender bone he was transforming into his flute with tools of copper as Nicolaus and Sergiusz played for his pleasure, their instruments and each other. With increasing frequency, Malachite would join him with a lamp and a book of his own, borrowed from the monastery or from Myca's own collection,

Ilias could not tell. Malachite, wisely, did not ask questions he did not really want the answers to when he saw Ilias working the first time they met in that fashion. Ilias, for his part, made no effort to discomfit the Rock of Constantinople, or disturb him in his reading. The conversations that passed between them were short and punctuated by long, thoughtful silences. A certain camaraderie began to grow between them, as they waited for a letter to arrive from Damek Ruthven, or for Myca to rejoin their society.

"Where did the bone come from?" Malachite finally asked one night, as the crafting of the flute neared its end, the length of pale bone elegantly shaped in the way that Danika had shown, inscribed with tiny, nearly invisible sigils scripted in the tongue of spirits.

The Rock of Constantinople had a book open across his knees. He sat, comfortably enough, in a nest of pillows he had built up over the nights to adequately support his back and brittle joints. He had not even pretended to read that night, Ilias noticed, but refrained from commenting on the matter.

"It is my own." Ilias replied, bending silver wire carefully into ivory grooves carved for holding it. "I removed it from my own flesh. When all is done, I will wash it in my own blood, as well, to seal the enchantments on it and make it my own."

Malachite was silent for a long moment. If that revelation horrified or repulsed him, it never showed on his face, which remained calmly impassive. Of course, it was a mask, for he rarely showed his true, leprous face to Ilias, but the *koldun* suspected the expression was his own. The look in his great, dark Byzantine eyes was grave, but not censorious. "Is all your magic so painful?"

"Not all of it, no." Ilias smiled slightly. "All of it demands a price, though, for something cannot be accomplished for nothing. If one wishes to command the spirits, or beg favors of them, one must be prepared to provide what they ask in return."

Malachite nodded, and was silent again, turning back to his book. Again, no pages turned.

Ilias bent the last of the silver wire into place, sealing the ends beneath a thin layer of bone to help hold it in place. "Do you truly believe that Nikita is a childe of the first prince of the Blood?"

Malachite replied without even glancing up, no doubt at all in his voice. "Yes, I do."

"Why?" Ilias wrapped the flute in a silken cloth and replaced it in its wooden box.

"For this is where my search for the Dracon has led me. To Nikita. There must be some connection there, even if we cannot see what it is as yet." Slowly, Malachite raised his head and fixed his unblinking dark gaze on Ilias again. "Why do you ask me this?"

"Because I wished to know the truth of the matter from your own lips." Ilias met his gaze squarely. "You are much different from Myca in this, you realize. For Myca, there is no simply *believing* something to be true. He is not much inclined to accept a thing on faith alone. He must always have proof—irrefutable, ironclad proof—before he will judge a thing to be true. He will not, I think, accept that Nikita is of his own line without such a proof. Nor will his sire." Malachite glanced away. "Lord Symeon has already said as much."

Ilias nodded slightly. "It is frustrating, I know. For what it is worth, you have my sympathy—I have been pounding my head against that particular wall of Draconian stubbornness since Myca and I first met. He is very..."

"Headstrong," Malachite muttered, or something like it.

Ilias felt the corners of his mouth twitch, and permitted the expression to emerge. "Strong in his own convictions. It is a fine trait to have, of course, so long as you share those convictions. I am mildly fortunate in that regard." He tucked the box in the crook of his arm and rose carefully—he had taken most of the bone mass from one of his legs, and the healing went slowly. "Would you accompany me, my Lord Malachite?"

The Rock of Constantinople tilted his head quizzically. "Accompany you?"

"I think it is past time that I checked the integrity of the wards binding Nikita, and that you were given the chance to look upon him with your own eyes." And, so saying, he offered Malachite a hand up.

For a long moment, Malachite did nothing but gaze up at him, his expression wholly opaque. Then, he accepted Ilias' hand and levered himself to his feet. Together, Ilias leaning slightly on the taller man's arm, they made their way down into the lowest level of the haven. The door to the storage room that had become Nikita's prison was, naturally, bolted from the outside and, within, all was dark. Fortunately, they had thought to bring their own lamp, and they lit the candles scattered closest to the door.

"Be careful not to cross the wards," Ilias cautioned his companion, pointing to the delicate tracery of blood and salt burnt into the floor, still faintly visible even to untrained eyes. "Because I cannot guarantee that I could drag you back up the stairs without someone noticing."

"I will keep that in mind," Malachite assured him, dryly, and kept a respectful distance as Ilias stepped closer to the edges of the circle, extending his hands to touch it.

The mere brush of his spirit-senses was sufficient to show Ilias what he needed to know—the wards stood firm, a bastion of stone containing the quiescent force of Nikita's substantial personality. To his eyes, they showed no signs of degradation, despite that he had not been present to monitor them constantly and maintain their upkeep. It occurred to him that, just perhaps, Nikita had made no attempt to wear at them in his absence. He sang a query to the spirits bound in the circle and, after a moment, stone grumbled a quiet reply. Nikita slept deeply, very deeply, divorced from his own grave-earth, sunken deep inside himself. That made sense, and Ilias murmured his thanks, coming back to himself, stepping away from the circle.

Malachite stood watching him an arm's length away, his face inscrutable yet again. Ilias rubbed the last of the afterimages from his eyes and asked, "Is it him?"

"Yes." Malachite replied, without hesitation. "This is the same man that I met in Paris or, at least, it is a man wearing the same face. I would know him by his voice, as well."

Ilias nodded. "Perhaps, once we speak to Damek Ruthven, we will have the chance to hear his voice.

Perhaps." Malachite murmured quietly, and there was

something in his tone that Ilias could not entirely place. It was only hours later, as he lay in the bed he shared with his fitfully dreaming lover, still awake despite the pull of daylight, that he realized what it was.

Fear.

Chapter Twenty-One

...My lord Damek Ruthven, to honor the old and long acquaintance between himself and Velya, and the honor that he owes to the scions of the Eldest's favored childe, offers the hospitality of his house to stapân Myca Vykos syn Draconov and his companions. The customs of his court are many and complex, and so herein you will find a brief discussion of those customs. An interpreter and guide will also be provided....

The journey to Sarmizegetusa was a journey of several weeks, most of which managed to pass in the vague semblance of comfort. The winter weather remained uncharacteristically dry and, while the roads froze solid, no snow actually fell. Ilias, after several nights of communion with the spirits and contemplation of their answers, suggested it was the result of the renewed intensity in the struggle against the Tremere. Both sides, it appeared, we working the weather in their own ways, with consequences wider-ranging than perhaps they had all intended. He could not predict when the weather-bind might finally break. Myca, balancing the honor of being invited to peruse Damek Ruthven's genealogical library against the potential discomfort of being trapped away from home all winter, decided that the risk was worth taking. They departed Brasov on a cold, clear day, all three packed in lightproof conveyances, accompanied by a double-handful of guards and a smaller handful of servants.

Sarmizegetusa lay high in the mountains further south even than the domain of Ioan Brancoveanu, further south even than

Ceoris, on the side that sloped eventually down into the vast Danube delta and, from there, to the sea. No road led directly to its ruins, though several simple trade roads snaked through the hills below it. Once the capital of the Dacians before the coming of the Roman Empire and, afterwards, the provincial capital of the Roman conquerors, the high fortress of Sarmizegetusa had long been abandoned, the hills and valleys around it occupied only by simple villages and the folk that made their living from the mountains and the forests. The important functions of trade and government had long since moved north of the great mountain wall, to face and deal with the Magyars and the Saxons, or south to contend with the Byzantines. Sarmizegetusa itself was little more than a picturesque ruin in the forest, the remnants of greatness clinging to the heights, the old walls of fortresses, the old wooden and stone columns of a dead faith, a vanished people.

Sarmizegetusa, for the Tzimisce, was far more than that. Its master, the eldest surviving descendant of the *bogatyr* lineages whose founders had guarded—and, some said, still guarded—the resting place of the Eldest, had dwelt and ruled there since before the coming of the Romans. Among the clan, he was famed in his own right, as scholar and *koldun*, as war-leader and wise counselor, and his many childer had showered honor and renown on his name and that of his house. He had, of his own merit, won favor in the eyes of the Eldest, it was often said, and the tales of how he had done so were many. Myca and Malachite both went to pains to learn the most common, and the most flattering, of them on the trip south to Sarmizegetusa, and Ilias was happy to provide what he knew. His own sire, dead for many years, was a descendant of a Ruthven distaff line, the several times removed grandchilde of Damek Ruthven, whose daughters had, over the years, been many. The petty lords whose domains they passed through en route told them tales, as well, and suggested in whispers that the Eldest had returned, after many years, to the bosom of the mountains that cradled Sarmizegetusa, the place he had once resided for centuries.

Myca was not entirely certain how much credit he was prepared to give that, and neither was Ilias. The Eldest had not made his presence felt among the clan in centuries—not, in fact, since the terrible year he sent his personal envoy to Constantinople to warn his most-favored childe against the Embrace of the boy called Gesu. That Myca knew for an absolute truth, for his own sire had been Embraced in the aftermath of that diplomatic visit, and a war had raged between the Dracon and his northern kin that had led to his own Embrace. What significance could actually be attached to the Eldest's long silence, Myca could not even guess, and he wasn't entirely certain he dared do so. There was an old aphorism among the clans about letting sleeping gods enjoy their rest, and his own in particular took pains not to disturb the sleep of the ancients by even thinking their names too loudly. He wasn't sure he believed that one could think a being's name too loudly, but, treading close to the place that might be the Eldest's own homeland, he found he wasn't quite daring enough to put it to the test, either.

They approached Sarmizegetusa on foot, leaving their vehicles and the horses that drew them in the care of a nameless village lower on the mountain, climbing steep and slender trails that led upward through the forest. Tabak Ruthven's letter had included a map, the route they should travel carefully marked in red ink, which they clung to tenaciously. It took more than one night, as Tabak suggested it might, and they took shelter for the day in the shadow of a partially fallen wall, heavily grown over by winter-bare trees, marked on the map as a remnant of the old Dacian fortress. The next night, they reached the boundary of Damek Ruthven's domain, marked by two tall wooden plinths bearing aloft a pair of sculpted iron wolf-heads that moaned and whined as the wind passed through them. There, the party stopped for a time, and Ilias went on ahead, unaccompanied, to announce their coming. He was clad in his ritual vestments, his unadorned white tunic and his golden crown of flowers, barefoot and unarmed, carrying only a lamp to light his way and the heavy parchment scroll they had prepared in accordance with the old customs of Damek Ruthven's court, of their names and their formal lineages, and their request to enter their host's domain. It had been written on the skin of a virgin girl, whom Ilias had been at great pains to acquire and keep virginal, and who was now among the mortal servants accompanying them on the journey. He had also gone to great pains to keep her alive, a fact which Myca found rather strange and unnecessarily time consuming, until Ilias explained, delicately, that Damek Ruthven evidently had a taste for virgin girls.

Myca endeavored to cultivate calm and patience while they waited at the gate for Ilias to return, reminding himself that this was merely a ceremonial formality, that the permission they craved had already been granted. He tried, with some difficulty, to remind himself that Damek Ruthven was old and powerful and that his age and potency entitled him to respect. His eccentricities were nothing more or less than a remnant of the oldest and most formal customs of the clan itself, and that yielding to those customs ultimately cost him nothing. He watched the path leading back down the mountain, the paved and terraced path that wound its way among the grassy mounds that covered ruined walls and the copses of trees that had stood since before the fall of the Roman Empire, with all his senses refined, looking for the slightest trace of light or motion. Malachite, he could not help but notice, was affecting an unconcerned posture that ultimately did very little to disguise his intense watchfulness. Not for the first time, Myca wondered precisely when his lover had begun winning the goodwill of the Rock of Constantinople, and how he'd managed to do it.

A flicker of white moved among the trees, and Myca permitted the tension making an iron rod of his spine to loosen a fraction. Ilias descended the path, carrying his lamp in both hands, accompanied by a handful of dark-robed figures, most of which were an arm-span and more taller than him. Behind him, Myca heard a brief, muffled sound of fear and surprise from one of the servants, quickly hushed. The guards and the two most experienced servants—Teodor and Miklos, he thought their names were—gathered up the baggage and prepared to move again without being ordered. The three remaining servants, all of them girls at the edge of adulthood, huddled close together in wise, fearful silence, waiting to see what happened next.

Ilias and his companions reached the bottom of the stair

and approached, pausing a few paces above the gate.

"Lord *taraboste* Damek Ruthven has accepted our request to enter into his presence." Ilias announced with perfect serenity, his expression as smooth as water on a windless night. For some reason, Myca found that vaguely disturbing. "Come with me. I shall lead the way."

Myca and Malachite exchanged a brief glance, then approached, passing through the gate, the servants following a respectful six paces behind. Ilias turned before they reached him and led the way, as he said he would, his hair swaying with the grace of his stride. Watching him move, Myca thought he saw something strange in it. Ilias was, for the most part, startlingly graceful and smooth in all of his motions but, tonight, something in that grace seemed a trifle... off. He could not place precisely what it was that caught his eye, but the more he watched, the more it faded away and the language of Ilias' body belonged solely to himself again, and the length of his stride slowed accordingly as they approached the entrance into Damek Ruthven's house.

Myca was faintly surprised to discover that entrance was little more than a round hut, its walls wooden plinths cemented together with clay, its roof a high cone also of wood. Within the small house, a pair of stone plinths stood, on which candles burned, illuminating a great pit that filled the center of the building, and the shallow steps descending into the mountain on which they stood.

"He awaits us below." Again, Ilias' voice was serenely devoid of expression. "Come."

And so they descended.

Damek Ruthven was almost precisely what Myca imagined him to be. He sat on a throne carved entirely of fused and reshaped bones, draped in thick, dark furs. The skulls of his defeated enemies ringed the dais on which that throne stood, and only a few of them were other than Cainite. The man himself sat tall and did not rise as they entered his presence. Myca guessed that, should he stand, he would be more than seven feet tall, clearly not the size he had been as a mortal man, but otherwise lacking any signs of obvious reshaping for he did not choose to present himself as entirely inhuman, either in beauty or repulsiveness. Damek Ruthven was not Embraced in his youth. His face was high cheeked and his pale eyes deep set, lined with care and toil. The long, brown beard and the curls spilling over his shoulders were both liberally streaked with white and iron gray. His enormous hands were scarred and rough, his limbs knotted with muscle. He wore antique garments of a type Myca had seen only in illustrations in the older books of the Library of the Forgotten, a cap of fur and felt, a long tunic that left his arms bare, baggy trousers and leather sandals, all without the slightest trace of ornamentation. He wore no jewelry or any other obvious signs of his status. The force of his personality filled the throne room with the awareness of his power more completely than any physical symbol could hope.

Kneeling next to one side of the throne, completely eclipsed in her master's shadow, was a woman. In truth, she was little more than a girl, her hips slenderly boyish, her breasts barely budded. She was a Cainite, Myca could tell from the glacial hue of her skin and her absence of breath in her lungs, though he could not guess at her age. She was almost entirely naked, but for the length of her own honey-golden hair and the beaten gold jewelry she wore. A queen's ransom in amber and rubies weighed down her hands and wrists and encrusted the collar at her throat and the rings encircling her erect nipples. She did not look up when they entered, but instead kept her eyes fixed firmly on the floor. The resemblance, in her submission, to his sire's advisor Eudokhia was somewhat unnerving. Standing on the opposite side of the throne was a second male Cainite, clad also in simple, antique garments, though somewhat more richly colored than those of his patron. His hair was darker, true black, though his eyes were fair. His face was a blandly perfect blend of characteristics that, even looking at him, refused to fix themselves in Myca's memory.

Ilias knelt and, setting aside the lamp he still carried, bowed smoothly to the floor, pressing his forehead against the stones. A few seconds later, Myca and Malachite followed suit, and waited for their presence to be acknowledged. It pleased Damek

Ruthven to let them wait. His voice, when he spoke, was a low rumble, speaking a tongue none of them knew. An instant later, a second, lighter voice translated this speech into clear and precise Greek. "Rise our guests, and our honored kin. Rise son of the Great Dragon, rise beloved of the gods, rise steadfast servant of the Great Dragon. You are welcome in our house, by the covenant of Earth and Sky, and by the Waters of Life and Death which bind us all."

Myca gave Ilias a count of five to rise first, then lifted his own forehead from the stones, leaning back on his legs to kneel, and from there to come to his feet. Ilias already stood, completely composed, and replied, also in Greek, "We give greetings to you, *taraboste* Damek Ruthven, and gratitude of the gracious hospitality of your house. To thank you for your greatness, we offer you these gifts, to do with as you will."

From the hall leading into the throne-room, the three girl-servants they had brought with them were ushered in, in the company of one of their black-robed guides. All three wore the glassy-eyed look of mortals drugged into quiescence as they were herded forward and directed to kneel for their new owner's delectation. He gave them all a cursory glance, his gaze lingering longest on the tall, fair one in the middle, before directing a curt command to the girl kneeling at his side. She rose, gathered up the gifts, and led them out. Damek Ruthven turned his pale, piercing gaze back upon them, and addressed them all in the tongue of his court, the ancient language of Dacia, which the interpreter again translated for them.

"You are welcome to reside in our domain for one month, by the reckoning of the moon, and search the library as you will, so long as you remove no volumes from my house. Tonight, we will feast together, and tomorrow you may begin your task." The interpreter smiled a thin-lipped smile. "I am Tabak Ruthven, childe of Damek, and I will be your assistant."

Damek Ruthven's library-archive was vast, contained in a single, enormous underground hall, and Myca fell instantaneously in lust with the place, lover of the word that he was. Malachite, Ilias saw clearly, was hardly less impressed, astonished by the size and scope of the project. Here, in the warm and well-lit hall beneath the ruins of Sarmizegetusa, lay much of the collected history of the Tzimisce clan, writings dating from its oldest nights, including some—so swore Tabak Ruthven, as he toured the high stone and wooden stacks with them—that his sire said came from the hand of the Eldest himself. Ilias did not doubt it. He felt the echoes of an ancient intellect in this place, a mind far older and even more abstracted from his own than Damek Ruthven, felt it keenly enough that it was nearly disturbing.

Myca, clearly having to physically resist the urge to dive headfirst into the historical tomes that made up fully half the library, exerted his enormous sense of intellectual self-discipline and turned instead to the genealogical scrolls, with the able assistance of Malachite and Tabak Ruthven. For the first time in months, he dreamed no disturbing dreams, suffered no painful, involuntary convulsions of mind or spirit. Perhaps it was because he was fully mentally engaged in his task, but something in Ilias doubted that was the whole explanation. He had been fully engaged in his tasks during the weeks they had spent at home, as well, and his concentration had not protected him then. A suspicion began to blossom in the back of Ilias' thoughts and a quiet request to Tabak one evening found him being escorted to the region of the genealogical archive that contained the records pertaining to the Moldavian lines of the clan, the lines to which Velya himself claimed to belong. A thorough search found no mention of the Flayer among those kinlines, a fact that disturbed Ilias more than slightly, and so he widened the scope of his own search accordingly.

He found Velya at last among the scrolls pertaining to the northern Tzimisce kin, the lines that dwelt still for the most part in the region of Poland surrounding the city of Szczecin, on the scroll of the *koldun*-prophet Triglav and his kin. A chill slid from the base of Ilias' spine and into the back of his thoughts, settling there and laying in roots. Triglav, sire of Velya the Flayer, was dead. Triglav, sire of Velya, had been dead for many, many decades, destroyed by the hand of the Dracon, the sire of Gesu, the sire of Symeon, the sire of Myca Vykos syn Draconov. He cursed himself quietly for never, in all the years of his acquaintance with Velya, asking him of his sire, or of his other existing kin. The conflict between the Draconian Tzimisce and the kin of Triglav had never truly ended, not to his own sure and certain knowledge. Myca, he knew, was Embraced in the midst of it, by Symeon when he had come north to raid the territories of his grandsire's enemies, to water the earth with their blood in retribution for a crime that had never been proven, and had long since ceased to matter. Eventually, the kin of the Dracon had simply stopped their raids and turned inward as the threat to their city had taken precedence to the pleasures of bloodvengeance. The kin of Triglav, exhausted, heavily thinned, had been forced to suspend their hostilities, as well. On the scroll he held, whole kinlines were black-bordered, wiped out root and branch, with no survivors known to exist. Only Velya, of Triglav's elder childer, survived.

What this knowledge truly meant, Ilias was not sure, but the possibilities chilled him to the core. Blood-feud was not a game among the Tzimisce. The murder of sires and childer and bloodkin was not a crime easily forgiven, or forgotten. It had taken an extraordinary political opportunity coupled with years of intensive diplomatic effort by the Obertus to bring Rachlav and Lukasz to a point where they would agree to lay down their hatred of each other. No such effort had been made between the descendants of the Dracon and the descendants of Triglav. That conflict had not ended, it had merely rested for a time. And, Ilias feared, suddenly, sharply, changed its shape. Slowly, he rolled the scroll shut, and replaced it in its leather case.

A prickle of unease raised the hairs on the back of his neck and, not for the first time in these last weeks and months, he felt himself not alone, and watched. It had troubled him off and on since their arrival in Sredetz, and had not abated since their departure from that city. Whatever it was, it tickled at the edge of his senses, played at the corner of his eyes, vanishing entirely when he tried to focus on it. Tonight, when he turned to face it, it did not wholly evaporate, but neither did it become any clearer. He felt, instead, a silent entreaty, a tug in his blood that urged him to follow, to walk, to leave the underground entirely and seek... something else.

Ilias picked up his candle-lamp and followed that impulse, his curiosity and his apprehension equally roused now.

Damek Ruthven's haven was a labyrinth of narrow corridors and small, boxlike rooms, clearly patterned on the layout of the fortress that had once stood above it. Of all of them, only the halls immediately surrounding the library-archive, easily the largest series of rooms in the entire structure, were actually well lit. Ilias moved carefully through the corridors beyond that space. Tabak had intimated that some of the halls terminated in traps and prisons for unwary invaders, but Ilias suspected that might have simply been an attempt at intimidating guests. Damek Ruthven hadn't struck Ilias, during any of their infrequent meetings, as the sort of person who appreciated random wandering, particularly in the halls of his haven. Ilias therefore attended his intuition closely as he made his way through the underground, avoiding servants, and coming at last to the base of a narrow stairway. It was not the stair that they had used to enter the haven—that one was wide and obviously constructed. This one almost seemed grown. The "steps" were mostly odd-shaped stones growing out of the side of the hill, packed earth, and the occasional tree root. Ilias climbed it, careful of where he placed his feet. A breath of cold wind stirred his hair and the flame of his lamp before he reached the top, nearly blowing out his light. Being careful not to place his hand too near the flame itself, he did his best to shield it, and continued on. The "stair" emerged at a large, triangular aperture formed by the space between two huge, heavy boulders. It might have even once been a shallow cave, Ilias thought. Outside the sky was clear, and the moon almost perfectly half-full, shedding enough light to see by.

A temple.

A long colonnade of stone and wooden columns led down from the threshold, widening into an enormous circle at its far end. Standing in the middle of that circle was a tree—a massive, wide-spreading tree, a true grandfather of the forest, still in leaf despite the winter, the wind hissing softly through its branches with a sound like distant whispers. Ilias almost thought he heard a voice in it. He felt the age and power of this place hanging in the air, rooted deep in the earth, before he even stepped foot on the path. Once he did so, that power rose up to seize him, to fill him, making his mind reel with the vast, incomprehensible age of it, stirring his blood as few other things ever had. He had felt it before, when he had climbed the path to present their petition. He had felt it walk with him and within him, and had known no fear or pain then, either. His lamp fell from his hand, and the candle extinguished itself in its own wax.

A god dwelt here, or a being close enough to divinity that the differences hardly mattered. Ilias was not aware, precisely, of walking down the path to the tree. He experienced the sensation of motion distantly, nearly outside of himself. He knelt among the roots of the tree, the ground beneath it scattered with fallen leaves, their scent sweet like dried blood. He was not surprised to find the bark of the tree, untouched by axe or flame or lightning-strike, to be warm beneath his hands, or that it felt like skin. He laid himself against its bole, large enough around that ten men standing hand-to-hand might not have been able to encircle it completely, and rested his cheek against it. The god welled up within it—welled up within him—like sap rising with the spring. He felt it touching him from within, moving in his blood and soul, running its fingers through his thoughts. Then, it spoke, softly, urgently, the same voice he had heard that night in his own sanctuary, as he dreamed a dream that filled him with fear, for no reason that he could understand. The same voice, and the same unfathomable tongue, the same sense of insistence, of an urgency so strong it was nearly fear. He begged it, silently, to make what it needed of him clearer. But it did not seem to know how.

Its withdrawal was as sudden as its rise. It pulled away from his spirit so swiftly he nearly followed it, drawn down by the wake of its motion. He became reacquainted with his body so swiftly and so hard his whole being reeled, and he fell hard away from the bole of the tree, weakened and shuddering. He felt as though he had been fasting for weeks, his hunger sudden, sharp and fierce, and his limbs too weak to pick himself up.

Cold hands caught at his shoulders, and he realized he was no longer alone. He exerted a Herculean effort and forced his head to lift, and his eyes to focus. Kneeling above him, Damek Ruthven did not look entirely pleased with him, but he supposed that was only just, all things being equal. Then he found himself being gathered into his host's massive arms and he let his head fall against the wool-clad chest, too tired to hold it up any longer.

"What did you see?" In Greek, directly beneath his ear, and Ilias smiled slightly to see that Damek was willing to bend on the use of languages, were his curiosity great enough.

"Nothing," Ilias replied, too weary to bother with embellishments. "I heard... his voice. Is that—?"

"Yes." Damek's voice, under his ear, was uncharacteristically tender. "You will need to eat. He has forgotten how to be gentle... and even I cannot say if he understands, or remembers, how fragile we are any longer."

Somehow, Ilias did not find that comforting.

"There is nothing here," Myca finally admitted, three weeks and a hundred scrolls of southern Tzimisce lineage trees later, as he and Malachite sat together in the library.

Malachite, very much to Myca's irritation, chose not to offer any permutation of 'I told you so,' and instead nodded gravely. "Perhaps we should take a different approach."

"You think we should check the lineage scrolls of the Eldest's childer." Myca replied, bluntly, thoroughly displeased. They had had this argument before.

"My opinion on that matter has not changed, Lord Vykos." Malachite did not stoop to obsequiousness but he often retreated into formality in the face of resistance. "And our time dwindles."

Myca was silent for a moment as he considered and struggled to control his irritation with the situation. Malachite, damn his eyes, was correct—their extensive search of the regional archives had yielded nothing at all. Assuredly, there were Tzimisce named 'Nikita' in the scrolls they had researched but none of them were *the* Nikita of Sredetz, the Archbishop of Nod, whose deeds would have been recorded like any of the others. And Malachite had not wavered at all in his belief that they would find the truth of Nikita's lineage elsewhere in the archive.

"Very well," Myca said softly, and summoned a servant to lead them to the appropriate section of the library. The scrolls pertaining to the immediate lineages of the Eldest's childer were stored in their own room, along with the volumes of clan histories and tales that pertained to them particularly. Some of these collections were larger than others; some of the Eldest's childer were nearly as enigmatic as he himself. The Dracon was not precisely one of them, no matter how little Myca himself knew of his great-grandsire, but neither was his existence entirely transparent. There were more myths of him than there were solid pieces of history, before or after his involvement in the Dream of Constantinople. Myca was entirely aware of this, based on the fear of the Dracon that persisted among the clan, a fear that often compelled cooperation where none might otherwise be offered.

The servant came, small and brown-robed, and led them through the halls to the room of the elder princes of the blood, then lit the lamps. It did not take Myca and Malachite long to realize that something was amiss. The folios pertaining to the Dracon's history were still present, neatly arranged in what appeared to be chronological order. Beneath those books, which were somewhat fewer than Myca expected, sat the leather cases in which the lineage scrolls were stored. The leather cases, however, were empty. All of them.

"Impossible," Myca whispered, genuinely shocked.

Malachite was equally stunned, and swiftly moved around the room, opening other cases and examining their contents. Quickly, Myca joined him, seeing what he was trying to do. The rest of the lineage scrolls were intact. They were also correctly attributed.

"It seems, Lord Vykos," Malachite murmured as they stood together, a dozen lineage scrolls belonging to everyone except the Dracon spread across the table between them, "that someone has gone to a very great effort at obfuscation on behalf of Nikita of Sredetz."

Myca was forced to agree.

Chapter Twenty-Two

Damek Ruthven was, predictably, more than slightly wroth when Myca and Malachite informed him of the theft that had taken place beneath his very nose, in his own library. They departed four nights later, subdued and very much under a cloud. Damek Ruthven made it clear through Tabak that he did not consider them responsible, but they had succeeded in wearing out their welcome. As they passed back over the mountains, the weather finally began to grow damp, and by the time they reached the monastery outside Brasov, snow was beginning to fall for the first time that winter.

Myca withdrew almost completely, assailed again by dreams and by doubts that gnawed at his confidence. He had refused to even contemplate the possibility that Malachite might be correct—that some true connection existed between his ancestor and the Archbishop of Nod. It seemed beyond credit, given the level of contempt the Cainites of Constantinople had always showered on the adherents of the Cainite Heresy, and the depths of personal antipathy that had lain between the founders of the Dream and the late, unlamented Narses of Venice. Now, it seemed, all the evidence—or, more precisely, the lack of evidence and the careful eradication of any that might exist—bolstered the Rock of Constantinople's claims in ways that troubled Myca deeply. It defied logic. It defied everything Myca knew about his great-grandsire. And it was beginning to appear correct.

It irritated him like a hair shirt against his skin, but he could find no means to refute the possibility that satisfied even himself. He was almost ready to unstake Nikita and twist the answers he now fiercely desired out of the oily little bastard. His Beast counseled violence and the distribution of a considerable amount of pain to quench his frustration. The only thing that stayed his hand, beyond the arguments by Ilias and Malachite against it, was the fear of what he would learn if he did so.

Several times after they returned to the monastery, he sat in his study as the snow piled up against the walls outside, and wrote to his sire, begging his help, his wise counsel, a word of comfort. Each of those letters he burned before the ink finished drying. Pride moved his hand in that, and an insidious fear that had had been growing in his breast since his visit to Velya's house, since the dream he had there, since those dreams continued, almost without cease. The bond between himself and his sire was strong, deep, untainted by the compulsion of the blood, a mark of respect that Myca had cherished all his unlife after the contortions of will he had seen imposed on his contemporaries. Now, he feared, feared with a deepening horror, that that respect was ephemeral, that he had been subjected to a violation as terrible as the blood oath itself, at the hands of the man he trusted nearly as much as he trusted himself.

Malachite returned to the monastery and tried with all his will not to sink into the same morass of pain and doubt that he sensed consuming Symeon's childe. He did not entirely succeed, despite the efforts of Ilias cel Frumos to draw them both out of themselves. Too much doubt had lived too close to him, for too long. Too many years of fruitless searching had passed, since the fall of Constantinople, since the destruction of nearly all the symbols of the Dream itself. He wished to have hope, but he could not find it within himself.

For good or for ill, he sensed the end of his long quest approaching, and as it did, he found himself increasingly reluctant to continue its pursuit. A terrible fear of where this road was leading him had begun to form, and moved him to argue against it when Myca Vykos, in an uncharacteristic display of open impatience, suggested that they release Nikita when they returned home and pry answers out of him. He feared that

Nikita held the key to finding the Dracon, and he feared what would happen when he and the Dracon met again. He feared what the Dracon would say to him this time.

He feared that those words would be, "The Dream is dead. Let it die."

And so he held his peace, and offered no suggestions, as he and Symeon's childe wrestled with their fears alone.

Ilias cel Frumos knew fear, and his fear was not for himself. He watched, helplessly, as Myca and Malachite withdrew into themselves, wrestling with their own demons, their own worries of what would come next, their own doubts.

Myca was dreaming again. He refused to speak of it, of the misery they caused him, and his temper was too uncertain to confront him about it. More often than not, he did not linger in their bed longer than he had to, rising and bathing and dressing with less than a dozen words passing between them. It struck him one night, as he sat alone in their chamber, that Myca was taking no comfort any longer from his touch, from the bond between them, and that filled him with a pain sharper than any he had thought possible. He had had consorts before this. He had left lovers, and been left by them, before this. He felt himself losing this lover and, for the first time, the thought of it paralyzed him with anguish.

Myca was not the only one who dreamed, or whose dreams disturbed him at a deep and primal level. He did not dream every night but, when he did, it was the same dream. The god-tree at the heart of Damek Ruthven's fortress, and the voice that spoke to him in his mind, in his blood, and his soul. Sometimes, in the dream, he was not alone. Sometimes, Nikita was present as well, bespeaking the god, in a conversation to which he was not privy. On those nights he woke utterly exhausted, drained almost to the edges of his strength. He killed while feeding more than once when he did not intend to, simply to maintain his flagging strength. The lack of control aggravated him. It was one thing to kill because he desired the pleasure of doing so, and quite another because he could not prevent himself from doing otherwise. No amount of effort on his part allowed him to extract more meaning from the words that filled his mind, and nothing he did prevented the dream from returning.

A malaise, spiritual and physical, settled on the monastery and persisted through the winter. It did not help that the mood of the three vampires bled over into their blood-bound servants, or that the weather in no way cooperated to lessen the gloom. After spending most of the summer and autumn bone dry, the snows came on with a vengeance, piling high against the monastery's stout walls and drifting even higher. Father Aron was forced to ration food among his charges, as the harvests had been less than expected. Fortunately, the reserves held until spring cleared the roads enough for the monks to descend into Brasov to barter for supplies.

Of the monastery's three Cainite residents, Ilias shook off the winter and the dark uncertainties it witnessed with the greatest ease. The spring was, after all, his season, and he descended into the woods and fields to tend to his own flock of adherents as soon as it was practical to do so. It was not in his nature to brood overlong and he felt that more than a month of poor humor and nagging anxiety was entirely too self-indulgent, even for a priest of indulgence. After a while, he even managed to coax Myca out of his study, if not wholly out of his mood, dragging him almost bodily out of the monastery and into the forest sanctuary of the god. There they walked among the greening trees and Ilias worked a subtle magic of his own on his lover.

Myca's heart was not so hardened against him as he feared. Myca's body, properly invited, quickened beneath his touch. They made love with a desperate ferocity of passion that neither had truly felt in months, beneath the stars in the circle sanctuary. Something inside Myca finally cracked open as they lay twined together afterwards, half-covered in someone's discarded mantle. Ilias cradled his lover gently as he wept freely, his pride at last giving way to the need for true comfort. Ilias held him, and let him cry, and when his lover was done, kissed away the tears.

"I have been a fool," Myca whispered against his neck, some

small time after that, "to turn away from you for so long. I have missed you more than I can say."

"We have both been foolish." Ilias stroked the still-trembling muscles of his lover's back, soothing them gently. "But if neither of us were ever fools, think of how bored we would both be."

Myca laughed weakly. "You are too kind. I..."

"Hush. Do not judge yourself too harshly." Softly. "I am here, my flower. Speak to me, please."

"Not yet. I cannot speak of it yet. But I will soon. I promise you."

"As you wish."

"We have all been... distracted this winter," Myca said, two weeks later, as the three vampires sat together in the oriel room. "But now that the spring has come, we must decide what to do next."

Malachite nodded slowly from where he sat on the opposite side of the gaming table, the remnants of a game of backgammon spread across it. The Rock of Constantinople was not susceptible to Ilias' finest charms but, after half a season spent in the solitary contemplation of his own fears and failings, he could be lured out of hiding by well-timed pleas for both company and sanity. "Are we agreed then, Lord Vykos, that there is little more that we might learn from the resources currently at our disposal?"

Myca had joined them halfway through the game and watched, with faint amusement, as Malachite chased Ilias around the board until the end. "We are agreed. Which leaves us, ultimately, with only a few legitimate options."

Malachite nodded again, picking up a game counter and rubbing it between his fingers, the first sign of a nervous gesture he had ever shown. "Nikita himself."

"Yes." Myca accepted that without hesitation. "I think it deeply unwise to attempt awakening him ourselves. If he is, in truth, a childe or even a grandchilde of the Dracon, he will be more than a match for any of us individually or together when he wakes. He is substantially weakened and restrained, yes, but he is not powerless, and I doubt that he will wake in a good humor."

If Malachite felt any triumph in hearing those words from Myca, it did not show in his expression or his voice. "What do you propose?"

"I will write my sire, with a detailed report of our conclusions to date, and ask his permission to move Nikita's body from Brasov to Oradea." Beneath the table, Ilias watched his lover's hand curl into a fist, and laid his own atop it silently. "If there is any who might assist us, it would be my sire, and he has the force of will and blood necessary should Nikita require more restraint that we alone could provide."

"Have you received any word from your colleague?" Malachite, it seemed, had an almost superstitious dislike of using Velya's name, and employed alternatives whenever possible. Ilias marked it, and thought it not unwise.

"Not yet. I am forced to assume that he has not made significant progress, or else he would have reported it to us by now. It would not help to rush him. Velya does things in his own time, though I believe he understood my urgency in this issue." Beneath Ilias' hand, Myca's own fingers straightened out, some of the tension in his frame bleeding away.

Malachite laid the little wooden counter back on the table. "I received a letter with the last courier from Oradea. All of our options might not yet be exhausted."

Myca inclined a questioning brow, and gestured for him to continue.

"The letter was from Markus Musa Giovanni." Malachite informed them, his tone bland. Beneath it, Ilias sensed a certain hint of distaste. "You know of him, Lord Vykos?"

"Of him, yes. We did not mingle in the same circles in Constantinople but there were, of course, rumors. I seem to recall that he and Alexia Theusa did not exactly embrace each other as brother and sister." Myca's tone was faintly wry, a little smile twitching at the corner of his mouth. "Other than that, I know very little of him."

"Be glad." The distaste no longer lurked. "He is quite—persistent in the pursuit of those things he desires. He has been pursuing me, almost without pause, since we both left Constantinople, possibly at the behest of the Oracle of Bones."

Ilias sat up straighter. The fame of Constancia was such that even he had heard of her, the enigmatic priestess of holy Mount Erciyes. "I have done my best to avoid him, for I am not convinced that further enmeshing myself in Constancia's plots or Markus' will aid me in my goals… but in this case, there may be something to be gained from letting him catch me."

"A necromancer." Myca murmured. "I had not considered that. Few among my blood practice those arts, for all the veneration of the Waters of Death, as well as Life."

"You see my thoughts on the matter." Malachite replied quietly. "Most of those who knew Nikita best—his colleagues and confederates among the Cainite Heresy—are dead now. Perhaps, the answers we require lie beyond the grave."

Chapter Twenty-Three

Myca sent his invitation south as soon as the roads cleared enough for his messengers to travel. By the early summer, the matter was settled. Rather than putting themselves to the arduous task of traveling to Venice, an excursion that Myca had looked forward to with approximately the same enthusiasm as having his limbs chewed off by a feral *vozhd*, the necromancer would come to them. In preparation, Myca moved his household to Alba Iulia, the better to facilitate communication between all parties. Letters were exchanged and permissions requested. Symeon granted his leave to host Markus Musa Giovanni at the Obertus Order's "mother-house" in Oradea, and to personally guarantee the peace of the meeting. Unhurried preparations for the trip to Oradea were subsequently made, as no one expected the necromancer to reach the city before later summer or early autumn.

This time, Ilias refused to be left behind. His resolve was immovable and, eventually, he prevailed. This time, he would go to Oradea with Myca and Malachite, and finally meet the sire of his lover, a prospect he regarded with some pleasurable anticipation. Myca, for his part, didn't regard the prospect with any pleasure at all and merely hoped that they wouldn't loathe (and attempt to murder) each other on sight. Despite the sliver of pain and doubt that had worked its way beneath the surface of his soul, Myca still hoped that his dreams were only dreams, and that his sire had never betrayed him in word or deed. In the deeps of the night, during that summer they spent in Alba Iulia, he finally told Ilias of his dreams. Ilias, speaking with the voice of wisdom, warned him that sometimes the Beast was wily and subtle, and its voice would prey on fears deeply held as well as the feral instincts; in walkers of the ways of desire, that was often true. He also advised that Myca tell him should the dreams grow strong and constant again, and he would do what he could to prevent them from troubling him, though Myca did not quite understand what Ilias thought he could accomplish on that score.

Ilias kept his fears about Velya to himself, since they were only that—fears based on supposition, and not fact. Myca accepted unsupported guesswork poorly, even when every instinct in Ilias' own being shouted of the danger after he was told of the dreams, and their nature. He did not tell his lover that a sufficiently skilled, and malicious, *koldun* could manipulate the spirits of the earth to inflict maledictions and madness on their victims. Instead, he quietly prepared those countercharms of which he knew, the defenses used to turn such curses back on their casters, and seeded them throughout the grave-earth they carried with them on the journey. Mostly, they were tiny disks of bone and clay, inscribed with signs of protection, braided cords that he sewed carefully into the hems of Myca's sleeping garments and the pillows they both shared.

Myca's dreams eased and, eventually, ceased altogether.

Symeon's house had, at last, reached its final form—the great Byzantine villa, surrounded by a constellation of lesser buildings, guest homes for visiting dignitaries, the servants' quarters, outbuildings for storage and beasts of burden. They were taken into it without the rigors of formal Tzimisce manners, welcomed home with open arms, and it was almost enough to make Myca weep with relief to find his sire exactly as he remembered him, not the shadowy tormentor of his dreams. Symeon was in perfect form, greeting Malachite with the pleasant blend of geniality and formality that characterized most of his relations with other Byzantine Cainites, welcoming the Rock of Constantinople as an old friend of whom he saw too little. Myca was, of course, granted pride of place as first-born and favored childe, with an evident warmth that Symeon otherwise showed to no one.

It was clear from the start that Symeon and Ilias understood one another perfectly. Myca was uncertain whether to consider that alarming or reassuring. Symeon treated Ilias with the precise and perfect amount of respect that he was due as a *koldun*, using the most formal and polite forms of personal address, rarely condescending to use his name, preferring his title. Ilias responded in kind, digging up proper forms of respectful address that Myca himself hadn't even realized existed and employing them with a peacemaker's skill. Neither made any great pretense of warmth, but neither did they make any open show of personal detestation or contempt. They very pointedly refrained from discussing any religious differences that would invariably cause friction between them. Symeon politely ignored the realities of the relationship between the heathen *koldun* and his favorite childe. Ilias was uncharacteristically restrained, and refrained from flaunting that relationship beneath Symeon's nose. It was, Myca supposed, the best that he could hope for.

Myca also noted the conspicuous absence of Sir Landric, the hostage who had remained behind to stand surety for Jürgen of Magdeburg's good behavior. When he inquired with Symeon concerning the matter, his sire coolly responded that the situation in the west had reached the point of stalemate. Jürgen, as predicted, had responded poorly to demands, and returned Symeon's envoy in a small wooden box. Symeon had, in return, repatriated Sir Landric in two carefully preserved pieces. Neither had made any further hostile moves, but a confrontation between them was now only a matter of time. Symeon did not even appear to fear or regret that eventuality. In fact, Myca sensed a certain anticipation on the part of his sire. Not for the first time, he recalled who first shaped his sire's personality. Antonius the Gaul had been both an astute politician and a warrior; so, too, was Symeon of Constantinople, Antonius' childe in all things but blood.

Markus Musa Giovanni arrived in Oradea with the last of the late-traveling trade caravans, as the summer slowly yielded to autumn. It rolled into the city by day, its leaders the servants of no less a man than Andreas Aegyptus, whose skills as a caravanmaster and conveyor of Cainite passengers were famed throughout Christendom, east and west. They carried with them a full load of trade goods—expensive silk brocade from the south, spices from the east, dainties and luxuries to tempt the locals, whose purses were fat with a full summer's profit—and a number of Cainites traveling to various points in the east. Symeon and Jürgen were both receiving ambassadors from all over Christendom and the Levant, and many of those dignitaries made use of Andreas' services; his face was familiar in Oradea and Magdeburg. When word came of their arrival, Symeon made a point to formally invite not only Markus Musa Giovanni to his house, but Andreas Aegyptus, as well, along with his childe Dehaan and his sister-in-blood, Meribah, both of whom traveled with him as companions. Andreas regretfully refused, having a tight schedule to meet, but promised that he would winter in Oradea if he was able, and pay a visit then when he could.

Markus Musa Giovanni rode to the gates of Symeon's house with the sort of train usually managed only by visiting princes and the first-made childer of Methuselahs. The man himself rode on a horse enormous enough to accommodate his own considerable size, its saddle and bridle decorated in the fashion of tastelessly wealthy merchants, followed and surrounded by a dozen guards in the livery of his family. None of them were other Cainites—Myca knew that certain highly ranked elders of the Cappadocian clan often traveled with Cainite bodyguards, but Markus did not appear to be one of them—though many were ghouls. A half-dozen ghoul body-servants also trailed along, leading a train of pack animals and a small cart loaded to the top with equipment carefully lashed down with ropes and tarpaulins.

Markus Musa Giovanni, Myca was forced to admit, possessed quite a vivid personality, as well. He dressed himself as a merchant prince, in richly colored and embroidered silk velvet, his doublets trimmed in ermine, his thick fingers weighted with gold and gems. About his throat he wore several long, heavy chains, the sight of which made Ilias hiss quietly. Even Myca was sensitive enough to sense the aura of power that surrounded the necromancer and, so, once Markus' presentation and welcoming feast was complete, he drew his lover aside and questioned him about it.

"The necklace he wears—did you look at it closely?" Ilias responded tersely, his hair rippling slightly in a breeze that found its way down the hall.

"He did not make it much visible, but I did see that there are... images appended from it. It is much like the necklace that Ioan wears, I thought," Myca replied carefully, noting Ilias' agitation but not quite ready to guess as to its source.

"It is similar. It binds something, but I cannot perceive entirely what. Likely several..." Ilias swallowed with some difficulty. "There are not many necromancers among our kind, Myca, because the *koldun* have been taught that the land of the dead is often also the realm of the gods. A wise *koldun* offers respect and reverence to the souls of the dead, and does not make them servants, nor bind them away from the gods and the rest they have earned. If this man were a dead-speaker, as the Lady Constancia is said to be... but he is not. He is an abomination."

And, thereafter, Ilias made no pretense of cordiality toward Markus Musa Giovanni. He was icily correct in his observation of the forms of hospitality, and in no way honored their spirit.

"I am given to understand from my Lord Malachite that you may have some use for my talents, Lord Vykos."

Myca understood, immediately, why the restrained and elegant Alexia Theusa found Markus Musa Giovanni detestable. The man was so unctuous Myca was privately surprised he didn't leave an oil slick on top of his bathwater. "That is true, Lord Giovanni."

They sat together in one of the smaller private meeting chambers on the first floor of Symeon's house, its doors closed, locked and guarded. The one small window was likewise shut, its shutters closed so tightly that not even the faintest whisper of the autumn breeze passed through them. A cluster of comfortably padded chairs was gathered about the low square table where they sat across from each other, and a lamp burned between them. A single servant attended each. Markus' man gave the distinct impression of being older than his apparent years, his pale watery eyes darting about in much the same manner Ilias displayed when he was perceiving spirits no one else could see. A tongueless scribe sat unobtrusively in one corner, awaiting the signal that his services were required.

"If you do not think me bold, Lord Vykos, I confess myself surprised and somewhat bewildered on that score." The necromancer had an admirable lack of nervous gestures, though he affected to run a ringed hand through his thick red beard when he wished to project the image of thoughtfulness. "It is the understanding of my family that sorcerers in plenty exist here in the east, and that they may practice some variation of the *nigrimancies* of my own kin. In fact, is there not a sorcerer among my lord's own retinue?"

"There are sorcerers here in the east." Myca admitted, blandly. "I cannot, however, speak for all of them, or of their skills. And it has always been my understanding that, should one wish to speak with the dead, one should seek the aid of a Cappadocian. Thus, your presence here."

Markus Musa Giovanni was also, pleasantly, not entirely a fool. His eyes narrowed slightly at what that response said and did not say, and nodded slightly. "You are wise, Lord Vykos, to seek the aid of one who knows his business in the necromantic arts. Such things should not be left to… amateurs."

"I am certain." Myca kept his tone serenely level, and admitted nothing. "Lord Malachite suggested to me that you were quite ably armed in those arts and, unlike many, willing to engage in commerce."

"That I am." The necromancer, Myca noted, was not immune to flattery but neither did flattery actually disarm him. "I admit it was curiosity as much as the possibility of remuneration that led me to answer your request, my Lord Vykos."

"I do not doubt it." Myca let a faint hint of a smile play around the corners of his mouth briefly. "I shall, of course, satisfy your curiosity if I may."

"That would be extremely kind of you, my Lord."

"I have, at the request of my sire, been investigating the Archbishop of Nod, Nikita of Sredetz. The Archbishop managed to entangle himself in a number of delicate diplomatic affairs that impacted the activities of the Obertus Order, and induced in us a desire to learn more about him." Myca watched the necromancer's reactions. He had a passable mask, but the occasional gleam in his eye and subtle change in his expression tended to betray his interest. "That has proven somewhat difficult."

"It is my understanding that the Cainite Heresy is in some disarray," Markus observed, wryly.

"Even so. Much of the Crimson Curia, those Cainites who might best shed light on their leader, are either in hiding, in torpor, or destroyed. Our efforts have been close to stymied." That yielded a glint of calculation in the necromancer's dark eyes. "Thus, when your letter reached Lord Malachite, he suggested that the unique talents of your family might be of use to us. For suitable recompense, of course."

Markus Musa Giovanni, quite refreshingly, did not even pretend not to be interested, or engaged, in commerce. "I confess myself intrigued by the possibilities inherent in this commission. My family has no particular love of the Cainite Heresy or its rulers, either, as I am certain you might guess."

"I had thought that possibility might exist, yes." Myca admitted. "I understand that numerous forms of profit may well arise for all involved in this enterprise."

"Yes." Markus stroked his beard slowly. "Yes, my Lord Vykos, I see it, as well."

Myca motioned the scribe forward. "The details must, of course, be recorded and reviewed."

"Indeed. This would, perforce, be a commission of some duration, as I cannot insure immediate results—and there is always the possibility of continuing consultation." Markus smiled a decidedly greasy smile.

"Very well. Shall we say a period of no less than half a year, with the possibility of extension as the matter requires?" Myca rather hoped to have Markus loaded on a southbound caravan no later than spring, if for no other reason than to preserve his own temper. He could, unfortunately, clearly imagine himself violating several Tzimisce laws of hospitality if required to keep company with the man longer than that.

"Half a year is an appropriate interval," Markus allowed the point with a nod, and the scribe, a length of parchment spread across his portable desk, recorded it promptly. "I shall provide all of my own tools and my personal expertise in the matter of necromantic consultation, and provide my own means of travel should the investigation require us to take to the road."

"Agreed. You shall receive, in return, provision for your material survival in the form of shelter and provender, which will be provided by my sire or myself, as well as the hospitality and protection of the Obertus Order during our travels, if any result." Myca paused. "Other material compensations shall be made—expenses, at the very least, and a fee commensurate with the duration of the commission and the degree of your personal involvement in the enterprise."

"Acceptable." Markus named an amount, which Myca thought stopped just short of outright extortion.

He motioned for the scribe to record it. "I shall present the request to my sire for final consideration and negotiation. Is there anything else that you may require?"

"Have you given any thought, my Lord Vykos, as to the disposition of the good Archbishop's mortal—and immortal—remains, should our investigations result in his final demise?" Markus' hand strayed, this time, to the heavy chains his throat. Out of the corner of his eye, Myca saw the man's servant shudder, quickly, and then force himself still.

"I admit that I had not." Myca replied, carefully.

"Ah." There was a faint hint of satisfaction in Markus Musa Giovanni's tone. "In that case, yes, my Lord Vykos, there is one last provision I would request for review. In the event of the Archbishop of Nod's final death, I would ask for the opportunity to claim any remnants that remain, for the service of myself and my family."

Myca pointedly did not request clarification on the idea of 'remnants,' and instead nodded to the scribe. "We shall see if my lord sire finds that request acceptable, Lord Giovanni. If so, I have no objections of my own."

Myca provided the materials that Markus thought would have

the greatest potential use in his rituals, a handful of letters from deceased members of the Cainite Heresy, several of them from the Crimson Curia, and a tiny sample of Nikita's grave-earth. Ilias did not approve on that issue, and seemed quite prepared to draw lines of clan between Nikita and Markus Musa Giovanni. Nikita, dangerous enigma though he was, was still Tzimisce, and Markus was still nothing more than a necromancer with no proper reverence for the dead. It took a considerable amount of effort on Myca's part to calm him on the matter and Ilias' ferocity in Nikita's defense startled him more than a little. Granted, Ilias had less contempt for tradition than most of his faith, but even he rarely invoked custom as the sole reason *not* to do something, particularly if he had no other options of his own to offer. Myca rather thought it best to keep the full details of the arrangement with the necromancer between himself, his sire, who approved them without reservation, and Markus Musa Giovanni, who at least had the sense not to gloat.

The necromancer's preparations required some time. A small room on the ground floor of the main house was provided for his use, which he promptly went about making ready, having the furniture carted out to storage and cleansing it from top to bottom. Those granted the privilege of attending the working itself gathered there on a night with no moon. Myca wondered if that had any particular significance—as such timing seemed to in Ilias' workings and within the bounds of Tremere sorcery, as well—or if Markus Musa Giovanni simply had a showman's flair for the dramatic. Markus had invited four watchers to witness the event: Myca himself, Malachite, and to Myca's surprise, Symeon. The fourth, Ilias, declined an invitation to attend the actual summoning of the ghost or ghosts quite pointedly, and withdrew from company whenever the matter was discussed. Symeon, Myca knew, found the idea of a sinner-priest with scruples that well defined to be more than a little amusing, and took no offense from Ilias' surliness in the matter. For that, Myca offered a quiet word of thanks to whatever gods were listening.

A certain amount of drama was present as they entered the room, which was entirely empty of furniture but for a smoldering brazier and a number of wrought iron and carved wood candle stands, each burning a tall, thick candle of decidedly unhealthy hue. Myca decided, eying them, that he wouldn't be surprised if they were composed of rendered corpse-fat. The flames leaping off the wicks were a glacially pale shade of blue. A series of overlapping circles, curved and straight lines, had been laid on the flagstone floor in chalk and salt and bone dust. The scent of the last was distinctive, even over the faintly sweet smell of the candles. Standing in the middle of this construct was Markus Musa Giovanni's flinchy little servant, whose name Myca had come to know as Beltramose, his watery eyes in constant motion, his expression and posture a mixture of well-worn fear and perfect resignation. He wore a long gray tunic that, coupled with his pale skin and virtually colorless hair, nearly gave him the aspect of a ghost himself.

The necromancer greeted them gravely, with a deep bow. He had dispensed with his usual selection of gauds for the ritual, clad in a somber black tunic and hose, his only adornment the chains he wore openly now on his chest, the links thick and heavy and hung with carved bits of bone and braided loops of hair. "My lord prince, Symeon of Constantinople and Oradea. My lords Vykos and Malachite."

"Lord Giovanni." Symeon bowed precisely, the corpse-lights striking fire from the gilt embroidery about his throat and cuffs. "I trust all has met with your satisfaction."

"Indeed, my lord prince, it has." Markus could not resist the urge to offer his most ingratiating smile, as well.

"Excellent." Symeon half-turned and nodded curtly to his seneschal, standing framed in the door, her expression so bland, her body language so perfectly correct, it practically shouted her disapproval aloud. She shut the doors carefully and, beyond them, they all heard her clear, crisp voice addressing the guards stationed there.

Markus Musa Giovanni arranged them in a loose semi-circle around the outer edge of his summoning circle, the best to watch the show, Symeon in the center, with Myca and Malachite flanking him on either side.

"I warn you, my lord prince, my lords, that some of what you see and feel may be disturbing, but it will not be able to do you any harm. The circle will hold the shade, whichever one is able to appear, contained within its bounds. It will speak through my servant, and will be compelled to answer whatever questions you put to it, and answer them truthfully. I must, for the time being, ask your silence."

He received it. The ritual began simply, without drama or fanfare, no chanting or mumbling or gratuitous displays of perversity, such as Myca's imagination, at least, had been providing vivid examples. The room, already none too brightly lit, perceptibly darkened. Already none too warm, it cooled so sharply that Myca felt it through layers of embroidery-stiffened silk. The unfortunate mortal in the center of the circle, barefoot and bare armed, shivered and the breath escaped him in visible puffs of frost. Out of the corner of his eye, Myca watched the necromancer feed the first of the letters into the brazier, releasing a breath of foul-smelling smoke as it was consumed instantly, the coals flaring icy blue as they did their work.

The cloud of foul black smoke hovered for a moment over the brazier, remaining almost unnaturally coherent, swirling and eddying in the draft of spectral cold that rose from the brazier. Then, in shreds and tendrils, it was drawn toward the circle, its substance sucked away and bound, rotating counterclockwise, visibly agitated. Within the circle, the necromancer's ghoul shuddered and twitched convulsively, his eyes widening. Then, without warning, the smoky vapor surged inward, towards him, enveloping him, forcing its way past his clenched teeth, up his nose. The ghoul, shuddering and convulsing, fell to his knees, tearing his hair and clawing at his face, a low keening wail emerging from his throat. Malachite almost stepped across the circle, moved to bring the suffering creature some sort of aid, only to be held back by Symeon's restraining hand.

"The spirit is... eager." Markus Musa Giovanni observed, blandly, in an effort to mask his own surprise. "It wishes to be heard."

That was patently obvious. The ghoul thrashed and convulsed in the middle of the circle, babbling in at least two separate voices, as the spirit strove to take his body and use it as its mouthpiece. Finally, his struggles ceased and he lay still, panting for air. After a moment, even those struggles ended and his simply lay, staring blankly at the ceiling above him.

Then he shrieked.

It was a sound that transcended mortality. No purely human throat could have made it. Contained within it was a blend of tangled emotions—rage and hate, and a vast black despair. Myca knew, instinctively, that had there been no circle protecting them from its force, no subtle web of necromantic bindings, it would have flayed their souls open and broken their minds.

Markus Musa Giovanni raised his own voice, shouting over the din, *"Be silent!"*

Silence was so abrupt and so immediate that Myca's ears rang with the sudden absence of sound.

"Rise." The necromancer's voice brooked no defiance.

The ghost-ridden ghoul rose, crawling first to his knees and then to his feet, struggling not to stand in the flesh's customary hunch, fighting for the dignity of an unbent spine, a commanding posture. It did not quite succeed. The ghost's image shone from within, the ghoul's flesh nearly translucent as water, their features overlaying each other in a weird interplay of light and shadow. Myca's eye followed the pattern and he gasped aloud at the image that drew itself in his mind's eye. Symeon's hand caught his wrist, as well. Myca froze in place, fighting the flesh-crawling revulsion he suddenly felt at his sire's touch and the urge to jerk himself away from it.

"Name yourself, shade." Markus addressed the thing directly and without fear, armed about with his own protections and means of compulsion.

A low death-rattle laugh emerged from the ghoul. "Name myself? That whelp there already knows my name."

Markus worked a complicated gesture with his free hand, and the spirit howled, bloody froth pouring down the ghoul's chin. *"Name yourself."*

"Filth! Perversion!" The ghost frothed for a moment longer, enraged and agonized, but yielded just the same. "How thin the blood of the Dracon has become, not to recognize its own. I am Nikita, Nikita of Sredetz, childe of Zdravka, childe of the one called the Dracon, may the earth refuse his blood and the air his ashes!"

Now it was Symeon's turn to react, taking a half step backwards, shock coming and going across his face. "What?"

The shade of Nikita of Sredetz turned a baleful, night-black eye on the prince of Oradea, a sneer curling its lips. "Surely you did not believe that your line alone sprang from the lust of the first prince of the blood? Our grandsire was not as profligate as Noriz, who sowed the seed of his blood far and wide and with anything that would hold still long enough to let him, but he was more whore than saint, little Symeon of Constantinople. You yourself should know that well enough."

Symeon hissed between suddenly bared fangs, and Myca found himself clinging to his sire's elbow, as a token preventative measure, at least. He was relatively certain that if Symeon really wished to cross the circle and wring that ghoul's neck, he would, and Myca would offer all the deterrence of a cobweb. He also discovered, within himself, a certain lack of surprise.

Distantly, he heard himself speak. "How long have you been dead, Nikita of Sredetz? How did you die?"

The shade howled again, reaching up to harrow its borrowed face again. "How long? What is time to the timeless dead? In the thrice-tenth kingdom, nights are forever and days are eternal. Days or decades, they are the same to me, now, and neither ends." It wailed, its teeth grinding, and more bloody froth flowed down the ghoul's chin. "How? I lived, and then I did not. There is no how."

"Who then?" Malachite asked sharply. "By whose hand did you meet your final death?"

The ghost was silent for so long, Myca was privately certain that the bindings had failed and he would not answer at all. Then, in an icy hiss, it whispered, "You think I would not know how I died, but who killed me? Fools. Fools. As though you would not rejoice at my destruction, no matter whose hand was responsible. Self-righteous fools."

Myca ignored the slurs and turned to Markus Musa Giovanni. "Is what it says true? Could it truly have no memory of how it died, or what slew it?"

"It is not impossible." The necromancer replied, in the tone of a man most definitely hedging his bets. "I have seen such things, when the death was brutal enough, that the spirit-remnants have no clear recollection of their final moments. But the death must have been a terrible thing—or possibly inflicted by one whose power was so great the force of their will to keep such things unknown extended beyond even fleshly death, to scar forever the soul of the victim."

"Very well." Symeon said quietly, at Myca's inquiring glance. "If it cannot tell us that in specific, we have little further use for this thing. Do as you will, Lord Giovanni."

Markus Musa Giovanni bowed deeply in response.

Symeon rested his hand on his childe's shoulder, as the necromancer began the process of peeling Nikita's ghost from the flesh of his ghoul and binding it to the reliquary prepared for it. "I think, Myca, that it is well past time we discovered for certain what you have captive in Brasov."

Chapter Twenty-Four

From the journals of Myca Vykos:

We departed Oradea in the midst of the autumn rains, and made what time we could on the wet and muddy roads. We left in haste, and traveled with a large contingent of szlachta, the creations of my sire, and an equal number of revenant guardsmen whose appearance was such that they could at least pass for human. Symeon himself could not travel with us, which pleased him not at all, but neither could he abandon his duties as the Prince of Oradea and head of the Obertus Order, even for a mission as urgent as ours. The necromancer, Markus Musa Giovanni, also accompanied us, having successfully argued to Symeon that his abilities might yet be of some use. Malachite was of the opinion that the Giovanni would now stick to him like a burr to his saddlecloth, and would have followed us with or without Symeon's permission. I cannot say that he is incorrect. The man was extraordinarily forceful about not being left behind, and beneath his bluster, I sensed a genuine emotion, a sensation close to fear or pain, that Malachite might escape him again. Ilias agreed, loath though he was to spend more time with the necromancer than was strictly necessary, and prevailing reproachful as he was about the treatment of Nikita's ghost.

Ilias was also not entirely surprised to learn that Nikita was dead—I think he suspected, even before I did, that our prisoner was not Nikita at all....

The party retraced its path along the entirely overland route between Oradea and Brasov, racing against the onset of winter.

Ilias bespoke the wind-spirits regularly now, Myca noticed, and was of the opinion that the winter, when it arrived, would be a harsh one. The balance of powers between the warring sorcerers in the mountains of the south had shifted again, and there would be no long, dry cold this year. The folk of the towns and villages they passed through were of a similar mind, and were loath to sell them supplies this late in the season. Consequently, they made heavy use of the Obertus monasteries that lined their route, and the stores those monasteries kept.

It was in one of those monasteries, as they approached Brasov late in the autumn, that they received the last piece of the puzzle.

"A letter? From whom?" Myca asked, looking up from the journal in which he was scratching out his thoughts, and turning a sharp eye on the master of the tiny Obertus priory outside of Sibiu.

"My lord, the messenger did not say, nor would he accept our hospitality." The prior was, much like Father Aron, an ancient Obertus revenant, a transplanted Greek. "He left only the message, and the instruction that it should be yielded to you alone."

In his hands he held the hardened leather case in which the letter had arrived and offered it silently. Myca exchanged a glance with Ilias, who sat quietly on the bed they shared, working at a tiny bone disk with tools of copper, and accepted the case, nodding dismissal. The prior, who seemed to have some genuine piety about him, fled without a backward glance.

Myca opened the case and drew out the letter, which was by no means a slender missive, sealed in ribbon and a crimson wax medallion, the sight of which sent a surge of excitement through him. Ilias rose and came to his side.

"Velya's arms," Ilias observed, as Myca cracked the seal, his tone carefully neutral. "He could have written to Oradea—it's not as though your sire would have said anything of it, not now."

"Perhaps. Perhaps not. My sire, as you might have noticed, has not quite shed all of his prejudices just yet," Myca replied dryly. "It is just as well that he sent it here—I do not doubt that he scattered these on our route home, knowing one would likely meet us. There is probably one in Brasov, as well."

Ilias nodded silently, keeping his counsel to himself, as he often did these nights. Myca frowned slightly at it, and opened the letter, Ilias leaning forward to read over his shoulder.

The pages of Velya's letter, and the translated extract of the journals, fell to the surface of the desk. For a long moment neither said anything, as they digested what they had just read, then Ilias leaned forward and plucked the extract from the pile of loose pages with a shaking hand.

"*I love and I hate—*" Ilias breathed out raggedly. "The Dracon himself. The first prince of the blood. This cannot be, Myca. No power at my command could bind *him*."

Myca shook his head slowly. "I do not understand it, either, my heart. But..."

"No. *Listen to me.*" Ilias' hand dug into his shoulder. "This is madness, Myca. It cannot be. I do not know what game Velya is playing with this but I fear what will come of it." Myca turned to face his lover and found his face a mask of conflicted emotions. "Myca, I should have told you this before. I learned it in Sarmizegetusa, but I did not know what to do, or how to say it."

Myca reached up and took Ilias hand, caressing his palm gently. "Speak. I am listening, my heart. There is nothing you cannot tell me."

Ilias shook his head slightly, but continued. "I know this will hurt you, my flower. That is why I did not speak of it before. I know the friendship between you and the Flayer, who was your first mentor within the clan. I fear, I fear very greatly, that he has used you ill and may be using you yet. Velya the Flayer is a childe of Triglav, whom your grandsire destroyed, and whose kin your sire warred against for decades before he chose you."

Myca forced his grip to relax when he heard Ilias' bones creak beneath its force, and his lover caught his breath. "Blood feud, then." Softly. "You think this is some... contrivance... of Velya's, then?"

"The best lies and the subtlest manipulations have truths at their core. Velya is not a fool, and he knows that you would not succumb to pure deceit." He reached out and caressed Myca's cheek. "I fear you have been the object of his malice in other ways, as well, but I cannot prove it. I suspect that he has been trying, in ways great and small, to turn you against your blood-kin and use you against them. He may even have been attempting it when he brought us together."

"I do not know what to believe." Myca replied, softly. "Velya is not the only one seeking the destruction of the Dracon. Before I left Constantinople for the final time, I was approached by an emissary of a powerful western Cainite—the Bishop Ambrosio Luis Monçada. Have you heard of him?" Ilias shook his head slightly. "He is a Lasombra, and extremely influential within his clan. The current pretender to the rule of Constantinople is little more than his lapdog. Bishop Monçada offered me concessions, his personal support for the establishment of Obertus monasteries in the west, in return for my effort to locate and destroy my grandsire. I agreed to his offer."

"You *cannot* be serious."

Myca smiled wryly. "Of course I am serious. I agreed because I had no intention of following through on my end of this little bargain, but maintaining contact with Monçada gave me a useful insight into the political machinations of the man himself, and many of his allies—and his enemies. It allowed me to learn what I needed to know to choose my own position, should I ever become engaged on the political field of the west. It also taught me that my grandsire, and what he is capable of accomplishing, is feared more widely than I had previously guessed. Otherwise? Monçada is a fool and, like many of his kind, seems to think of our kind as short-sighted barbarians, easy to manipulate with honeyed words and promises of *eventual* support."

"The Lasombra," Ilias observed, acidly, "have ever reached for more than was within their grasp, and have never lacked in arrogance. He honestly thought you would murder your own kin for his favor?"

"Yes. And it strikes me now that the murder of my kin—the murders that they have committed and the death that others seek to bring to them—may lie behind a great many things that have gone on of late." Myca traced the lines on Ilias' palm thoughtfully. "I do not know what we will find when we reach Brasov, my heart. Do you think the wards are intact?"

"I cannot feel them. We are still too far from home." Ilias admitted. "But I would know were they broken, I am certain of that."

"Very well, then. We will continue as we planned. We will secure Nikita, or whoever he truly is, and bring him back with us to Oradea." Myca pressed a kiss to Ilias' palm. "I do not know how much of any of our fears are true, and how much is simply fear. I thank you for speaking to me. I know that was not easy for you, or you would have spoken before. Whatever is happening, or has happened, we will find the truth of it, and deal with it together. Are we agreed in this?"

"Yes, my flower." Ilias closed his fingers around his lover's own. "Yes, we are."

Myca had no love of Malachite, but if there was no love, there was at least respect. He went to bring Velya's letter to the Nosferatu and ask for his thoughts on the matter, hoping to avoid the necromancer if at all possible. Neither Myca nor Ilias thought he would be willing to settle for the binding of the ghost of Nikita of Sredetz when he felt himself still commissioned, with profit yet to be gained from his journey. Ilias pled a task of his own that required completion and then, when Myca had gone, he gathered up his small box of ritual gear and stole outside.

It was raining, and the grassy hill was slick with water and mud; Ilias slid several times and nearly fell more than once. But there was an appropriately dense grove of trees at the bottom of the hill next to a chuckling, high-running stream, and he had wanted to sit in that place since they arrived. Now, he wanted to go there because he needed the peace and the closeness of the earth, of tall trees standing over him as he worked. The ground beneath the trees was covered in fallen leaves and treacherous with roots, obliging him to move slowly, and his candle-lamp flickered in the rain and breeze as he drew the items he wanted out of his box. He closed the box, which more often than not doubled as his altar when he was on the move, and laid a white cloth over its wooden top, on which he set the candle lamp, a small bone-hafted knife, and a pottery bowl. From within his tunic, he drew out a small leather pouch he had worn on a thong around his neck since they left Sarmizegetusa, and emptied its contents into the bowl.

Nine pinches of his own grave earth showered out. Nestled among them was a tiny seed, deep crimson in color like the seed of a pomegranate, which Ilias had found clinging to his clothing after his encounter with the god-tree in Damek Ruthven's mountainside temple.

He knew a gift when he saw one, and also knew that then had not been time to use it.

Taking a deep, unnecessary breath, he unsheathed his knife, its sharp copper blade glinting, and sliced open his palm. He willed his hand to bleed until the liquid filled his hand, and poured it slowly into the bowl, watching as it soaked into the earth and bathed the seed. Aloud, he whispered, "My lord, I know who you are. I know your name. I know you as I know my own blood, as I know my own bone. You flow in my veins with the Waters of Life and Death, my flesh is yours and your flesh is my own."

The seed shivered and, to Ilias' eye, seemed to grow, drawing his blood into itself.

"My lord... who is called the Shaper... I know that you were trying to warn me of the danger that we would face. I fear that the danger is here, and that I am not its equal." Ilias swallowed with some difficulty. "I beg you, guide my hand."

He took the seed in his still-bloody hand and swallowed it. Deep within himself, within his blood and flesh, he felt something stir.

Chapter Twenty-Five

The monastery outside of Brasov was completely dark and still when they arrived—which, considering the hour that they did so, would not have been unusual for an ordinary monastery but was certainly out of order here. A messenger had been sent some time ago to order preparations for their arrival. Myca knew that they should be expected, and a night watch should have awaited them. Instead, the lamps outside the door were darkened, and no bustle of efficient Obertus monks and servants issued forth to greet them, or even open the doors. Fortunately for his temper, no one insisted on belaboring the obvious. They simply dismounted and allowed Myca to confer quietly with the captain of their guards.

A contingent of the guards remained outside with the Cainites, their weapons at the ready, while the remainder separated into groups and began trying the various entrances into the monastery itself. The front doors were, naturally, barred from the inside and none of the windows were large enough to admit a full-grown man, even if they weren't shuttered tightly against the weather. Myca watched for a moment, then turned to rejoin the others, who were standing watchfully themselves, tense and silent, even Ilias.

"Something is amiss," Myca informed them quietly.

"In what way, Lord Vykos?" Markus Musa Giovanni asked, fingering his several chains thoughtfully. "And is there any manner in which I may be of assistance?"

"Someone should have been awake to greet us." Myca replied, tersely. "That the monastery is barred against us is more than slightly odd." He paused, and considered. "Would it be possible, Lord Giovanni, to ask the spirits at your command to enter the monastery and determine the cause of this problem?"

Ilias shifted slightly, but made no objection to this request. He had been quiet for the last several nights, withdrawn thoughtfully into himself, but not sullen. He spoke when spoken to, but did not begin conversations, as was his usual wont. Myca wanted to ask him what troubled him, or what he was thinking of, but the process of making certain all the arrangements for their return to Oradea were in order consumed most of his time.

"It is possible. I would just require a moment of privacy. I must, of course, concentrate." The necromancer bowed slightly and, at Myca's gesture, stepped away from the others, taking only his servant with him.

"What do you think it is?" Malachite asked, in an undertone, once the necromancer had departed. Even his illusory face was creased in undisguised concern.

"I cannot yet guess." Myca glanced at Ilias, bundled inside an oiled leather cloak to keep out the damp. "The wards are still in place?"

"Yes." There was no hesitation in the *koldun*'s tone or manner, but Myca felt a low tremor of alarm nonetheless. "I have no explanation, Myca. It could be almost anything. For all we know, an illness might have struck."

Myca nodded slightly, unconvinced, but having nothing better of his own to add. A call rose, from somewhere beyond the circle of torchlight in which they stood, and in a moment, the captain of the guardsmen approached, bowing deeply. "Lord Vykos, the door leading into the refectory from the garden is unbarred and unguarded. Do you wish us to investigate?"

"Bide a moment. Keep your men outside until Lord Giovanni returns." The captain bowed a second time and retreated to issue orders to his men. "Lord Malachite, perhaps you should…"

The Rock of Constantinople was already at his baggage, extracting his little-seen sword from its oilcloth wrappings and belting it about his waist. Ilias, standing his head bowed in the depths of his hood, appeared to be murmuring softly to himself, perhaps interrogating the spirits. Myca thought it best not to disturb him and simply waited, measuring the tension among the men and controlling the slow but steady rise of his own alarm. After a moment, Markus Musa Giovanni rejoined their circle. He did not bow, and the expression beneath his beard was struggling for neutrality and failing to achieve it.

"My Lord Vykos, I fear that something has gone quite drastically more than amiss."

There was not a single living thing within the monastery walls.

Myca was silently stunned. The monastery had, from all appearances, not been assaulted or otherwise invaded. There were no signs of violent struggle, nor was the place an abattoir. No blood or fire stained the walls or the floor. No bodies littered the rooms. It was simply empty, its hearths cold, its braziers unlit, its halls untenanted. All of the pallets in the monks' dormitory were made, as though they had all risen for the first of the morning's devotions and then never lay down again. The refectory was in perfect order but for the lingering stench of perishable supplies long since gone to rot. Clothing set for washing and mending still sat in the laundry. In the scriptorium, half a king's ransom in ink and paints for the illuminations had gone dry for want of their containers being closed. Documents were still spread out on the desks and, in some cases, showed that their writers had ceased working in mid-sentence, mid-word.

The lower floors were similarly abandoned. None of Ilias' servants remained, their quarters cold and empty as tombs. Ilias took the news far better than Myca would have thought. He neither raged nor grieved, but Myca supposed there would be time for that later. The *koldun* instead took a handful of men down to the lowest room in the monastery to confirm that the wards were still intact and "Nikita" still imprisoned. Above, the ghosts bound by Markus Musa Giovanni's will continued exploring rooms and the men began lighting lamps and candles, setting a fire burning to chase away the chill damp that had invaded the walls, and continued searching for any sign of the monastery's missing inhabitants. Myca and Malachite assisted them, as best they could, searching for clues invisible to mortal eyes or beyond the range of all mortal senses entirely. There was, however, nothing to be found, even the old, well-worn sensations of daily habitation thinned and faded, like a painting rinsed again and again with water.

"I do not like this at all," Myca finally admitted, with some difficulty, giving voice to his unease as the three Cainites stood together in the monastery refectory.

"No more than I." Malachite agreed, grimly. "Where is Ilias? It does not take that long to climb the stairs."

"He is coming," Markus Musa Giovanni said quietly, speaking for the first time in several moments, the abstraction that came over him when he spoke to his own spirits fading. "He is in the long hall with the men—"

The refectory door opened, and Ilias' bodyguards entered ahead of him, one of them carrying his dripping cloak and hanging it by the fireplace to dry. Ilias approached slowly, his hands tucked into the long sleeves of his tunic, his face an inscrutable mask. When he spoke, his voice was pitched low, so that none of the mortals present could hear it. "The wards are broken. Nikita is no longer imprisoned." He withdrew his hand from his sleeve, pouring a long stream of ash from his palm. "And I believe that I have found the monks and my servants."

Myca was very much of a mind to order everyone out of the monastery, down the hill to the chapter house outside of Brasov, and then have the place leveled. If he could have accomplished it safely in the time they had and with the force at his command he would have done so. He was forced to settle for ordering the men, all the men, inside to perform a thorough search of every room in the monastery, supported by the reconnaissance efforts of the necromancer's ghosts. Neither effort found any trace of Nikita and with the dawn now approaching swiftly, he was forced to accept the one option he wished to avoid—sheltering in the abandoned monastery by day.

The four Cainites made the best of the situation that they could. Rather than sleep in separate chambers, the oriel room was made ready with bedding and pillows, pallets laid out and the entire structure, above and below, heavily guarded. Myca, not at all comforted by these precautions, paced the halls until the nearness of sunrise forced him to seek the oriel room and his pallet, pulled close to Ilias' own. Malachite and Markus Musa Giovanni were already abed with their servants close by them. Ilias sat cross-legged and awake, awaiting his return, serenely composed despite the many oddities of the night. Myca found that tranquility soothing almost in spite of himself, shedding his shoes and cloak, and laying down beneath the mass of furs and coverlets that Ilias had prepared in his absence. His lover curled close against him, arm across his belly, head resting on his shoulder, and Myca drew comfort from the closeness, as well, nuzzling the copper-blonde hair brushing his chin.

For a moment, they lay together in companionable silence. Then, Myca whispered the question that had gnawed at the back of his thoughts all night. "How did he break the wards without you feeling it?"

A moment more of silence passed before Ilias made his reply, his tone thoughtful. "I do not know. I should have felt it immediately. The spirits should have spoken to me at once, unless they were commanded otherwise. That is not impossible." Softly. "If he is truly the Dracon, it is not outside of his power to do so, were he somehow freed physically, but any physical breach of the wards would have warned me, as well. It is a puzzle, my flower."

"Too many puzzles," Myca muttered, and drew Ilias closer. "My sire will not be pleased to learn that we have lost him, if, indeed, he is even lost. But it seems likely. None of the men, nor the ghosts, found any trace of him."

"And the spirits could tell me nothing." Ilias murmured sleepily.

"We should have acted sooner." Myca stared blankly up at the shadowed ceiling far above, trying to think of how he would phrase it in the letter he would have to write.

"Perhaps. Perhaps we have done all that we could do." Ilias reached up and brushed Myca's eyes closed gently. "Sleep, my love. We will think of what to do next in the evening."

Myca pressed a kiss into his lover's palm. "As you wish."

He walked between columns of blue marble. To his right was the sea—a vast dark expanse he could hear and smell more than see, the waves crashing against the breakwater dozens of feet below, the salt-breeze stinging his eyes, catching in the unbound spill of his hair, the trailing lengths of his clothing. To his right was a garden, full of rare and wonderful night-blooming plants, scattered with statues and fountains, crossed by gravel paths and lush expanses of well-tended grass. It was a beautiful place, serene and elegant in the manner that all of Byzantium was elegant, gracefully designed and pleasing to all of the senses, not just the eyes.

He wished to appreciate all of those beauties for their own value, but his efforts to shorten his stride were half-hearted at best. He was, after all, not walking for his own pleasure. He was, again, about to enter into the presence of the most beautiful thing in Constantinople: the lover from whom he had been long parted, and to whose arms he had only lately returned...

This is not real, *Myca told himself within his dream.*

This is not real. This never happened.

He threw back his head and cried out aloud, bloody tears of joy running down his cheeks. Beneath him, his lover's back arched, pressing their bodies more closely together, palely glowing hands clutching at his thighs. He sat astride his lover's loins, their flesh united, rocking slowly on his knees, wringing every sensation he could from the places their bodies touched, stroking his hands across his lover's chest and belly. When they were together in this way, they both remembered what it was to live and love, to burn with desire and quench that desire in another's flesh, before the more divine union of the blood. Heated from within by a wild passion, he strove to make his lover scream, to cry out, and, finally, cry out he did—moaning a name, his own name.

That is not my name, *Myca told himself within the dream.* This is not me, though I feel his touch burning me still. I was not the lover of...

Michael the Patriarch. Michael the Archangel. Michael, in whom the Dream was made flesh. They lay together afterward, bodies entwined, flesh and blood still singing with ecstasy. Michael's golden head lay on his breast, Michael's hand cupped his loins and caressed his belly, making him quiver with renewed desire. Michael's fangs pierced his throat and exalted him with passion that was truly divine. Michael's flesh entered and claimed his own, and Michael's thoughts spilled into his mind through the bonds of blood and desire between them.

"You wear his face, though you are not him—your spirit, even reshaped as it is to please me, is your own still. You are not him..." *The Patriarch, the angel, whispered gently into his mind.* "But there is much of him in you, I see that, at least. They chose well, did my faithful Gregorius Dimites and your sire Symeon, when they chose to gift you with his form and his aspect, and send you to me, as a gift of their love. And you... you are worthy for your own sake, for you alone have come to spend my last nights with me, and give to me the comfort that the one who came before me never knew. To you, I shall give what no one else shall ever possess. To you, I give my Dream."

Myca woke, suddenly and completely, as many things became clear.

He remembered.

He remembered the night that his sire had summoned him to a house outside of the Obertus mother-house in lost Constantinople. He remembered their conversation, and feeding on a servant whose blood was thick and sweet with a substance he did not recognize. He remembered falling into his sire's arms, and being carried to a room, where he was stripped bare and reshaped into another's image. He remembered the maddening voice of the Muse, Gregorius Dimites, speaking in his thoughts, twisting his mind, striving to obliterate his identity and leave him with only one thought, one truth: that he was the Dracon, returned to the city in its darkest hour, returned to give aid and comfort to his failing lover. He remembered the nights of passion spent in the arms of the Patriarch—and remembered, in the end, that the Patriarch knew him for who he was...

Knew him for who he was...

And used him, nonetheless.

He wanted to scream. A gentle hand touched his hair,

stroked loose strands back from his face, soothed him silently.

"It seems," the voice belonging to the hand said quietly, an unfamiliar lilt to each word, "that many of us have been wearing faces not our own of late. Is that not so, my childe?"

Myca opened his eyes.

The Archbishop of Nod knelt in the center of the oriel room, unmoving and unspeaking, a lamp burning on the bare floor next to him. On either side of him lay a servant—the necromancer's servant, his head twisted at a decidedly unnatural angle, an expression of perfect peace etched onto his face, and Malachite's servant, who had evidently perished with a good deal less equanimity. Markus Musa Giovanni himself crouched against the far wall, clutching his chains. Malachite stood opposite him, sword in hand, and visibly unwilling to use it. Myca sat up quickly and cast a glance at Ilias—and found himself staring at a stranger in his lover's clothing.

A certain undeniable physical resemblance joined the silent Archbishop and the sorcerer kneeling peacefully at Myca's side. They were both dark of hair and dark of eyes, fine-boned and graceful. The sorcerer had the long-fingered hands of an artist and his face a more than vaguely feral cast, sharp chinned and high-cheeked, his auburn eyes angular. The Archbishop of Nod had the perfect beauty of Malachite's icon if not its fair coloring, the interplay of shadows and light over his features lending them an air of depthless weary melancholy. Before Myca's eyes, he bowed his forehead to the floor, once, and rose again to his knees, his voice soft but resonant in its reply. "You are… not wrong, my sire."

Myca very much wanted to leap to his feet but found his muscles too weak to manage it, and settled for scrambling an arm's length or two away from Ilias-who-was-not-Ilias. "What is going on here?"

His question went unanswered. Ilias-who-was-not-Ilias rose from his place among the bed-furs and crossed the room to kneel at the side of the Archbishop of Nod. He made no move to reach out to the Archbishop, who returned the favor. They sat together in a silence that none dared to break for a long, long moment. Then, Nikita-who-was-not-Nikita slumped over his knees, his spine bending, the mask of his face crumbling, and Ilias-who-was-not-Ilias took him in his arms.

Myca leaned back, found a wall, and pushed himself up it, leaning hard against the stone to support his watery legs. He wanted to shout a number of things, not the least of which was, *Who are you and what have you done with my lover?*, but could not quite find the depth of foolishness necessary to do so. Instead, he made his way laboriously around the edge of the room, until he came to the side of the necromancer, Markus Musa Giovanni.

"What is this," Myca hissed between clenched teeth, not quite giving it enough inflection to make an actual question.

The necromancer shot him a wild-eyed look. He extended a shaking hand towards Nikita-who-was-not-Nikita's bent back. "When I woke he was here. I do not know how he came to be here... or where the guards might be."

Myca somehow suspected that the absence of guards was the least of their worries. "He is... that is... Nikita..."

"He is the Dracon." Malachite's voice, clear and strong, filled the oriel room. "I know that face better than I know my own. I have carried it with me since I left Constantinople."

"Faithful Malachite." A soft, hoarse whisper. "You should have listened to me the last time, Rock of Constantinople. Truth has no one shape, no one symbol. All eyes see it differently. All tongues speak it differently. Nothing—nothing—exists unchanged forever. Not even we." Nikita-who-was-not-Nikita straightened himself, though he did not rise. "Do you see it now, faithful Malachite? Do you understand it now? The Dream—"

"The Dream is not dead," Malachite answered, quietly. "The Dream has only changed its shape. It cannot die, even if all of its symbols crumble and fall to dust. The Dream is a thing with its own life. Do you give it so little credit, hidden one?"

"I give it all the credit it deserves," the Dracon whispered tiredly. "The Dream will survive all who first saw it blossom, and helped give it its first form. My time as its custodian is at an end. The last task I set myself is done. Michael is avenged. Those who sought to diminish and sully what he created are dead or undone. Narses is destroyed, and the Heresy destroyed with him." He bowed his head again, a curtain of dark hair falling across his face. "And I am so tired."

Somewhere, Myca found his voice. "You did this… you murdered Nikita of Sredetz and stole his form… You went to an effort that I cannot even imagine… to destroy the Cainite Heresy?"

"Yes." The Dracon's head came up again and he half-turned, the expression on his face somewhere short of pleasant. "Would you not do the same to avenge *your* lover, Myca Vykos, born of my blood?"

Myca took a ragged breath, cast a glance at Ilias-who-was-not-Ilias, and decided not to answer that question. "Why did you let us hold you? Why did you let *Jürgen* hold you? Why did you let him take you in the first place?"

A rise and fall of slender shoulders. "Jürgen disappointed me. I hoped he would destroy me. He did not. He sent me to *you*."

"Destroy…" Myca began, absolutely appalled, only to be interrupted by an unlikely source.

"Destroyed?" Markus Musa Giovanni asked, softly, his eyes gleaming with an unpleasant light.

Across the room, Malachite stiffened with visible alarm.

"This is outside of your purview, Lord Giovanni," Myca ground out through bared fangs. "And outside of your commission."

"Outside of the commission I hold from *you*, Lord Vykos," the necromancer replied, coolly. "But in this matter I do not serve you. I serve my Lady Constancia of Erciyes, whose prophecies have never failed in their guidance. The Rock of Constantinople knows of what I speak."

Myca flicked a glance in his direction. "Malachite?"

"Constancia of Erciyes," Malachite murmured, his gaze fixed unwaveringly on the necromancer, "has prophesied that the Dream must die. It cannot, for the Dream is more than the sum of its symbols, as she, wise as she is, must realize."

"Perhaps," the necromancer countered, his fingers knotted in the lengths of chain about his throat. "But those symbols may be undone, and the Dream itself forgotten for an age and more if needs be, bound away and kept hidden from all eyes and all minds."

"Do not be a greater fool than you have to be, Giovanni—" Myca snapped—and recoiled, quickly, to avoid be splattered by the blood.

He had not even seen Ilias-who-was-not-Ilias move. One moment, he was kneeling at the side of the Dracon. The next, he was standing before Markus Musa Giovanni with his hand buried to the wrist in the necromancer's chest.

"Constancia of Erciyes," He said, he biting off each word clearly, "has the unhealthy habit in meddling in matters which do not concern her, and sending others to die for her." The hand twisted, and wrenched itself free.

Markus Musa Giovanni crumbled to dust without even a scream, his empty clothing and many chains falling to the floor in a heap. Myca retreated another handful of steps, too shocked to speak, and stopped only when he bumped into the far wall. Ilias-who-was-not-Ilias licked his fingers clean, and casually crushed bone fragments and braided locks of hair underfoot, rending the necromancer's chains and fetishes he used to bind and command his ghost-slaves.

"Constancia," the Dracon whispered into the ringing silence that followed, "knows me well. She knows what I desired."

"You desire death," Myca said softly.

"I desire an *ending*." There was endless, depthless weariness in that admission. "You cannot imagine it, childe of my blood, and I hope you never have cause to. I hope that you do not see the night when you have outlasted everything and everyone that you have ever loved, and watched everything that you tried to preserve crumble around you."

"Everything?" Ilias-who-was-not-Ilias asked softly.

Silence. Ilias-who-was-not-Ilias crossed the room and knelt again at the Dracon's side. Within himself, Myca felt his blood stir and pulse in his veins, a sharp contracting pain filling his chest, reaching up to pound at his temples. Shock—for it was shock that had kept him from any other reaction—gave way to fear, and fear to a sudden, painful anguish. They were speaking to one another, he realized with dizzying suddenness, speaking to each other in a speech that required no clumsy words, that offered no barriers to perfect comprehension. He understood, then, what Ilias had been trying to tell him about his visions, about the agony that dwelt in the spirit of Nikita-who-was-not-Nikita, in Nikita-who-was-the-Dracon, the soul-devouring pain and loss that consumed him, even deep in the sleep of ages. He understood how one could be eternal, as old as the mountains, and still long for the peace and silence of death, how one could be touched by divinity and find divinity wanting.

Ilias-who-was-not-Ilias held out a hand to him and, almost against his will, he stepped forward, and took it. In that moment, he was lost, and knew it to the core of his soul.

"Bear witness, Rock of Constantinople." Ilias-who-was-not-Ilias whispered, and drew Myca down.

It was pleasure. The hands that touched him, that remade him to suit its need, saw no need for the deliberate infliction of agony. Myca felt that, had nothing of Ilias existed within them, simple indifference would have caused him mind-shattering pain and thought nothing of it. But Ilias was in those hands, at least in part, and so he felt only pleasure as his body was reshaped, opened and made ready to receive.

He watched from a vast mental distance, every nerve singing with resonant joy, as Ilias-who-was-not-Ilias turned from him to his ancestor, who waited, silent, face bowed. He watched the perfect flesh distort and malform, discoloring, rippling. Liquid. He was becoming liquid, Myca realized, distantly, and could not bring himself to care, or fear what would happen next. Ilias-who-was-not-Ilias gathered the ball of liquid into his hands, held together by the thinnest layer of skin, and swallowed it, taking it into himself, transforming it, solidifying its essence. Myca knew—he felt the knowledge of what was happening within the flesh and blood of his lover filling him wordlessly.

He parted his legs, and cried aloud in pleasure as their bodies joined together again, at last.

His lover moved inside the reshaped passages of his body and, if he thought he had known pleasure before, it was nothing compared to what he felt now. It overwhelmed him in less than a heartbeat, drawing him down into a sweet, blood-colored, blood-scented whirlpool of ecstatic sensation, rapture so vast it consumed all his senses. Distantly, he knew that this was not an act of love, but of violation, a rape committed against his body and his soul, to save the existence of one who wished only for death. He could not bring himself to care. In the terrible rapture cleaving his soul and his flesh, he felt Ilias, he felt his lover striving to spare him pain, felt his lover's soul wrap about his own and endure the pain of this defilement for his sake, and his alone. He knew that, in some way, love touched him and protected him, even now, and died for him as the pleasure peaked.

He felt the seed spill into him, hard and thick, anchoring itself inextricably into his being, into his soul, blood, and flesh. He felt the last of Ilias' soul gutter and die within him, consumed at the last, and the searing agony of violation as his body sealed itself around the intruder, the dragon-seed of his ancestor, the container of its essence, polluting his own being with its alien presence. He felt the fine ash of his lover's dissolving body fall across his own blood-sticky flesh, scorched to destruction from within by the force of the being that had spoken and acted through him. Myca Vykos threw back his head and screamed.

Interlude

I cannot adequately or accurately define the full meaning of the bonds between my sire and myself. Not even to myself, for my own satisfaction, can I pull the threads of the tie between us apart, examine and analyze them, describe them in words that are safe and painless. The strength of that bond is such that it transcends the descriptive capacity of language; words alone cannot convey it.

But because I am who I am, I must try.

Does it matter how we first met, who I was, and who he was, at that long-ago time? Does it matter where we were, and the words we said to one another, and the language that we spoke? I do not think it does. That place no longer exists in any way that matters. Its villages are buried rubble, its people scattered and lost in the greater sea of humanity, its language forgotten before it could be written.

What were we, what are we, to each other?

Perhaps the more important question.

He was not, was never, my lover, though I know that many of the ancients took their childer for the sake of pure lust, out of a desire borne in blood. That was not the way between he and I. Our bond is deeper than any tie that arises from transient desire, infatuation with a pretty face or a sweet voice. In fact, I do not know all the reasons why he first chose me, and I do not think that I want to know them. Some things, even between oneself and one's sire, are better left unexplored. I know that he made the decision for the first time when I was little more than a child, and that he held to it as I grew to manhood. Unlike many of his childer, he offered me a true choice when the time came—not the deadwater or death, as so many of our kin do in these degenerate nights, but the gift of his blood or the right to live and die as a mortal, a life in which he would not interfere.

Why did I choose as I did? I could offer a thousand facile rationalizations of my choice, but all of them would be just that—rationalizations, self-justification coated in layers of pride and regret. I will say, instead, only this: when I made my choice, of my own free will and knowing what I would both gain and lose by so doing, I believed that it was the right choice to make, the right way, the path that I had been born to follow. Was I wrong about that choice, or was I right? Even I do not know any longer. I am not entirely certain that I care any longer. It has been too long since I made that choice. The reasons no longer matter, and the consequences are ceasing to matter, as well.

There are those who say that I am my sire's first-chosen and favorite. They are only partially correct. The pride of place for the first-chosen rightfully belongs an elder brother whose name is now all but forgotten and whose line has so dwindled that if it contains a dozen childer, I would be surprised, indeed. But favorite? Yes, I was that. I say it, and claim the truth of it, without pride and without pleasure. My sire loves me, not as a man loves his lover, but as a father loves his son. You cannot imagine how terrifying that is, how heavy a weight it hangs upon my shoulders, to know that in me resides the sum of my sire's remaining humanity, the remnants of his ability to feel and comprehend human emotion, the womb of his rebirth as a thing only barely human any longer.

It is almost true, that he cannot die. So long as one of his blood exists, he exists. So long as the world does not fall to ash, he may make himself whole again. It happened once. His flesh perished, but his essence lived on, lived on and found purchase within me to remake itself. I felt both things, almost at once—the shock of his death, rippling through the blood in my veins, and the second, greater shock of his life, quickening within the blood that he had given me, within my very flesh. I felt him reshape me to host himself, building a nest within me of blood and soft tissue, to cradle a tiny seed of recovering consciousness. I felt him grow, slowly, as he drew the scattered pieces of himself, the fragments of his identity, back together again, growing stronger and *more coherent as the weeks stretched into months. Nine months, of course, nine the number it takes to create miracles of new life. My belly swelled with him and within myself, I felt him move, I felt him caress me from within, lovingly, trusting me in his vulnerability as he trusted no one and nothing else, even his bogatyr witch-warriors. I knew how a woman must feel as her babe grew beneath her heart, and it nearly drove me mad to discover that same depth of love within myself for my sire, whose soul I carried within me, whose blood and flesh were as much my own as his.*

He birthed himself on a moonless night, as my body contorted with the demands he made on it, yielding flesh and blood as he required. I know there was pain, but the pain is not the most intense memory I have of that night. Rather, it was laying there afterwards, panting and as exhausted as any woman who had birthed her first child, with him laying on my hollowed-out belly, small and red and wrinkled. He mewled, hungrily, as any infant would, and I took him in my arms, gave him suck from my own throat—and when I looked into his eyes, I saw that his effort to recreate himself had failed.

There was nothing human in his eyes. I had birthed a monster, whom I could not even strangle in the cradle, whom I could not even expose for the sun to burn to ash and the wind to scatter. Blood has passed between us for months—nine months, the time needed to make miracles—and the bond between us was tight. I loved the monstrous thing I had birthed as much as I loved the scholar who had fed my mind, the seer who had advised me with wise counsel, the sire who had let me find my own way, as he had found his. The horror of it choked me, and I could not even flee it. Instead, I took him back to the place that he had claimed as his own, and gave him to the care of those who could care for him, and then I ran from the sight of him and the knowledge of what had become of him, and built myself a home across the deep salt sea where I hoped to escape the pull of him, the desire to return to him. I threw myself into esoteric studies and, then, into the arms of my lovers, in hopes of building something better than I had first given birth to. In all of these things, I failed.

Epilogue

Madrid, 1235

The messenger arrived in Madrid by night and made his way unerringly to the house of Bishop Ambrosio Luis Monçada. The bishop's servants admitted the messenger, eventually, for they did not like the look of him—weary and travel-worn and clearly not of gentle birth, or else he would not have been traveling like a common vagabond. The messenger paid the superciliousness of the bishop's servants no heed and delivered his message to the bishop's secretary, pausing to accept no refreshment, nor to meet with the bishop himself, who was engaged in business that night.

When the bishop received the message, he was considerably irritated with his servants for not taking the messenger's name or detaining him for further questioning. He did not, however, punish them as harshly as he could have. He suspected that attempting to detain this particular messenger against his will might have cost him a number of well-trained functionaries. The letter came from the east, from the domains of the Obertus Order, and was, the bishop thought, characteristically short and to the point, consisting of only one line in an elegant hand.

The matter that we discussed has been accomplished.—M.

He might have doubted the veracity of that claim, given that he had no way to confirm it otherwise, had it not been for one thing. Pressed into the wax medallion at the bottom of the message was not the imprint of a seal, but the seal itself, a heavy golden signet, its image deeply incised into the metal. A brief perusal among his own records showed the bishop that the signet had left its stamp on a half-dozen pieces of ecclesiastical correspondence over the years, most of which were more than two hundred years old.

Bishop Ambrosio Luis Monçada was uncertain whether he should be personally pleased by this development or not. Instead of dwelling on the matter, however, he instead wrote several letters of his own, and began putting plans long held in reserve into motion.

The visitor came to the house of Velya the Flayer in the spring, traveling simply and alone, unaccompanied by servants or bodyguards. He arrived early in the evening and was received with all due ceremony, offered viands and all the comforts of an honored guest, which he accepted graciously. The letter he presented upon his arrival was carried to the master of the house and, in due course, the Flayer roused himself sufficiently to attend his visitor as a guest of his eminence and rank deserved.

Myca Vykos was mildly amused to see that Velya had obviously not enjoyed an entirely restful winter. Beneath the Flayer's cultivated air of genial elegance lurked exhaustion so deep he could not entirely conceal it, no matter how smoothly he crafted his face or carefully he carried his body. Myca rose and embraced him as a kinsman and hid his pleasure in the time-honored rituals of greeting.

"You surprise me, Myca," Velya admitted, once they had made themselves comfortable. "It is somewhat unlike you to travel unannounced and without companions. Where, dare I ask, is fair Ilias?"

"Ilias is dead."

Silence. Velya's face was as still as a lake on a day without wind. Myca reached into his dalmatic and drew from an inner pocket a small bone disk, which he held up, allowing the lamplight to play over the symbols incised in its surface. To his credit, the Flayer showed no reaction on his face, though his hands curled on his thighs as though he wished to tear the charm from Myca's hand, and possibly the hand along with it.

"He was more powerful than he knew, and more beloved of the powers he commanded," Myca said, softly. "His workings, some of them, survived the death of his flesh." He closed his hand, the charm shattering beneath his fingertips, crumbling to dust.

Velya the Flayer visibly slumped in his chair as the magic he had labored under for months dissipated, the counter to his own *maleficia* undone.

"I know what you did, Velya." Myca whispered. "Before he died, Ilias told me of it. He sensed what you were doing and moved to protect me from it, and he even knew from where it came. It pleased me to let you suffer as I suffered, at least for a time." He rose. "I came to tell you that, and to tell you that your punishment is ended, and I am satisfied by it. That, and your quarrel with my family is ended."

Velya rose, as well, his eyes narrowed. When he spoke, his voice was a hiss in which Myca clearly heard the Beast speaking. "It is not for you to decide such things."

"Oh, but it is, Velya. It is. If you raise your hand to me or mine again, I will finish what I started, and I will begin with *you*." The words, and the voice that spoke them, were not his own but, for the moment, Myca did not care. "Death is clean, Flayer. Death is an ending. There are worse things, and I know all their names."

Silence descended again. Myca turned, and strode toward the door. As he touched the handle, the Flayer spoke again.

"What are you?"

"An apt choice of words, my old friend." Myca opened the door. "I am not what, or who, I was before. I am not yet certain what, or who, I am becoming. You showed me truths that have changed me, and will continue to change me. For that, and for the... friendship... we have shared in the past, I am grateful. For that, I am willing to overlook the means you used to show me those truths. But do not cross me again, Flayer. If a reckoning is to be made against the blood that created me, that reckoning will be wrought by *me* and for *my* purposes, *my* vengeance. Be content with what you have gained already."

He closed the door behind him and walked out into the waiting night.

About the Author

Myranda Kalis (an alias she uses to protect her relatively innocent husband) has been writing incessantly since the age of twelve, honing her skills as a slinger of verbiage on bad space opera. She did, however, nobly refrained from angsty Goth poetry, even when she was an angsty Goth. *Dark Ages: Tzimisce* is her second novel (*Dark Ages: Brujah* was the first) and she has, over the years, contributed to several roleplaying game supplements for the *Dark Ages* setting of the *World of Darkness*, as well as fiction pieces and the odd essay here and there. Myranda lives in Pennsylvania with her husband, Anthony.

Acknowledgments

The author would like to offer her profound thanks to Philippe Boulle, Joshua Mosquiera-Asheim, and Lucien Soulban, without whom this book would likely never have been written.

She would also like to thank her husband, Anthony L. Sarro III, for tolerating her protracted disappearances into the writer's hermitage over the last year or two, and for all of his help and encouragement.

Curious about other Crossroad Press books?
Stop by our site:
http://store.crossroadpress.com
We offer quality writing
in digital, audio, and print formats.